Martha creates charming stories that give her readers exciting adventure and timeless romance. If you're looking for a solid, faith-based historical, I encourage you to try Martha Rogers.

—TRACIE PETERSON
BEST-SELLING AUTHOR OF STRIKING A MATCH SERIES,
INCLUDING EMBERS OF LOVE AND HEARTS AGLOW

Summer Dream is a sweet, heartfelt, and well-written story about faith in action and a love that never fails. I can't wait to read the rest of this series.

—ANDREA BOESHAAR
AUTHOR OF UNEXPECTED LOVE
AND UNDAUNTED FAITH

Martha has done it again, written a compelling story with a charming, no-nonsense plotline. I trust you'll love Rachel and Nathan's story as much as I did.

—LYNN COLEMAN
BEST-SELLING AUTHOR

SUMMER DREAM

SEASONS
of the HEART

BOOK ONE

SUMMER DREAM

SEASONS
of the HEART
BOOK ONE

MARTHA ROGERS

REALMS
A STRANG COMPANY

Most Charisma House Book Group products are available at special quantity discounts for bulk purchase for sales promotions, premiums, fund-raising, and educational needs. For details, write Charisma House Book Group, 600 Rinehart Road, Lake Mary, Florida 32746, or telephone (407) 333-0600.

Summer Dream by Martha Rogers
Published by Realms
Charisma Media/Charisma House Book Group
600 Rinehart Road
Lake Mary, Florida 32746
www.charismahouse.com

All Scripture quotations are from the King James Version of the Bible.

The characters in this book are fictitious unless they are historical figures explicitly named. Otherwise, any resemblance to actual people, whether living or dead, is coincidental.

Cover design by Studio Gearbox
Design Director: Bill Johnson

Visit the author's website at www.marthawrogers.com.

Library of Congress Cataloging-in-Publication Data:
Rogers, Martha, 1936-
  Summer dream / Martha Rogers.
     p. cm.
  ISBN 978-1-61638-360-2 (trade paper) -- ISBN 978-1-61638-437-1 (ebk.)
  I. Title.
  PS3618.O4655S86 2011
  813'.6--dc22
                                    2011002914

11 12 13 14 15 — 9 8 7 6 5 4 3 2 1
Printed in the United States of America

Acknowledgments

+ To the 19th Century ACFW writing friends who encouraged me and supported me all along the way. They answered so many questions and helped me get my research right.

+ To Jenea King for her support in carrying my books in Corner Books and promoting them.

+ To my family for buying and reading my books and giving them to friends. You are the best. You really encourage me.

+ To my editors, Lori and Deborah, who helped take this story to new levels.

+ To my husband for putting up with my odd "working" hours and my disappearing for hours at a time.

To every thing there is a season, and a time to every
purpose under the heaven.
—Ecclesiastes 3:1

And we know that all things work together for good
to them that love God, to them who are the called
according to his purpose.
—Romans 8:28

CHAPTER ONE

Briar Ridge, Connecticut, February 5, 1888

*W*HY DID PAPA have to be so stubborn? Rachel Winston stared at the gray clouds outside her window and fought the urge to stomp her foot like a spoiled child. However, young women of twenty years must behave as befitting their age, as Mama so often reminded her. Perhaps she should have shown the letter to her mother first. Too late for that now; Papa would tell Mama as soon as he had the opportunity.

The back door closed with a thud, and Rachel shuddered. Papa had left for the church. His departing meant she needed to finish dressing or she'd be late, and then Papa would be even more upset with her. It wouldn't do for the preacher's family to be late for the services.

The paper in her pocket crackled when she moved toward

the bed to retrieve her boots. Rachel fingered the crumpled edges of Aunt Mabel's letter. There was no need to read it again, for she knew the words by heart. Her aunt's invitation to come to Boston for an extended visit had arrived at a most inopportune time with the winter weather in the northern states at its worst. Even so, she shared the letter with Papa, hoping he might be agreeable to the visit.

A metallic taste soured her mouth, and she swallowed hard in an attempt to squelch it. Papa argued that the unpredictable weather of February made travel from Connecticut to Boston dangerous. If only one of the many Boston trains came to Briar Ridge. Aunt Mabel meant well, but her timing left something to be desired. Papa didn't even want her going to Hartford or Manchester to board a train. It took over three hours by horseback to make the journey to Hartford—longer in bad weather.

She grasped the wrinkled letter in her hand and pulled it from its resting place. "Oh, Auntie, why did you wait until now to invite me for a visit?" she said to the letter, as if Aunt Mabel could hear her. "Last spring when I graduated from the academy would have been perfect, but you had to travel abroad." A deep sigh filled her, then escaped in a long breath and a slump of her shoulders.

Aunt Mabel believed that a young woman should go to finishing school before she thought of marriage and had offered to pay for Rachel's tuition. Papa had frowned on the idea, but her mother finally prevailed. For that, Rachel was most grateful, and she wouldn't have traded those years at the academy for marriage to anyone. But now that she was twenty, she found that the pool of eligible bachelors in her area was slim to nonexistent. Going to Boston would have provided the opportunity to meet more young men.

Rachel sat on the bed to ease off her slippers and bent over for the winter boots that would protect her feet from the slush. The frozen ground outdoors called for them, but they were not the choice she would have liked to wear to church this morning. Rachel shoved her feet down into the sturdy boots designed for warmth, not attractive appearance.

Of the eligible young men in Briar Ridge, only one came to mind, but then Daniel Monroe didn't count. His sister had been Rachel's best friend since Papa came to be pastor of the Briar Ridge church nearly seventeen years ago. Daniel treated her more like his sister anyway. Two years older, and just starting out as a lawyer, he was far more knowledgeable than she, and keeping up a conversation with him took more effort than she deemed it to be worth. Rachel had finished at the seminary with good marks, but Daniel's conversation interests leaned more toward science and new inventions like electricity and the telephone than things of interest to her.

Rachel's anger subsided as she pulled on the laces of her boots. As she reflected on her father, she remembered that he loved her and wanted only the best for her. He had promised that when spring came, he'd talk to her about the trip. Until then she would be the obedient daughter he wanted her to be and dream of the trip ahead. The Lord would give her patience, even though that was not one of her virtues.

She smoothed her skirt down over her hips and picked up the letter to place it on the table beside her bed. A response to Aunt Mabel would go out with tomorrow's mail to express her regrets in not being able to accept the invitation. Papa would probably write to her as well, but Rachel wanted her aunt to know how much she appreciated the invitation.

If Seth were here now, he could give her good counsel. He'd always been the one she'd turned to when things didn't go well with Mama and Papa. She loved her older brother and missed him, but he'd be home from the seminary in May, and she could talk with him then. Since he studied to be a minister like Papa, he'd most likely leave Briar Ridge if his ministry took him elsewhere after his graduation.

She'd met a few young men while at school, but the strict rules and regulations set forth at Bainbridge Academy for Young Women in Hartford had given her few opportunities to develop a relationship. Not that she would have considered any of them, but she would have appreciated the chance.

Mama called to her, and Rachel hurried to the front hall. She noted the firm set of Mama's jaw and braced for the scolding that would be in order. "I'm sorry to take so long, Mama." She grabbed her cloak from its hook.

"You know how your father hates for us to be late to church. It is unseemly for the minister's family to be the last to arrive." Mama turned and walked outside, her back ramrod straight.

Rachel breathed a sigh of relief. No time for a scolding now. She set a dark blue bonnet firmly over her hair and fastened the ties. She followed her mother out to the carriage, where the rest of the family waited. As usual, Papa had gone on ahead to open the church and stoke the two stoves to provide heat on this cold winter morning. Rachel climbed up beside her sister, Miriam, and reached for the blanket.

"What delayed you, Rachel? There's no excuse for not being ready with everyone else." Mama settled in her seat beside

Noah, who had taken over his brother's responsibilities until his own departure for college next fall.

"Time slipped away from me." No need to tell her everything now. Rachel tucked a blanket around her legs and glanced at Miriam beside her. Miriam's eyebrows lifted in question, but Rachel shook her head.

Micah piped up from the front seat. "Did you make Papa angry?"

"Micah! Of course not." Rachel glanced at her brother Noah and noted the smirk on his face. She frowned to let him know she didn't approve.

His gaze slid to her now. "Oh, then why did he stomp through the kitchen and ride off without a word to anybody?"

Mama clucked her tongue. "Now, children, it's the Sabbath. Papa was late and in a hurry to get to the church." But the look in Mama's eyes promised she'd speak to Rachel about it later, especially after Mama learned the real reason for the tardiness.

Even though his decision disappointed her, Papa simply wanted to protect her from danger. She should be grateful for his love and concern, not angry because he said no. The promise of a trip to Boston when the weather improved would have to be enough to get her through the remainder of winter.

A recent snowfall still covered the frozen ground. Most of it in the streets had melted into a hodgepodge of brown and black slush caused by carriages and buggies winding their way toward the church. Rachel breathed deeply of the clean, fresh air that seemed to accompany snow in winter and rain in the spring.

If not for the inconveniences caused by ice and snow, she would love this time of year, even when the leafless branches of the trees cracked and creaked with a coating of ice. She gazed toward the gray skies that promised more snow before the day ended. If it would wait until later in the day, she might manage a visit with her best friend Abigail this afternoon.

However, a warm house, a cup of hot tea flavored with mint from Mama's herb garden, and a good book might entice her to stay home on this cold, winter afternoon. Tomorrow would bring the chores of keeping the woodpile stocked and the laundry cleaned. She enjoyed the winter months, although this year she wished them to hurry by.

Miriam snuggled closer. Rachel smiled at her sister, who had recently turned thirteen. "I see you're wearing your Christmas dress today. Is there a special occasion?"

Miriam's cheeks turned a darker shade of red. "Um, not exactly."

"Then what is it…exactly?"

Miriam tilted her head to one side and peered up at Rachel. She whispered, "Jimmy Turner."

So her little sister had begun to notice boys. "Well now, I think he's a handsome lad. Has he shown an interest in you?"

Miriam nodded and giggled. Rachel wrapped an arm around her sister as the buggy slowed to enter the churchyard. She stepped down onto the snow-covered ground muddied by all the wagons crossing over it. Now she was thankful for the thick stockings and shoes she wore to protect her toes. She then reached up for Micah while Miriam raced ahead.

The little boy pushed her hands away. "I can get down by myself."

Rachel couldn't resist the temptation to laugh. At seven, her younger brother expressed his independence and insisted on doing things for himself. He jumped with his feet square in a pile of snow and looked first at his feet then up to Rachel. She shook her head and grabbed his hand to go inside the building. How that little boy loved the snow. He'd be out in it all day if Mama would let him.

When she entered the foyer with Micah, she spotted Miriam already sitting in their pew with Jimmy Turner in the row behind her. Rachel hastened to sit down beside her sister. Miriam stared straight ahead but twisted her hands together in her lap.

When had Miriam grown up? Even now she showed signs of the beauty she would one day be. Thick, dark lashes framed her brown eyes, and her cheeks held a natural pink glow. Papa would really have to keep an eye out for his younger daughter.

Rachel glanced around the assembly room and once again admired the beauty of the old church built not long after the turn of the century. Instead of the quarry stone and masonry of the churches in Boston and even New Haven, Briar Ridge's church walls were of white clapboard with large stained-glass windows along the sides. On bright days, sunlight streamed through them to create patterns of color across the congregation.

Brass light fixtures hung from the high vaulted ceilings, and the flames from the gaslights danced in the breeze as the back doors opened to admit worshippers. As much as she loved her church here in Briar Ridge, she remembered the electric lights she'd enjoyed in Hartford, one of the first cities to have its own generating plant. How long before electricity would become as widespread in Briar Ridge as it was in the larger cities? Probably awhile since Briar Ridge wasn't known for its progress.

When the family first came to town, Rachel had been three years old, so this was the only home and church she could remember before leaving for school. Familiar faces met her everywhere she gazed. A nod and smile greeted each one as she searched for her friend Abigail and the Monroe family.

Unexpectedly a new face came into view a few rows back. A young man with the most incredible brown eyes stared back at her. Rachel's breath caught in her throat, and the heat rose in her cheeks.

She felt her mother's hand on her arm. "Turn around, Rachel. It's not polite to stare."

With her heart threatening to jump right out of her chest, Rachel tore her gaze away from the stranger seated with the Monroe family. Papa entered from the side door and stepped up to the pulpit. The service began with singing, but Rachel could barely make a sound. Everything in her wanted to turn and gaze again at the mysterious person with the Monroe family, but that behavior would be unseemly for the daughter of the minister.

However, her thoughts refused to obey and skipped to their own rhythm. Rachel decided that whoever he was, he must be a friend of Daniel's because Abigail had never mentioned any man of interest in her own life. In a town like Briar Ridge, everyone knew everyone's business. She hadn't heard any talk of a guest from Daniel or her other friends yesterday.

A prickling sensation crept along her neck as though someone watched her. She blinked her eyes and willed herself to look at Papa and concentrate on his message. However, her mind filled with images of the young man. Who was this stranger who had come to Briar Ridge?

Nathan Reed contemplated the dark curls peeking from beneath the blue bonnet. When she had turned and their eyes met, his heart leaped. He had never expected to see such a beauty in a town like Briar Ridge. His friend Daniel's sister was attractive, but nothing like this raven-haired girl with blue eyes.

When she turned her head back toward the front, he stared at her back as if to will her to turn his way again. When she didn't, he turned his sights to gaze around the church, so much like others he'd once attended. He wouldn't be here this morning except out of politeness for the Monroe family. He'd arrived later than intended last evening and welcomed Mrs. Monroe's offer to stay the night with them. The least he could do was attend the service today.

Nathan had no use for church or things of God. He believed God existed, but only for people who needed something or someone to lean on. God had forsaken the Reed family years ago, and Nathan had done quite well without any help these four years away from home.

He shook off thoughts of the past and concentrated once more on the blue bonnet several rows ahead. Perhaps Daniel would introduce him. She would be a nice diversion from the business he must attend to while in town. He blocked the words of the minister from his mind and concentrated on the girl's back.

The little boy seated next to the young woman seemed restless, so she lifted him onto her lap. The child couldn't be her son. She didn't look old enough. Then the older woman next to them reached for the boy and settled him in her arms. In a few minutes the boy's head nodded in sleep.

Nathan resisted the urge to pull his watch from his pocket and check the time. Surely the service would end soon. Potbellied stoves in the front and back of the church provided warmth, and the additional heat of so many bodies caused him to wish he had shed his coat. He fought the urge to nod off himself. Oh, to be like the young lad in his mother's arms.

Finally the congregation rose, and the organ played the final hymn. It was none too soon for Nathan, for he had grown more uncomfortable by the minute. Long sermons only added to his distaste for affairs of the church. The singing ended and people began their exit, but he kept his eye on the girl in blue until the crowd blocked her from view.

He stayed behind the Monroe family, who stopped to greet the minister. Mrs. Monroe turned to Nathan. "Reverend Winston, this is Nathan Reed, our houseguest from Hartford this week and a friend of Daniel's."

The minister smiled in greeting and shook Nathan's hand. "It's very nice to have you in our services today, Mr. Reed. I hope you enjoy your stay in Briar Ridge and that we'll see more of you."

"Thank you, sir. I look forward to my visit here." But the minister wouldn't be seeing any more of him unless they possibly met in town.

When they reached the Monroe carriage, Nathan turned and spotted the girl coming down the steps. He watched as Daniel waved to the young woman and she waved back. Abigail ran to greet her, and the girls hurried over to where Nathan stood with Daniel. Abigail tucked her hand in the girl's elbow.

"Nathan, this is my best friend, Rachel Winston. Rachel, this is Daniel's former roommate in college, Nathan Reed."

Rachel Winston? Nathan's hopes dashed against the slushy ground on which he stood. Could she be the preacher's daughter? He didn't mind a young woman being Christian, but he drew the line at keeping company with one so close to the ministry.

When her blue eyes gazed into his, a spark of interest flamed, and it took him a few seconds before remembering his manners. "It's a pleasure to meet you, Miss Winston."

Her cheeks flushed red, and she glanced away slightly but still smiled. "Thank you. I'm pleased to meet you too, Mr. Reed. Perhaps we'll see each other again if you're in town long."

Rachel's smile sent a warmth into his heart that caused him to swallow hard. Although the length of his stay was uncertain, his desire to see the lovely Miss Winston again might just override his pledge to avoid anything or anyone with ties to the church.

CHAPTER
TWO

*E*ZRA WINSTON STOOD by his wife's bedside, where she had retired to rest after Sunday dinner. "Is there anything I can get you, Felicity?"

She raised her hand to pat his arm. "No, dear, I'm only a little tired. I don't seem to have the energy I once had."

He placed his hand over hers. "Perhaps I should have the doctor look in on you."

"Oh, no, we don't need to bother him. I'll be fine after a bit of nap time." Then she furrowed her brow and squeezed his arm. "What did Rachel do that had you so disturbed this morning?"

Ezra hesitated. He'd rather wait until Felicity felt better, but since she'd asked, he must explain. "It wasn't Rachel but my sister Mabel. Sometimes I wonder if she has any sense of time or season. She invited Rachel to visit with her in Boston in a few weeks. She seems to think Rachel will have more opportunity to find a suitable young man for marriage there." Sometimes his sister's meddling led to more trouble than it was worth.

"In the dead of winter?"

Ezra perched carefully on the side of the bed with his long legs supporting most of his weight so as not to disturb his wife. "I'm afraid so. Of course I said no, and that is what had Rachel so upset." He understood his daughter's eagerness to go to Boston, but not in February.

"I see." She patted his hand. "I'm sure she'll get over it in a week or so. Daniel has taken an interest in our daughter, so perhaps it won't be necessary for her to travel to Boston."

He placed his hand over hers and raised it to his lips. "Daniel is a fine young man. Of course, Mabel may be trying to make up for not being able to keep Sarah from marrying that young Muldoon boy and traipsing off to Texas before she had a proper introduction to society."

Two years older than Rachel, his niece Sarah had exhibited her independence and let love, not her mother, dictate her life. Rachel had voiced her own desires on several occasions, but not in the headstrong manner of her cousin.

Ezra rose and walked to the window, where he stared out at the snowflakes silently covering the ground. "I promised her she could go in the spring or summer to visit. A trip like that is something which she can look forward to in the months ahead, and it will help her to get over her disappointment."

"That was a splendid idea. Summer is much better for travel."

Her voice sounded weak, and it alarmed Ezra. He hurried back to her side. "I'm sorry, dear. I'm disturbing your rest. I'll go back down to my study and begin reading Scriptures for next Sunday's sermon." He leaned over and kissed her cheek. "Take your nap and get a good rest. I'm sure Rachel will take care of preparing a little supper for us later."

"Thank you. I appreciate that."

He pulled the curtains closed and then stepped out of the darkened room. Worry lines creased his brow. If Felicity didn't improve and get her energy back soon, he'd have to make a call to the doctor and have him come to check on her.

For nearly twenty-five years of marriage she'd been hale and healthy with nary a day of sickness. The only time she had ever taken to her bed was when she gave birth to their children. Even then, Felicity didn't stay down long. Running her household had been more important. Now he prayed she wouldn't be paying the price for her long years of working without ceasing.

Downstairs he found Rachel and Miriam in the parlor, their heads bent toward one another as Rachel showed her sister how to embroider a pillow slip. He stood in the doorway observing them for a moment. Rachel had grown into a beautiful young woman, with her blue eyes an unusual contrast to her dark hair. Miriam's hair also had a darker hue, but she had inherited his brown eyes. She too would one day be a very attractive young woman. Already her smile and sparkling personality attracted people to her.

Rachel glanced up and saw him. She bent to say a word to her sister then strode over to him. "Papa, I wish to apologize for my behavior this morning. It was quite childish of me to be so upset with your decision. I shall be pleased to wait until summer comes to go to Boston."

"Apology accepted, Rachel. I'm sorry my sister has such poor timing, but with weather like this, travel is all but impossible. Boston will be much more appealing in warmer weather."

He placed a hand on her shoulder. "You have become a young woman before my very eyes, and you are sure to attract the attention of many young men. Your mother and I pray daily for you to find a fine Christian man who will be your companion throughout life."

She blinked her eyes then cast her gaze to the floor. "Thank you, Papa. I pray I am worthy of such a young man."

Of that he had no doubts. Not only was she a faithful Christian girl, but she was also one with many talents, one of which he would partake now. "With this cold weather, a cup of tea or hot cocoa would be most welcome. I'll be in my study." He turned toward the hallway but stopped and turned back with a grin on his face. "And a few of those cinnamon cookies you baked would be a nice accompaniment."

Rachel's heart raced, but she stood still until her father closed his study door. Relief that he'd accepted her apology swept through her, and he had smiled. Being on Papa's bad side was not a pleasant position. Best now to take care of his request. "Miriam, I'll be in the kitchen. Papa would like some hot cocoa and cookies."

Miriam jumped up from her place on the sofa. "Oh, please, may I help and have some too?"

"Of course, and if I'm not mistaken, our brothers will be down when they get a whiff of what we're doing." She wrapped her arm around her sister, and together they strolled to the kitchen.

Rachel handed Miriam a pan and told her to measure milk

into it then set it on the stove. After getting down the sugar and cocoa powder, Rachel made a mixture to add to the milk after it warmed. As she waited for the liquid to heat more, Rachel gazed out the window at the swirling snow. Though not as heavy as two days ago, it still kept her inside rather than visiting with her best friend Abigail.

A commotion at the door caused her to turn with a stern look at her brothers Noah and Micah. "No need to fight to get through the door. There's plenty for everyone. Please be quiet and sit at the table, and I'll fix yours. Mama is resting, so no loud noises."

Although ten years separated the two brothers, they enjoyed roughhousing with each other and sometimes didn't realize how much noise they made. She finished the beverage and poured three mugs for her siblings and set a plate of cookies on the table. "I've put two for each of you, so you won't spoil your appetite for supper."

She prepared another plate for her father and poured the steaming cocoa into a pottery cup. After placing both on a tray, she turned to her brothers and sister. "I'm taking these to Papa. When you've finished your cookies, please put your dishes and cups in the sink. Miriam, if you'll be so kind as to wash them, I'll dry them when I return."

Miriam scowled and her bottom lip protruded. "Why can't Noah do that? I want to finish my needlework."

"Because your brother has to get the wood for the stove so we'll have plenty for supper and the fireplaces. Micah, you could help Noah with that."

The child's face lit up, and he bounced in his seat. "Can I, Noah? Can I?"

Rachel left them talking about their chores and went to Papa's study. She knocked on the door, and at his bidding to come in, she stepped inside. "Here is the refreshment you requested, Papa." She noted the open Bible and his pen. "Are you working on next week's sermon already?" She set her tray on his desk.

He laughed and picked up the cup of cocoa. "Yes, my dear, it's never too soon to be prepared."

She started to leave but hesitated. "Papa, I'm concerned about Mama. She hasn't had much energy and has needed me to help her with more tasks than usual. Is she ill?"

Papa furrowed his brow and pursed his lips before answering. "You are a very astute young lady. I believe with you here to help her, your mother will be better in no time. However, I would like for you to watch and make sure she doesn't overextend herself with household chores."

"Of course, Papa, I'll make sure to take on more responsibility. I don't mind at all. I enjoy helping Mama." And she truly did. Seeing the house clean and dust-free with everything in place gave her a great sense of satisfaction. She'd help make Mama's load lighter for the next few days or however long it took.

When she returned to the kitchen, her brothers and sister had disappeared. Miriam had washed the dishes, and they now sat on the counter waiting for Rachel to dry them. A smile crossed her lips. Miriam may complain, but she usually did as instructed and did it well.

Rachel grabbed a towel and began drying the cups. She glanced out the window at the snow. It had stopped falling, but it was too late for a visit with Abigail, even though she wished for a closer look at the Monroe's houseguest. Such a handsome young man was a rarity in Briar Ridge. Abigail said he had been a classmate of Daniel's. That meant he must be a lawyer too.

Nathan Reed. She liked that name. A good patriot's name and well suited for a barrister. Whatever his business happened to be here in Briar Ridge, she hoped it would be long enough for her to see him again. Something she didn't quite understand had tugged at her heart when their gazes had met in the churchyard.

Nathan sat with Daniel, conversing in the parlor. Mr. and Mrs. Monroe and Abigail had retired to their rooms for the afternoon. Drowsiness threatened to overtake Nathan, but he resisted the urge to close his eyes. He needed information from his friend.

He'd begin first with good manners and then move on to his real interest after that. "I say, that was a fine meal your mother served. Being a bachelor and on my own, I don't get many home-cooked meals like that. My compliments to the cook."

Daniel chuckled. "I suppose we do take Ellie's cooking for granted. Mother has done well with our household staff. Now tell me about your reasons for being here in Briar Ridge. You did say it had to do with a matter of law."

Let him talk and ask questions. When Nathan's queries came later, Daniel would be more obliged to answer. "Mrs. Cargill has asked our firm to dispose of her property holdings here, as she plans to remain permanently in Hartford. We have an interested buyer for her house and land, so I'm meeting with him tomorrow to set terms."

"Ah, yes, the Widow Cargill. She recently went to Hartford to visit with her children. I had heard she planned to live there to be close to her grandchildren. I can't blame her for that."

"I look for the settling of the matter to take several days. I do believe I was sent here because I'm the newest in the firm, and travel isn't as pleasant in the winter. Of course I didn't mind, because it meant an opportunity to visit with you and your family again."

"And we're glad to have you." Daniel changed positions in his chair and peered at Nathan. "I sensed you were somewhat uncomfortable in church this morning. If I remember correctly, you didn't attend very often while at Yale."

Nathan smiled politely. "You're right. As a child and a young boy, I had great faith, but I've neglected God for so long that I'm sure He no longer has an interest in me or my affairs, and I certainly don't intend to bother Him with them." He had shared some of his past with Daniel, but his friend had pried for no more information than what Nathan had been willing to reveal. Respect for Nathan's privacy had sealed their friendship.

"Sometimes it's really better to bother God. Some things only God can handle."

The words bounced off Nathan's heart like raindrops on oilskin. He'd done quite well on his own and didn't intend to change now. Time to change the subject. "Your sister and Miss Winston appear to be good friends."

"They have been close since childhood. They even went to Bainbridge Academy for Young Women and studied the same courses in Hartford. Of course, I've known her for that long myself." Daniel leaned forward as if in a conspiracy. "Please keep this quiet, but I plan to ask Reverend Winston if I may call on Rachel in the coming days."

Nathan hid his disappointment at that news, but then he should have no real interest in Rachel himself since she was the minister's daughter. It was just as well Daniel had expressed his interest in her because a religious girl like Rachel didn't belong with a man like himself.

"Nathan," Daniel continued, "Mother has expressed a desire to host a dinner party while you're here. She's hoping you'll be in town long enough for her to plan one for this coming Friday night. I told her I would inquire as to your possible length of stay."

"That's very kind of your mother, and I would be honored. I'll plan to stay through the week. I'm sure I can come up with enough to keep me busy here in Briar Ridge." And it would afford another opportunity to see Rachel Winston. He could still admire her from afar and not express interest, for the last thing he wanted to do was to hurt his best friend.

CHAPTER THREE

$\mathcal{M}$ONDAY AFTERNOON RACHEL opened the door wide. "Oh, Abigail, I'm so glad you're finally here." She rocked on her heels as her friend removed her cloak and hung it in the entry hall. As she labored over the laundry that morning, Rachel had been anticipating this time with Abigail.

"I wonder what could have you so excited for my visit today?" Abigail's eyes twinkled when she turned to Rachel.

"Oh, please, do tell me everything about that handsome young man staying with you. Where is he from? How long will he be here?" She grasped her friend's arm and led her into the parlor. "Is he a lawyer like Daniel?"

Abigail grinned and shook her light brown curls. "Why, Rachel Winston, I haven't seen you this interested in a man since that last cotillion at Bainbridge. It's as though you've never seen a man before."

"I haven't. I mean, not one like Mr. Reed. I could drown

in those eyes. They're the color of Papa's coffee without cream." She eased down onto a brocade chair.

"Hmm, I must agree with that." Abigail sat on the sofa and arranged her skirts. "I truly don't have much to tell you. Daniel spoke of Nathan Reed only a few times while they were at college. I do know he came to Connecticut from North Carolina, and now he is with a law firm in Hartford." Abigail clasped her hands in her lap.

"So he is a lawyer, just like I suspected. But he's from North Carolina, you say? How unusual. I wonder, why did he come this far north for an education?" Rachel waved her hands. "Never mind that. He is quite handsome, don't you think? But why is he here in Briar Ridge?" Rachel's eyes opened wide. "Oh, Abigail, I didn't even think. Is he here to see you?"

Abigail's laughter rang out. "Oh, that would be a good one. Daniel informed me in no uncertain terms that Mr. Reed is not the man for me."

"Oh, dear, why would he say that?" Rachel's heart plummeted. Was he already betrothed to another? Most young men his age were if they were not already married.

Her friend shrugged. "Oh, you know how Daniel is. I don't think there's a man alive he would consider suitable for me. He's as bad as Papa. He may be only twenty-two years old, but he acts like an old man sometimes."

"Well, then, tell me about Nathan Reed." Rachel smoothed her skirt and settled back in her chair. The man intrigued her more by the minute.

"He's in town to take care of the Widow Cargill's estate. Remember, she moved to Hartford to live with her son and his family? Anyway, she wants to sell her house and property here in Briar Ridge. He's here to see to that. I think he'll be here the remainder of the week and perhaps the next." Abigail sat back with a smug grin.

Rachel leaned forward. "There's something you're not telling me."

Abigail's eyes danced with merriment. "Hmm, yes, there is." The grin became a broad smile. "Mama is planning a dinner party in Mr. Reed's honor on Friday. The invitations will be delivered this afternoon."

"A dinner party? Oh, how lovely." Rachel mentally checked each garment in her closet for one formal enough for the event. Aunt Mabel had been most generous in sending proper attire to Rachel while in school in Hartford. Mama would help her choose the best one. She clasped her hands. "Do tell me more about the party. You said nothing about it after church yesterday."

"Mama hadn't made the plans then. She and Papa decided yesterday that a party would be in order. You know how Mama loves to entertain."

Invitations to Mrs. Monroe's dinners were highly regarded. The Winston family always attended the affairs, as Mrs. Monroe thought the presence of a minister added to any social occasion, and she wanted her church affiliation to be known. "Any party your mother plans will be one to remember. What do you plan to wear?"

The next half hour, as they discussed the latest fashions and the upcoming event, Rachel's thoughts returned to the prospect of seeing Nathan Reed again. His brown eyes, square jaw, and brown hair filled her mind.

Abigail stood. "It's getting late, and I promised Mama I'd be home to help her decide about floral arrangements for the tables on Friday."

"If you have anything to do with them, they will be lovely. You have such good instincts when it comes to that sort of thing." Abigail had won all the awards and accolades for her domestic endeavors in those classes at Bainbridge. She needed to find a young man and settle down so she could use her skills. Rachel led her friend to the front hall and reached for Abigail's cloak. "I hope we have time for more visits this week."

"I do too, but Mama is likely to keep me busy with her plans. She may not prepare and serve the food, but she certainly pays a great deal of attention to all that goes into the meal and decorations." Abigail tied the ribbons of her bonnet then pulled on her gloves.

"And that's why her invitations are coveted and all her parties are so well attended." Rachel hugged Abigail then closed the door behind her. Resisting the urge to shout, she raced up the stairs and into her room. A search through her gowns revealed a royal blue silk she had worn last year at the academy. No one here had seen it. She reached for the dress and held it under her chin. Mama could add a bit of lace here and there, and it would be perfect.

A knock sounded on the door below. Rachel rushed out to the hall and leaned over the banister. A young man handed her mother a white envelope then departed. Rachel bounded down the stairway. "Is that the invitation to the Monroe party?"

Mama opened the envelope and glanced over it. "Yes, it is. This Friday evening. That doesn't give us much time to prepare." She held the envelope to her side. "Before we talk about the party, I want to discuss what happened with your father yesterday."

Rachel's heart sank. Since the subject had not been mentioned, she thought the matter would be laid aside. Of course, she should have remembered Mama wouldn't speak of anything that may cause an argument on a Sunday afternoon.

"Come into the parlor with me."

Rachel followed her mother into the room just vacated by Abigail and sat on a side chair. She ran her hand over the smooth cherrywood armrest and bit her lip.

Mama cleared her throat. "My dear, your father told me about Aunt Mabel's letter of invitation to visit in Boston. I must agree that it came at the worst possible time."

Rachel nodded but dared not say a word lest her feelings from yesterday returned.

"Your aunt and I have been in frequent correspondence since you graduated. We both agreed that you would have a better chance of finding a suitable young man in Boston, but since she was out of the country last summer, she could do nothing about it. With her own daughters grown and away from home, she'd love to have you come for a visit with her and meet the sons of her friends. However, I had no idea she'd send an invitation so soon."

Rachel slumped back in her chair. So discussions had been going on all along. No wonder Papa had been even more adamant than usual. "I had no idea. Aunt Mabel showed me great kindness when I was the academy. And I do want to visit her."

"Of course, and your father and I both agree that when the weather warms up and the roads are more easily traveled, you will get your trip to Boston. Mabel has also extended an invitation for Abigail to come with you."

"Abigail can go with me?" Happiness now tickled her insides, and all the anger she held for her father yesterday disappeared like fog under the sun. She should never have doubted that he had only her best interests at heart. And now those interests had expanded to include her best friend.

"Yes, and I've already discussed it with Mrs. Monroe, and she and Mr. Monroe have given their permission for Abigail to travel with us, but they will not approach the topic with her until later in the spring. We had hoped to tell you this a little later as well, so you wouldn't have so long to wait, but Papa didn't expect his sister to write directly to you. He said you were very angry and upset yesterday morning before church and decided I should tell you now, but please don't say a word to Abigail until her parents discuss it with her."

"Oh, I won't, I promise. I was upset with Papa, and I'm so sorry. He only had my best interests at heart because travel this time of year can be so dangerous." Her parents did want her to be happy, but they also wanted her to be safe.

"Yes, and your father spoke to me of your apology yesterday. I am proud of you for doing that because I know how hard it is for you to admit a mistake."

Mama did know her too well, but the apology would work in her favor later. Now joy flooded through her soul. Rachel jumped up and bent over to hug her mother. "You and Papa are the best parents in the whole world. I can hardly wait until summer comes."

Mama laughed. "Well, the party Friday night will help the wait to be more pleasant." She handed over the invitation.

Rachel clutched it to her chest then read it. A seated dinner. How wonderful. That meant she just might be placed next to Nathan Reed for the better part of the evening. She whirled around in glee. This had turned into a most perfect day.

Mama tilted her head to one side. "Well, my dear, I'm glad you are excited about attending. Could it be the presence of Mr. Reed that has caught your interest?"

Heat rose in Rachel's cheeks. She could never hide anything from either of her parents. "Oh, Mama, he's the most hand-some man I have ever seen." With that she spun around again and hurried up the stairs. "And I found just the dress to wear," she called over her shoulder. The perfect dress for the perfect evening. The dinner party couldn't come soon enough to suit Rachel.

"I appreciate your mother's hospitality, but a formal dinner party is not necessary, Daniel. I don't want your mother going to such trouble on my account." Nathan wrinkled his brow and studied the invitation in his hand. This had turned into much more than he expected when Daniel first mentioned the event yesterday. Now, relaxing with Daniel in the parlor after a day of meetings with Mrs. Cargill's lawyer, he wondered if he should be staying on so long, but all indications pointed to a week's worth of work in evaluating Mrs. Cargill's estate and transfer-ring all her business to his firm in Hartford.

Daniel waved his hand. "Don't be concerned about that. Mother would rather give a social than just about anything else.

She'll find any excuse for throwing a gala, and you happen to be her excuse for this one."

"I see." Nathan's mind filled with the image of the girl he had met at the church. Would she be invited? Abigail had introduced Rachel as her best friend, so surely she would be included on the guest list. Of course, with Daniel's interest in her, any admiration must be from a distance.

"And I have just the young lady to seat you with that evening." Daniel smiled with his arms crossed against his chest.

Nathan smiled. "And who would that be? Your sister, Miss Abigail?"

Daniel frowned. "What? Oh, no. She has a partner, and Miss Winston will be mine." He rocked back on his heels and grinned. "You haven't met Miss Amy Hill yet. She doesn't attend our church as regularly as we do, but Amy and I were in school together before I went off to Yale and she went to Amherst."

Nathan's interest perked up. "She was in school with you and an Amherst graduate? Then she must be near our age." He'd never expected to find someone so educated in Briar Ridge. Perhaps he should have visited his former roommate sooner.

Daniel laughed again. "Yes, she is, and a most attractive young woman. Her father is a prominent businessman and handles many of the investments for our citizens."

"Then I most definitely look forward to the evening." Perhaps another young woman, more suitable than Miss Winston, would keep him from thinking about dark curls and blue eyes. Of course, it is always that which is out of reach that is more appealing.

He slapped Daniel on the shoulder. "I must say, old friend,

that I had no idea your town boasted such beautiful young women. If I had, my first visit would have been much sooner." He paused, then asked, "When do you plan to ask Reverend Winston for permission to court Miss Winston?"

Daniel's eyebrows rose before a satisfied smile graced his lips. "Soon, I hope. Rachel and I have known each other since we were children. A minister's daughter would make a most respectable wife for a lawyer."

"I daresay she would, and if she doesn't return your attentions, that would be disappointing. As for me, you know how I pledged in college to stay away from women who are believers! All they do is try to convert you. It's most tiresome." He paused, then asked with forced lightness, "But what does Rachel think of you? Do you think she returns your interest?"

Daniel stroked his chin. "Of course, I have no idea whether or not she will return my feelings, but given time, I hope she does. Knowing what a woman thinks is quite the puzzle. Just when you think you have her figured out, she does something completely different."

"Yes, I have found that to be the case as well." Nathan nodded. "At any rate, I am looking forward to meeting Miss Hill. She should be the perfect dinner companion. Thank you." And the perfect diversion to keep his mind from straying to Miss Winston. If all went well, perhaps he would be granted permission to call upon Miss Hill on other occasions. If Mrs. Cargill's estate proved to be the assignment it promised to be, he could look forward with pleasure to more visits to Briar Ridge.

At that moment Abigail stepped through the door with a tray of refreshment. Her flushed cheeks led Nathan to believe she'd overheard their conversation. No matter. If Miss Winston heard from her friend that he wasn't interested in dating a believer, that would make his task of avoiding her charms all the easier.

CHAPTER
FOUR

*F*RIDAY FINALLY ARRIVED, and anticipation of the evening filled Rachel with excitement as she prepared for the dinner. She fingered the new lace trim Mama had added to her dress. Mama could do wonders with fabric and trim, especially with her new sewing machine. Rachel patted a curl into place, then smoothed the front of her silk gown and smiled. The dress may not be what the young ladies of Hartford wore, but the smaller bustle did fit the style of the day and was most appropriate for tonight's social affair. Besides, it would be much easier for her to handle, and women in Briar Ridge were not as fashion conscious as those in Hartford.

She planted her hands at her waist. At least she didn't have to wear a corset like her Aunt Mabel laced up when she dressed for special occasions. The one time Rachel had worn one, she'd nearly passed out from lack of breath. Women these days may speak of freedoms and rights, but when it came to dress, they certainly submitted themselves to the restrictions of proper attire.

Mama opened the door. "Oh, my dear Rachel, you are beautiful. That blue is the perfect color for you." Her nimble fingers straightened the braided silk that trimmed the skirt and bodice.

"Thank you." She peered at herself in the mirror. If only Nathan Reed would see her as Mama did. Of course, he had been busy with his duties for Mrs. Cargill all week, and she had no occasion to speak with him since their meeting on Sunday.

"Come, your father and Noah are waiting in the carriage." Her mother's silk taffeta skirt swished as she turned and walked out of the room. Rachel had to smile at her mother's slightly plump figure. She didn't bother with a corset and preferred the simpler mode of dress without the stylish bustle, as it fit her role as a minister's wife.

Rachel followed her mother out to the street and allowed Noah to assist her in boarding the surrey. She settled herself on the seat and glanced at her brother. He looked quite dashing himself in his black suit and coat. His light yellow hair had darkened over the years to a golden brown that complemented his ruddy complexion. He smiled, and she noted the sparkle of mischief in his dark blue eyes. He'd have the younger ladies vying for his attention all evening.

Not many social occasions occurred during the winter months, but no new snow had fallen since Sunday, and the cool air felt rather pleasant. She anticipated the dinner ahead with an eagerness that caused her heart to beat faster the closer they drew to the Monroe home. Mr. Reed was by far the most exciting thing to happen in Briar Ridge all winter. Sometimes she wished that young women could be more forward with their words and actions around young men.

Sitting with her gloved hands clasped in her lap, Mama drew Rachel's attention away from her reverie. "Mrs. Monroe always puts on the loveliest dinner parties. I'm sure tonight will not be an exception."

Papa nodded. "Yes, the food and company will be quite enjoyable." He peered at Rachel. "I met Mr. Reed at the bank this week. He seems to be a well-mannered young man. He is here only until his business is concluded, but it is quite hospitable of the Monroes to host this dinner for him."

Why was Papa looking at her that way? If Papa liked Mr. Reed, then why did his eyes send a message of warning? Did he suspect her interest in Nathan Reed? Surely not. She had been quite careful in curbing her enthusiasm for this evening's festivities in front of her parents. Only Mama had mentioned it on that first day, but not since then. Of course, Mama would have discussed it with Papa, and he only thought of Rachel's well-being.

Her father pulled into the line of buggies waiting to empty themselves of passengers. When they reached the front stoop, a young man offered his hand to help the ladies step down. Papa handed the reins to another attendant responsible for hitching the carriages that did not have a personal coachman.

As one of the grandest homes in all of Briar Ridge, the Monroe house now gleamed with light from the high arched windows along the front. Rachel glimpsed men and women dressed in their finest gathered in the drawing room of the mansion, and anticipation tickled her nerves. The Monroes had spared no expense in putting on this affair.

A butler stood in the entry hall waiting to receive their outer coats and hats. Rachel handed her cloak to him, then gazed around the front entrance. Greenery wove its way up the stairway to the second floor with pink and white camellias imported from the South nestled among the leaves. Rachel marveled at how well they had survived the long trip.

Silver and crystal sparkled in the candlelight from the dining room on the right, and guests mingled in the drawing room on her left. Rachel immediately sought out Abigail and hugged her. They walked arm in arm to the window.

"Oh, Rachel, you look so beautiful."

"Thank you, but so do you, Abigail. That shade of red is perfect for your golden-brown hair."

Pink tinged Abigail's cheeks. "It's my favorite." Then she bit her lip. "Rachel, I have to tell you something. Amy Hill is to be Mr. Reed's dinner partner tonight. You will be with Daniel."

Amy Hill? How had that happened? Amy was a year older and had been away at college. She should have remembered that Amy would be here. Rachel's hopes fell. Not that she wouldn't enjoy the evening with Daniel, but sitting with Nathan Reed would have been much more exciting.

She turned to her right at the sound of laughter. Amy and Nathan conversed with another couple in the corner. Amy laughed again and shook her head slightly, her blonde curls not moving an inch. Rachel's stomach became a bottomless, empty pit that nothing could fill. How would she ever compete with the educated, beautiful Amy? Rachel squared her shoulders. She had come to have a good time, and a good time she would have.

At that moment Nathan turned toward Rachel, and like a magnet, their gazes locked in with the same force that had been there last Sunday. Her breath caught in her throat, and time stood still.

A hand touched her arm. She blinked and found Daniel standing by her side. "Rachel, may I escort you to dinner?"

All around her others made their way to the dining room. She smiled. "Of course. I'd be delighted." She placed her hand in the crook of his elbow and walked at his side toward the other room.

As the gentlemen seated the ladies, Rachel drank in the beauty of the table set with Mrs. Monroe's finest china. The centerpieces of camellias and greenery gave testimony to her hostess's expertise with floral arrangements. The pink and white blossoms nestled among the leaves as though they had grown right there on the table.

Rachel sat next to Abigail, and they shared a quick clasp of hands and a brief smile before their escorts seated themselves. Rachel leaned close to whisper, "The centerpieces are elegant. It appears our class in floral arrangement taught you a great deal. You and your mother did a magnificent job."

"Thank you." Abigail grinned and squeezed Rachel's hand again.

As was his custom, Mr. Monroe called on Papa to say grace before the meal. Rachel listened with pride to her father's deep voice asking blessings on the food and the guests who were to receive it. She lifted up her own prayer to keep jealousy for Amy Hill at bay this night.

Nathan had become aware of Rachel Winston the moment she stepped into the parlor. Again her beauty took his breath away. He had imagined her all week as he had seen her on Sunday in church. Tonight a mass of dark curls trimmed with blue ribbons added to her beauty and shone in the light from the lamps and candles around the room. If it were not for Amy Hill, he'd never take his gaze away from Rachel. The moment their eyes had met on Sunday, something had happened, and again this evening, that same pull had drawn his gaze to hers. He must speak with her later.

He shuddered. Such thoughts must be banished out of respect for his close friend, not to mention the barrier of Rachel's father being a minister. In the past he found that women who were too absorbed by religion tried everything to change his beliefs. He wanted none of that. Besides, he would never try to woo her away from Daniel. He must keep reminding himself of that. Rachel was Daniel's partner for the evening and perhaps for a lifetime. It was only that she was forbidden that the attraction remained, but he must stand by his convictions.

Miss Hill better suited his purposes, and he settled on having her at his side. Although intelligent, she tended to focus on herself rather than happenings around her. Still, she was more like the young ladies he escorted in Hartford—blonde, pretty enough, talkative. She prattled on now about being president of some young ladies literary society. He listened with half an ear as his gaze drifted to Rachel across the table and a few seats down from where he and Amy sat.

Daniel certainly provided a more suitable escort for Rachel.

He had a stellar reputation and not a tainted one like Nathan's. A solid Christian lawyer with a natural gift for numbers, Daniel would make a fine husband for the fair Miss Winston.

"Am I such a dull dinner companion, Mr. Reed?" He became aware of the voice beside him and the hand on his arm.

Nathan smiled. "Of course not, Miss Hill. You are a most delightful young lady. I am honored to be your partner." What had happened to his good senses? He must keep his mind on his dinner companion.

Her pink-tinged lips pouted. "You'd never know by the attention you've lent me the past few minutes. I do believe you were off somewhere else rather than here."

Nathan felt the heat rise in his own cheeks. "I apologize, Miss Hill. My mind indeed strayed when it should be focused on my lovely companion."

"I accept your apology. I was inquiring as to how long you supposed you might stay in Briar Ridge."

Nathan had no answer to that. Everything hinged on how long it would take to sell Mrs. Cargill's property and settle her estate. He had run into a few unexpected glitches just in the last few days. "Only time will tell, Miss Hill. I do hope it will be long enough for me to call on you."

She batted her long, fringed lashes at him. "I think that would be a fine idea, Mr. Reed. You might ask my father before the evening is over."

And he would, but even as he made plans with Amy Hill, his thoughts filled again with Rachel Winston. He cut his gaze toward her as she bent her head toward Daniel. She was such a direct contrast to the fair-haired girl beside him. Both young women had complexions he'd heard referred to as "peaches and cream," although he couldn't see what fruit and milk had to do with one's skin.

Still, Rachel's dark hair and blue eyes set her apart and caused all others to pale in comparison. He had escorted women with blue eyes on more than one occasion, but never had he seen anyone whose eye color was so close to that of the sapphire ring Mrs. Monroe wore.

Amy spoke again. "Daniel says you and he were friends in college."

Nathan laughed. "Yes, we were. In fact, we lived together in the dorm at Yale for the time we were in law school."

"How interesting. I've known Daniel all my life, but it's nice to have another male in town." Again she batted her eyelashes.

Nathan smiled inwardly. Such a flirt, this Miss Hill. She didn't fool him for one minute. In her eyes, he was fair game. He wondered how Daniel and Amy would treat him if they knew the truth of his past. Daniel did know Nathan had come from North Carolina to seek his education, but the reason for his coming had been a well-kept secret.

Even if Miss Winston were not the daughter of a minister, his secret built a chasm between them that might not be bridged by polite behavior and good career prospects. Besides, her father would never allow her to date someone not of the faith. He bit the inside of his lip. How long would he harbor this attraction for Miss Winston when he knew it could lead nowhere?

The servants removed the dinner plates and then returned with pastries and coffee. He picked up the smaller dessert fork and, as he did, glanced again toward Rachel. Her gaze locked with his, and he felt chained to the spot. Her eyes held no guile, no flirtation, but simply plain, honest interest. He steeled himself to resist the temptation to return her smile, and his heart groaned in protest. If he believed in praying, his prayer at the moment would be to forget ever having laid eyes on Rachel Winston.

Daniel sat beside Rachel and admired her beauty once more. Perhaps this evening he could find a few minutes to be alone with the Reverend Winston and ask permission to call upon Rachel.

He glanced down the table where Nathan and Amy dined. They did make a handsome couple. Although Daniel had considered her as a possible future mate, Amy's lack of interest in things spiritual had kept him from pursuing a relationship.

He turned his attention to Rachel, a young woman much more suited to his position and beliefs. For a brief moment he saw a flicker of disappointment in her eyes. But it must have been his imagination, as she turned to him with a smile. "You mentioned earlier something about plans for a generating plant in Briar Ridge?"

"Yes. With Hartford so close, we should have no trouble connecting and getting electricity for our city. After all, the Hartford Electric Company is the largest of such facilities in our country. In fact, Father is investigating the possibility of having electricity in the bank within the next year or two if he can negotiate with our town council to have lines extended." And what a boon that would be for their town. More people would likely want to live there and bring in more business.

"How exciting. I know what a convenience electric lights

were in our room at the academy last year. To think we can flip a little switch and have light without matches, gas, or oil."

"Mark my words, it won't be too many years before we have telephones in Briar Ridge too. Father is looking into that invention as well. It would be quite valuable for him to be able to communicate with a bank in another city."

"It's all so amazing, Daniel. I'm glad we'll be around to see all the progress."

"Yes, it does appear that we will soon catch up to some of the larger cities, if not in population, then in modern inventions." The one big drawback at the moment was the fact that Briar Ridge had no connecting rail lines with any of the railroad systems in the state. It was now a three- to four-hour ride by horseback to Hartford, and that created an inconvenience in inclement weather.

Daniel's gaze once again traveled down the table to his friend. "It appears that Amy Hill and Nathan Reed are getting along quite well. She would be quite a match for him. I wouldn't be surprised to see him making several return trips to Briar Ridge."

"Is that why you didn't want Abigail to be attracted to him?"

Daniel's eyes opened wide, and he grinned. "Abigail told you, did she? Well, that's partly the cause." His expression sobered. "The other is that Nathan has no use for things of the church. I'm afraid Father would never allow Abigail to be courted by someone not of our faith."

Beside him, he heard a sharp intake of breath from Rachel. Again that gleam of disappointment flickered then vanished. A disturbing thought came into his mind. Surely Rachel couldn't be interested in Nathan herself. Reverend Winston would never allow it.

Those words sealed her destiny with Mr. Reed, and Rachel could do nothing about it. That must have been the reason for Papa's words in the carriage coming to the dinner. She lifted a forkful of pastry to her mouth and glanced again at the couple. How different things would be if Nathan were a believer.

She and Amy both had fine educations, but Amy's beliefs were much more liberal than Rachel's, especially on women's suffrage. Being from the city, Nathan probably appreciated a woman who had more modern views, as Amy did. Even if he were involved in things of the church, Rachel might not prove to be interesting enough for him after meeting Amy.

Rachel sighed and ate a bite of the layered torte covered with a rich creamy sauce, but it may as well have been paper. In her disappointed state the pretty dessert had no appeal.

From the corner of her eye she noted the couple as Amy bent closer to Nathan and said something that caused him to smile. A pinpoint of jealousy pricked Rachel's heart even with Daniel sitting beside her. How rude she must appear. What had happened to her manners? With a small sigh of resignation, she turned her attention back to her escort.

After dinner the guests again congregated in the parlor and drawing room. Daniel led Rachel over to Nathan and Amy Hill. As Daniel chatted with Amy, Nathan turned his attention to her for the moment.

"Miss Winston, Daniel has informed me that you attended

Bainbridge Academy for Young Women in Hartford. That is an excellent finishing school." His brown eyes regarded her with interest.

Heat rose in Rachel's cheeks. "Yes, it was. I learned so much there."

"And what was your major course of study?"

Rachel swallowed hard and hesitated with her answer. Her studies seemed trivial in light of his law degree. "I studied French, music, and domestic science courses."

"What was your favorite class?"

She blushed. "I would have to say floral arranging and entertaining. I love to see people enjoy each other's company over a beautiful table, as we did tonight."

He laughed. "There is nothing more important to women than presiding over coveted social events."

Was it her imagination, or did his gaze reveal increased interest in her? She turned to Daniel. "I think I need some fresh air." Anything to move away from the temptation of more conversation with Nathan Reed.

"Of course. If you'll excuse us, Nathan, Miss Hill." He grasped Rachel's arm and led her to the French windows overlooking the terrace in back of the house.

The cool air refreshed Rachel and stilled the warmth that had grown in the presence of Nathan. Here she had wonderful, loyal Daniel at her side, and she was attracted to a man who did not share either her background or her most cherished beliefs. What was the matter with her?

Chapter
Five

Rachel finished her chores after the noon meal then reached into the cupboard for the floral tea set and placed it on the table. Abigail had promised to come over this afternoon because there had been no time to talk since the dinner party.

While the water heated for the tea, Rachel placed a dozen cookies on a plate. Remembering what Daniel told her at the dinner party on Friday, she had not been surprised when Mr. Reed did not attend church Sunday with the Monroe family. She paused with a cookie in hand and knitted her brow. She must erase all thoughts of him from her mind, but no matter how hard she tried, she could not rid herself of his image.

Despite his lack of regard for things of the church, Rachel found herself drawn to Mr. Reed in a way she'd never experienced. She had abandoned her hopes of attracting him away from Amy, but still Rachel wanted to know more about him. His eyes seemed to hint of sadness that spoke of a deep hurt.

Oh, he hid it with his smiles and talk, but she saw right through that to the intense pain smoldering behind the façade.

Although he had been someone else's dinner partner, she couldn't escape the electricity that passed through her every time he glanced her way. Rachel sighed. That should serve as another warning. If he couldn't concentrate on the lovely Amy Hill, he must have what Papa called a "roving eye." Such behavior would never be tolerated by her parents, no matter what his faith or background.

The water came to a boil in the teakettle. She shook off her confusion and poured the hot liquid over the tea ball to let it steep. Nothing like a cup of mint tea and Mama's sugar cookies to soothe the nerves and calm her emotions. The dried herb Mama added to her tea leaves gave off a delightful aroma that filled the kitchen and mingled with that of cinnamon and sugar lingering after their bake session this morning. Someday Rachel would have her own herb garden, but until she could meet a suitable young man, her duty lay here. Even now Mama was bringing in the clothes they had washed earlier in the day, and although Rachel offered her help, Mama insisted she prepare for Abigail's visit.

Rachel hung her apron on the hook in the pantry, then strolled into the parlor. She straightened a knickknack, fluffed a pillow on the sofa, and walked to the window. No sign of Abigail yet. Her hand stayed on the lace curtain as she peered out at the street. When they had first arrived in town, the church and parsonage sat on the eastern edge of Briar Ridge with not much else around. Now houses lined both sides of the street, and it seemed each one had children or young teenagers in the family.

The scene reminded her of how she and Abigail had been the only ones their age for much of their school years.

The Monroe family owned the bank, the hotel, and a dry goods store. Their wealth exceeded others by a good margin and had been instrumental in bringing Reverend Winston to Briar Ridge all those years ago. Although Papa's ministerial wages were not high, the Winston family lived quite comfortably in the manse provided by the congregation.

She sighed and returned to the deep green sofa. Running her hand over the brocade surface, she saw once again the care Mama had taken to decorate this house. On a strict budget, she had chosen pieces to add to what she already owned and furnished a home that mirrored her charm and practicality. This room reflected good taste in its tapestry chairs that matched the sofa, rosewood tables, and glass lamps hand-painted with roses.

Rachel picked up her needlepoint and began work on the floral design. If she kept her fingers busy, perhaps time would go more quickly.

Mama spoke from the doorway, a basket of clothing in her hands. "Dear, I'm going up to put these things away, then lie down for a spell. Did you make refreshments for Abigail?"

"Yes, ma'am. I prepared a tray with tea and some of those cookies we baked this morning."

"That's fine. If I'm not back down when the children return from school, come wake me, please."

"I will." She gazed after her mother. Mama rested more often than usual lately. Rachel noticed how fatigue filled her eyes in the afternoon. Her mother worked hard without any servants to help. Rachel had taken on more of the chores as Papa suggested, but perhaps she and Miriam should take on even more of the household tasks to relieve Mama of the burden.

She remembered the tea and went to check on it. The pot still felt warm, but she added a little of the hot water from the pot on the stove. Papa liked to have a cup of herb tea whenever he happened to come home during the day, so Mama made sure the kettle stood ready to make it for him.

The knocker clanged on the front door, and Rachel raced to open it. "Oh my, Abigail, I'm so glad to see you." She reached for her friend's hand and all but pulled her inside.

"Rachel Winston, that's the second time in a week you've yanked me inside like this. I'm glad to see you too, but let me at least remove my cloak and bonnet." Abigail removed her hand from Rachel's clutches and flexed it. She reached up and untied her bonnet strings. "As if I didn't know why you're so anxious to visit today."

Rachel helped Abigail with her coat, then hung it on the hall tree. "You know me as well as Mama and Papa, but I pray they don't sense my interest in Nathan Reed. Papa would never approve."

Abigail sat on one of the upholstered chairs and arranged her skirts. "I'm afraid what I have to tell you won't make you feel any better."

Rachel's breath caught in her throat. What else could be wrong? She settled on the sofa and picked up one of the pillows and hugged it to her chest. "I knew it. He's fallen for Amy Hill."

"No, that's not it." Abigail's mouth drew into a frown.

Rachel jumped up. "Let me fetch the tea and cookies. Things always look brighter over tea." Besides, that would prolong the news Abigail had to share. If it was as bad as she intimated, then

Rachel wasn't sure she wanted to hear it. Dozens of scenarios ran through her mind as she poured hot tea into the china cups. Did he have someone in Hartford? Did he have some awful disease? Could he be a dishonest man? Had he truly fallen for Amy Hill? She shoved away those thoughts. If anything bad were true, Mr. and Mrs. Monroe wouldn't have honored him so.

She bit her lip, returned to the parlor with a tray, and set the refreshments on the marble-topped table in front of the sofa. Abigail reached for one of the cups and smiled. "It's not really anything drastic, but it will make a difference."

A difference in what? Rachel's hand trembled as she poured tea. Abigail held her saucer with the cup of tea until Rachel had poured hers. "Now, tell me your news."

"First of all, he was called back to Hartford. A wire came for him, and he left early this morning." Abigail sipped her tea and gazed at Rachel over the rim.

Rachel's heart sank. Most likely she wouldn't see him again anytime soon. But that in itself wasn't news. Nathan would have returned to Hartford anyway. Something else had to be going on.

As if in answer, Abigail said, "I had an opportunity to speak with Mr. Reed yesterday afternoon. I wanted to ask him why he had refused to attend church with us. He told me he didn't have any use for things of God or the church."

Rachel relaxed. That wasn't news to her, but Abigail couldn't know that. "Yes, Daniel told me that. If he could have stayed longer, perhaps we would have had the opportunity to show him God's love."

Abigail frowned. "I'm not so sure that would be possible. I

overheard Daniel and him talking. I really wasn't listening on purpose at first, but then I couldn't seem to stop myself."

"What did they say?" Rachel covered her mouth with her hand. "No, don't. It's not right of me to ask." This must be the real reason for her friend's visit.

"Then I won't tell you." Abigail bit into a cookie.

Curiosity poised like a caged bird ready to take flight in her soul, but Rachel refused to let it loose, even if she were about to burst with wanting to know. She had no right to know what had been meant as a private conversation. Her imagination ran wild again. What if he harbored some deep dark secret that tainted his past? Maybe Daniel knew the truth, and that was what they discussed. She could pray and work with the Lord if the only problem was his lack of faith, but she feared worse. Now his past intrigued her even more, and the bird of curiosity flapped its wings.

Abigail set her cup back on the tray and leaned forward. "I think you need to know this even though you say your only interest is to guide him to the Lord. He told Daniel that you would be a good marriage match for my brother, but as for him, he'd pledged in college to stay away from young women who were believers."

Curiosity thumped to the bottom of the cage in defeat. She slumped against the back of the sofa. "Oh, Abigail, how awful. What are we going to do? I like Daniel, but I don't care for him in the way a woman should for a man who is courting her with marriage in mind."

"I understand that, but it might be better if you simply forget your fascination for Mr. Reed and give Daniel a chance since he does have feelings for you." Abigail reached for her cup again and one of the cookies. "And I would love to have you as my sister-in-law."

"But Abigail, he's like a brother to me. I've known him almost all my life." Indeed, she had crossed him off her list right away. Having him as an escort for various occasions would be fine with her, but to seriously think of marriage, never. Somehow she must convey that to him without hurting his feelings or losing his friendship.

"Yes, and he's a wonderful man," Abigail said. "He's smart too. Father is very proud of the way Daniel fit right in with the law firm here. Having a lawyer in the family is always good for his business at the bank. I think Papa is counting on Daniel for free advice. Anyway, you won't find a better man in all of Briar Ridge."

Rachel stood and walked to the mantel. She picked up a porcelain figurine of a man and woman in colonial dress. "That's true, and I do care for him, but like a brother, as I said." She placed the couple back on the mantel and turned to face Abigail. "Why does life have to become so complicated once we reach our age?"

Abigail laughed. "Oh my, it's only complicated if you make it that way. And thinking of Nathan Reed as any more than Daniel's friend *will* complicate it." Abigail sipped her tea. She tilted her head to the side. "At least you have Daniel interested in you. Who is there around for me? George Simmons is the only other young man our age in town."

That was true enough. Because of his ill health, George had not been considered as a possible suitor for either young lady. Rachel had to admit he was usually pleasant to be around, but he had no imagination and at times could be most boring.

Her aunt's letter came to mind. She supposed she could tell Abigail the news as long as she left out Abigail's part in the plans. "Last week I received a letter from Aunt Mabel. She has invited me to come to Boston for the social season, but Papa insists that I wait. He said a trip might be possible when the weather improves and travel is less precarious."

A smile lighted Abigail's face. "Oh, that's marvelous. What a grand time you will have. But then why are you interested in Nathan Reed?"

A very good question, and one for which she had no clear answer. "I suppose it's because he's new and interesting. Of course, with the fact that he's not of our faith, I must quit entertaining thoughts about him." She sighed and sat on the sofa again. "I wish love could be simple and easy to understand."

"This reminds me of our school days when you had dreams about Laurence Keys."

"I remember, but then he up and married after school and headed out for Kansas." She broke a cookie in half, watching the crumbs fall to the plate. "This is different. I see sadness in Nathan."

"I've seen it too. It's as though some mystery or secret is there that he isn't willing to share."

A ruckus at the door cut off any further conversation. The noise announced the arrival of her siblings. Micah raced through the double doors and jumped onto Rachel's lap.

Abigail stood with her hand on her chest. "Gracious. School is out already. Mother will be expecting me home."

Miriam burst in with her hands on her hips. "I told you not to run, Micah."

"It's all right this time." Rachel snuggled the boy in her

arms. She loved the smell of the outdoors and fresh air clinging to his clothes and hair. Then she held him away from her. "My, your cheeks are red. Must be getting colder."

Rachel deposited her brother on the floor, then followed Abigail to the front hallway. "I'm so glad you came by. We must visit again soon. I miss our regular afternoon talks."

Abigail pulled on her cloak and fastened it. "I do too, but it seems we don't have as much free time now that we're home and not sharing a room at school."

"We'll have to make arrangements to meet at least once a week for chats like we had today." She hugged Abigail then closed the door after her.

Rachel turned to Micah and Miriam. "We made cookies this morning. Go on to the kitchen and have some, but no more than two each. We don't want to spoil your supper."

Noah poked his head around the doorway. "You always say that, but it shouldn't include me."

Rachel laughed. "No, I guess not. I know nothing will spoil your appetite." Then she spoke in lower tones. "When you go upstairs, be very quiet. Mama is lying down. I don't think she's feeling well."

The three nodded and disappeared through the door to the kitchen. Rachel gathered up the teacups and plates and placed them on the tray. Mama had said to waken her when the children arrived home, but Rachel didn't want to disturb her just yet. She carried the tray to the kitchen where her brothers and sister now sat with glasses of milk and cookies.

"Remember what I said about not spoiling supper. Two for each of you." At Noah's crestfallen look, she laughed. "All right, you can have more, but two extra should be enough."

Rachel left them to their refreshments and made her way upstairs. At her mother's door, she paused, worry knitting her brow. She needed a talk with Mama, but she hesitated to awaken her. Finally she tapped on the door with her knuckles. "Mama, may I come in?"

A weak voice carried through from the room. "Of course, dear."

She opened the door to find the drapes had been drawn. Rachel peered through the darkness. A weight of fear came over her as she hurried to her mother's side. "Mama, are you all right?"

"I'm a little tired, that's all. Did you need something? I thought I heard the others arrive from school." She sat up in the bed. "I must be about preparing supper."

"They're having cookies and milk downstairs. I...I wanted to talk with you if you have a moment."

Mama patted the rose-patterned coverlet on the bed. "I'm never too tired or busy for a visit from you, dear. Have a seat, and tell me what's on your mind."

Rachel moistened her lips and sat next to her mother. How should she begin? She decided to plunge ahead. "Mama, I wanted to speak with you about Nathan Reed."

Mama nodded. "I thought I saw a spark of interest whenever his name is mentioned, but what is the problem?"

Rachel picked at a piece of lint on her skirt. "He told Daniel he has no use for things of the church."

"Yes, your father told me that. He asked Daniel about him after he failed to attend church this past Sunday." Mama frowned and pursed her lips. "That isn't good, and you must not let your own attraction overshadow your common sense."

Rachel's throat constricted, and she swallowed hard. "I understand, but I want him to know the Lord and have the assurance of eternity in heaven."

Mama reached up to stroke Rachel's hair. "That's a noble thought, but you mustn't pursue the young man and try to convert him. You don't know enough about his background to know why he feels as he does. Any change in that must come naturally from the Lord. You can't force your beliefs on Mr. Reed."

Mama had so much wisdom. She'd have to let the Lord handle the situation, but it would be nice if He let her be part of it. Rachel hugged her mother then leaned back. Once again fear lodged itself in her heart at the sight of Mama's pale face and dark-circled eyes. "You rest a while longer. I'll go down and prepare supper. I'll send Miriam up for you when it's ready."

"Thank you, dear." Mama's voice sounded even weaker than earlier as she lay back down. Rachel hoped she hadn't depleted what little energy Mama had.

When Mama settled on the pillow and closed her eyes, Rachel tiptoed from the room. Her mother had to be all right. If Mama became ill, all responsibility would fall on Rachel, and she'd never be able to do as good a job as Mama.

Rachel descended the stairs and considered her mother's advice. She had no idea what the Lord had planned for Nathan, but Rachel did know God didn't want any of His children to perish without Him. If only she could match her mother's wisdom with patience, life would be easier, but patience was one virtue she had yet to achieve. At the moment she had no other choice but to wait for the Lord to work in His own time.

Nathan closed the folder on which he had worked since his early-afternoon return and shoved it across his desk. He glanced at the file cabinet on the wall next to him. It seemed wills and probates took up more of his time these days at Fitzpatrick, Clements, and Stone. Such affairs filled most of his hours, and sometimes he longed for a situation in which he could use the argumentative skills he had worked so long and hard to develop at Yale. Still, people's deaths did put money in his pockets. He fared better than some of his classmates who had chosen to go on their own to practice law instead of joining an established firm.

He had been most fortunate. With its population nearing the one hundred thousand mark, Hartford had much to offer him in the way of clients, friends, and, best of all, ladies. The city had more than its share of young women his age. Indeed, he received many invitations to social events where he met them. Even tonight he would call on one of them to take her to dinner and the theater.

The chimes from the clock in the reception area reminded him that he must leave now in order to arrive at the Harrington home in time for his evening with Miss Harrington. He waved good-bye to the firm's secretary and headed outside into the frigid air. Snow from a recent storm still covered the sidewalks, although most of it now lay in clumps of gray slush. At least the city did keep the streets clear for navigation by horse and carriage.

Nathan braved the six-block walk to his boarding house in a chill wind, thankful for his heavy coat and woolen neck scarf.

He tried to think ahead to the evening with Miss Harrington, but the cold seemed to freeze his brain. If it were not for his social engagement, a warm bed and a good book would be his choice on such a night.

Although Miss Harrington's beauty provided an excellent asset, her somewhat inane conversations offset her natural charms. No matter, her father held great influence among those clients Nathan wished to win to the law firm. He could endure the lady's company if it meant a new client or two on his credit.

When he walked through the door into the vestibule where he lived, warm air seeping in from other rooms greeted him. He mentally thanked his landlord for the heating system installed in the boardinghouse.

Nathan bounded up the bare, wooden stairs to his second-floor flat and unlocked the door. His hat landed on the bed covered by a patchwork quilt, and he draped his coat over a ladder-back chair. Only one room with sparse furnishings, but it served him quite well. Most meals were taken in the big dining room downstairs, but tonight he'd dine on restaurant fare.

After changing into attire suitable for both dinner and the theater, Nathan shrugged on his coat and picked up hat, gloves, and woolen neckpiece to brave the cold once again. A hansom cab waited at the appointed time by the curb. He'd spent more than he had planned on such a luxury, but tonight the extra expense would be worth it.

At the Harrington home, Nathan waited in the foyer and noted the elegance of the surroundings. The marble floor glistened in the glow from the electric lighted chandelier, as did the finely polished oak banister on the stairway. Nathan swallowed hard when Mr. Harrington stepped through the double doors on the right.

"Good evening, Mr. Reed. My daughter shall be down shortly." His mustache twitched as he grinned and extended his hand in greeting.

"Thank you, sir. It's an honor to escort her to dinner."

"Yes, yes." He nodded, then stroked the short beard covering his chin. "I plan to come by your offices tomorrow if you have time to see me."

"Of course. I'll be free in the morning." Even if he wasn't, he'd make the time for this man. Harrington could be the first of many important contacts.

The man's gaze shifted to Nathan's right. When Nathan turned, he observed Alice Harrington descending the steps. Her red-gold tresses shone in the glow from lighted sconces gracing the wall along the stairway. He heard the soft rustle of silk as she glided across the marble tiles to his side.

"Good evening, Mr. Reed."

"Good evening to you, Miss Harrington." He bowed slightly. "You look exceptionally lovely tonight."

She fluttered her eyelashes and smiled. "Thank you."

Nathan's thoughts suddenly went back to Amy Hill. Two ladies with the same initials, the same beauty, and the same flirtatious eyes. Was it simple coincidence, or unconscious choice in order to forget blue eyes and raven hair?

A servant appeared holding a fur-lined cape and gloves. Nathan shoved the question from his mind, retrieved the cloak, and placed it around Alice's shoulders. "If you'll excuse us, Mr. Harrington, we'll be on our way."

The stout man stepped back. "Of course." He smiled at his daughter. "Have a fine evening, my dear."

A few minutes later they sat in the cab headed for the restaurant. Nathan tucked a blanket into the corners of the seat. "I do hope you will be warm enough."

Again Alice batted her lashes against her cheeks, then gazed at him with wide-open green eyes. "With both my cloak and this blanket, I am quite comfortable, thank you."

Nathan's usual gift for conversation seemed to have disappeared. It wasn't that he didn't know what to say, but for some reason he didn't feel like small talk. Still, manners called for it. He tried in vain to recall what he knew about her from their encounter several weeks ago at another social gathering.

Alice smoothed out the bow formed by the ends of the sheer fabric covering her hair. "How was your trip for Mrs. Cargill?"

Nathan started. She remembered what he had said and where he had been. "Quite productive. Everything went well. Briar Ridge is a quaint little town."

"I wouldn't know. We haven't spent much time in smaller places. I much prefer New Haven, Hartford, or Boston. Small towns are rather boring, don't you think?"

Boring? Far from it. Briar Ridge had proved to be most interesting. Of course, it wouldn't hold the interest of a lady of Miss Harrington's standing. But at least she wasn't on his list of women he wouldn't court.

Alice's lips bowed into a pout. "Mr. Reed?"

"I'm sorry, my mind wandered there for a moment." If he were to be successful at his line of work, he must pay more attention to young women like Alice Harrington.

"Mr. Reed, I was saying my father is quite interested in

your law firm. Mrs. Cargill had nothing but high praises for you and how you handled her affairs. He and Mother discussed it at length the other night during dinner. I think that's why he wants to see you tomorrow."

All other thoughts and images left his mind. His goal loomed within reach. As a bonus, a lovely woman sat at his side. She could be the source of many pleasant evenings. Indeed, if he wanted to impress Mr. Harrington, all attention must be centered on the opportunities here in Hartford and not on what transpired in Briar Ridge. He smiled and turned his full attention to the attractive young woman at his side.

CHAPTER SIX

For the second morning in a row, Mama had not come down for breakfast. Rachel prepared oatmeal for her siblings and eggs for her father. A worried frown creased his face when he appeared in the kitchen. She opened her mouth to speak but snapped it closed when Papa shook his head.

Concern filled his eyes, and his gaze locked with hers for a moment before he turned away and spoke to Micah. "How's my fine young man doing this morning? Are you ready for school?"

Rachel turned back to the stove to fill her father's plate. Something must be terribly wrong. She served the meal without thinking about it, her thoughts fogged with worry over her mother. When Noah, Miriam, and Micah departed, Rachel sat down beside her father. "Papa, what is it? Is Mama still feeling ill?"

"Yes, my dear, and I'm worried. I'm going over to Dr. Thornton's straightway and ask him to drop by and see her. She is much too pale and has no strength at all this morning." He peered at Rachel from behind steel-rimmed glasses. "Can you take over her duties for a few more days?"

Rachel reached over and hugged her father. "Of course I can. Mama had the meals for the week planned like she always does. It'll be easy to fix them for us. I'll see to the dusting and the laundry too. In fact, I'll go up and tell Mama now not to worry because I can do all the chores."

Papa's sigh of relief touched Rachel. No matter how little she really knew about running a household, she would do her very best and assure her mother that everything would be taken care of.

Her father stood and placed a hand on her shoulder. "You've become a fine young woman, and I'm very proud of you for stepping in. Your mother will be glad to hear it too, but if she's asleep, don't wake her."

He strode toward the front hall. "I'm going now to fetch the doctor."

She listened for the sound of the front door shutting before turning back to complete the task of clearing the table and washing the dishes. Going for the doctor meant Papa's concern went deeper than he revealed. She bit her lip and decided she must see for herself. After Rachel put away the last of the breakfast dishes, she prepared a tray with two slices of toasted bread and a small cup filled with pear preserves. A cup of tea completed the light breakfast. She hoped her mother would feel up to eating.

Rachel climbed the stairs and stopped outside the bedroom door. Shifting the tray slightly, she knocked. "Mama, may I come in?"

A barely audible sound came from the other side. "Yes, dear, please do."

Inside the room, darkness again lay over the scene. Rachel shivered in the cool air. She set the tray on a bedside table and lit the lamp there. In its light, she peered down at her mother. Her eyes appeared as two dark sockets on an ashen face. Lines of fatigue crossed her brow. Fear wrapped its tentacles around Rachel's heart. What if something was seriously wrong with her mother?

She mustn't let Mama see her concern. "I brought you some tea and toast, Mama. We missed you at breakfast, and I thought we could have a few minutes now while you eat."

Her mother's hand reached across the quilt and clasped Rachel's. "I'm so sorry I couldn't come down and prepare the meal for everyone. I just don't seem to have any energy left in me. Can you help me with the chamber pot?"

"Of course, Mama." Rachel reached over to help her sit up, then brought over the vessel from its place in the corner. When she finished, Rachel helped her mother back into bed.

Rachel set the covered pot back in the corner. "I'll take this down with me and clean it for later. I do hope you'll eat a little. It will help restore some strength." Although from her mother's appearance, Rachel could see it would take more than a few meals to bring her mother back to good health.

Mama ate a few bites of toast and sipped her tea. Her hands shook ever so slightly when she set the cup back on its saucer. A chill inched its way down Rachel's back. What if Mama were more seriously ill than they first thought? A tear spilled down Rachel's cheek. Quickly she wiped it away and blinked to keep any more from escaping.

"Mama, don't you worry about a thing. I can take care of the meals, and Noah and Miriam can help with other chores." She'd sit them down and give them instructions this afternoon. They must be told of Mama's illness.

Mama shook her head. "Oh, my sweet girl, I don't want to burden you with all those responsibilities. I'm sure I'll feel much better in the morning."

That wasn't going to happen, but Rachel kept silent. When she decided her mother wasn't going to eat or drink anymore, she covered the remains on the tray with a napkin. "I'll take this down along with the chamber pot and leave you to rest." She bent over and kissed her mother's pale cheek.

Mama simply nodded then closed her eyes. Rachel set the tray on a table. She picked up a poker and stoked the logs in the fireplace to increase the heat and ward off the chill. When the flames blazed higher, she tiptoed from the room, first removing the tray, then the chamber pot. Downstairs she set the tray on the counter, then continued on to the outhouse.

As she completed her chore, Rachel envisioned the new homes being built with a separate room for such necessities as bodily functions and cleansing oneself. She hoped the mayor's idea of digging and placing sewer lines throughout the city would come to fruition soon. Even then, she doubted Papa could justify the expense of such a luxury.

Rachel sighed and hurried back into the house to get out of the cold. A few minutes later she heard the front door open and men's voices. Papa was home with the doctor. She washed her hands, dried them, and then hurried to greet the men. The two stood at the bottom of the stairway.

"Oh, Dr. Thornton, how good of you to come. Mama hardly

ate anything when I took tea and toast up a little while ago." Rachel reached out to greet him.

He grasped her hand. "I came right away when the reverend explained her condition."

Papa removed his coat. "He's going up to examine her. Could you prepare fresh coffee for us and have it ready when we come down?"

"Yes, I'll start on that now and have it here whenever you need it." Rachel turned back to the kitchen. Coffee was not one of her strong suits. She didn't really know how it should taste, as she drank only tea, but she had seen Mama do it enough to try it herself.

The next half hour was spent preparing the brew using the little measuring device she'd seen her mother use to make coffee. In a few minutes the aroma filled the room. At least it smelled like coffee should; she only hoped it tasted as good. She searched in the cupboard to find suitable cups. Her mother's china seemed much too dainty for Papa and the doctor. Finally she chose the crockery cups on the middle shelf and pulled them down.

Ezra held Felicity's hand as Doctor Thornton examined her. "How long have you been feeling weak, Mrs. Winston?"

Felicity coughed and said, "Well, maybe a month or so."

Ezra bit his lip. Why had he not noticed her condition before these past few weeks? She had gone about her responsibilities with nary a complaint. But that was Felicity. She never wanted to let people know she was not up to full strength.

Dr. Thornton listened to her heart, checked her pulse again, and shook his head. "I've been reading in some journals about a condition caused by lack of iron in the blood. Her symptoms fit the articles I've read."

Ezra's brow furrowed and his heart thumped. "What does this mean? Can you treat it?"

The doctor removed his glasses. "It means she will need rest." He reached for Felicity's hand. "My dear, I suspect your body is undergoing changes that occur as women come to the end of their childbearing years."

Felicity's eyes opened wide. "Oh, I've been having a great deal of blood loss in recent months. Could that be part of it?"

"Most definitely, because it would lower your red blood cell count." He raised his eyebrows and tilted his head. "Now, you will need to eat good, healthy foods. This is no time to skip meals because you don't feel up to eating. Make yourself eat, and I will prescribe a tonic that will help the blood build itself back up."

Ezra brushed Felicity's hair from her brow. "How long will it take for her to get better?"

The doctor closed his bag then wrote something on a white pad. He handed it to Ezra. "I'd say four to six weeks of rest, good eating, and this tonic will be sufficient."

"Don't worry, dear. Rachel is quite capable of taking care of your household responsibilities. She's done a fine job so far." She had surpassed even his expectations with the way she had taken charge of her brothers and sister in the past week. Even her cooking had improved.

"I'm sure she will, but I hate for her to have such responsibilities at her age. Of course, I will help her all I can from here."

Dr. Thornton picked up his bag and smiled at Felicity. "I'm sure you'll be a good patient and be up and about in no time." He turned to Ezra. "Just be sure to get that tonic started as soon as you can."

"I'll take care of it this afternoon." Ezra leaned down to kiss Felicity's cheek. "You do what the doctor says and get your rest now. I will bring a tray up for you and expect you to eat well. No excuses. Promise?"

"I promise. Be sure to tell Rachel to come to me if she has any questions or needs help."

"I will." He followed the doctor from the room. Although concern still laced his soul, with the Lord's healing hand and Rachel's care, Felicity would be fine.

The sound of voices drifted in from the hallway. Rachel hastened to fill the cups with steaming liquid and retrieved two muffins from the bread box on the counter. The coffee looked a little dark, but its aroma tickled her senses like it always did when Mama made it. She couldn't understand why something that smelled so good should taste so bad.

Papa pushed through the door. "Ha, I see you do have everything ready." He picked up a ginger muffin sprinkled with sugar. "Hmm, one of my favorites."

He tasted the muffin then smiled and nodded his approval. That was good, but was he planning to share Mama's condition or just leave Rachel to guess? Dr. Thornton picked up his cup, and she waited, barely breathing, for him to taste and comment or react.

The doctor downed a big swallow. He lowered the cup and stared straight at Rachel. "A little strong, but mighty tasty for a cold day like this." He took another sip.

Relief flooded Rachel. At least she hadn't ruined it as she had in the past. She stood with her hands folded in front of her. Her gaze flitted from one man to the other. Neither appeared very happy. Scenarios of her mother being extremely ill or dying raced through her mind. Finally she could bear it no longer. "What is wrong with Mama?"

Papa set his cup down. "Tell her what you explained to me."

Dr. Thornton brushed crumbs from his vest. "Well, now, it seems your mother has become severely anemic. That means her blood doesn't have enough red blood cells. Her pulse is somewhat slow too, but that in itself isn't bad. It just combines with the other to leave your mother without much energy."

Rachel stared at the doctor and gripped her hands together. What did this all mean? How long would Mama be ill? Rather than pound the doctor with these questions, she asked, "What do I need to do to help her?"

Papa leaned forward. "She must rest and take the medication Dr. Thornton prescribed. We'll also have to make sure she eats properly. I'll leave that to you, and I'll ride over to the apothecary and pick up the medicine."

Rest for Mama meant work for Rachel, but whatever tasks must be done, God would help her. Miriam and Noah would do their part too once they knew of Mama's illness.

Papa cleared his throat. "Rachel, Dr. Thornton, I suggest we pray for Felicity and her recovery right now." He reached over and grasped Rachel's hand. "Heavenly Father, our dear wife and mother lies up in her bed ill and weak. We seek Thy healing hand to be on her to restore the strength and vitality she's always had. She is Thy child and Thy servant, and Lord, Thou dost know how much she means to all of us. Protect her and guard her from further illness. Thy will be done in her life. We also pray for strength for dear Rachel as she takes over the tasks of providing for the rest of us. Give her a cheerful heart. We pray in Thy name. Amen."

Her father's deep voice and confident faith gave her courage. In this time of sacrifice she would do everything God gave her to do without complaint or argument.

Nathan removed his hat and coat and laid them across the back of the chair in his room. Mr. Harrington had been true to his word. He had visited Nathan's office, and now the firm had two new clients. If things went well with Mr. Harrington's personal affairs, he planned to hand over his business affairs as well. That meant more money for the firm, and Nathan hoped he'd be up to the task.

He picked up his last letter from Amy. She spoke of a great celebration in Briar Ridge planned to commemorate its founding and invited Nathan to join her. He pictured Amy and her fair beauty. Unfortunately it seemed so shallow. It didn't reach her heart as Rachel's did.

His hand jerked the letter, and Nathan blinked. Why had Rachel popped in uninvited like that? He'd managed to put her out of his thoughts since his date with Alice Harrington. But Amy Hill might be the better choice, as her father was quite influential in Briar Ridge.

Another trip to see his friend looked even more favorable now. He'd go tomorrow to see Amy and let her know he'd like to attend the Founder's Day gala with her as well as spend some time with her. He could leave early tomorrow and be in Briar Ridge in time to conduct one last bit of business concerning Mrs. Cargill's estate.

However, even as he planned to see Amy, Rachel would not leave his thoughts. Every time he pictured her, he saw the peace that shone through her eyes. Four years ago he had prayed for such a peace, but God had ignored his pleas.

He laid a valise on his bed and stuffed in a few items of clothing to take with him. The papers he needed lay secure in his satchel. With the nice weather of the past few days, the ride to Briar Ridge would be rather pleasant. He mentally checked his schedule for tomorrow morning, pleased that nothing pressing appeared for the afternoon.

As Nathan lay in bed, sleep eluded him. The words of the senior partner came to his mind and hovered there like a black cloud before a thunderstorm. Mr. Fitzpatrick had suggested that it was time for Nathan to be thinking of marriage. Married men gained more confidence from their prospective clients. Even though Mrs. Cargill had lauded Nathan's work, the men in charge deemed it better for him to have a wife.

He spent a restless night of considering Fitzpatrick's advice and thinking of the differences in Amy Hill, Alice Harrington, and Rachel Winston. Amy would be the proper choice for a wife, and marriage didn't have to be built on love. But then Alice had her good points also. When he finally fell asleep, his dream was a confusion of women's faces. He woke exhausted.

After a few hours in the office, Nathan sat astride his horse, headed toward Briar Ridge. Again his thoughts meandered over the young women he had met in the past few weeks. Any of them could be a gracious and capable hostess. Amy Hill, although beautiful, had little on her mind but frivolities and herself. Alice Harrington, on the other hand, had proven to be quite different than he first thought. She had both beauty and brains, but without that spark of life he had noticed in Rachel Winston. He admired Rachel's gracious manner and the pure joy in her face every time he had seen her. What made Rachel so different from the other two?

He stopped at an inn near an apple orchard for a late lunch. As he entered the establishment, rich aromas of apples and cinnamon as well as that of good, old-fashioned home cooking tickled his senses. A young woman showed him to a table and pointed toward a slate board with menu items printed on it.

"My name is Faith Anderson, and those are our specialties. If you would like to see additional foods, I can bring you a sheet with them on it."

He glanced at the board and shook his head. "What I see there is fine. I'll have the stew, bread, coffee, and apple dumplings."

Nathan gazed about at the homey atmosphere with red-and-white-checked curtains and tablecloths. A fire blazed on the hearth, and through an opening at the back he spotted shelves and racks of apple products. Through the window by his table, he saw row upon row of apple trees now bare of leaf and fruit. In a few months the field would be a cloud of white blossoms. Then in the fall, luscious red fruit would burden the limbs. No wonder the menu here contained so many dishes with apples as an ingredient.

Faith returned in a few minutes with a steaming bowl of thick, hearty stew and a chunk of still-warm bread. A mound of butter accompanied the bread. She then poured him a mug of coffee. "Enjoy your meal, sir."

He thanked her and scooped a spoonful of thick sauce laden with meat chunks and potatoes. The food turned out to be delicious and just what he needed on a cold day. Just as he finished the stew, Faith appeared again with the dumpling. It lived up to its appearance and aroma. He made a mental note to stop over here again on his trips to Briar Ridge.

A young man stood by the door as Nathan prepared to leave and pay his tab. "This is a fine establishment," Nathan said to him. "Are you employed here?"

"Yes, my father owns the orchards, and in the winter months I help out when we're open. Did you enjoy your meal?"

"I certainly did, and I'll be returning on future trips. Tell your cook that the apple dumplings are delicious." Nathan shrugged on his coat.

"I will, sir. My sister and mother are the cooks, along with a cousin or two." He extended his hand. "Name's Jonathan." Then he grinned at Nathan's raised eyebrows. "Yes, like the apple. Ma said it was a good biblical name as well, but I do get a reaction every time I tell someone."

Nathan shook hands. "Well, Jonathan, this has been a most pleasant dining experience."

"And it's a pleasure to have you dine with us, and just in time. We'll close down for a few weeks next weekend. Because of the snow and ice this time of year we have fewer customers in the restaurant, but our store remains open."

"That's interesting. Oh, my name is Nathan Reed. I'm

from Hartford on my way to Briar Ridge." His interest in the orchards piqued. "What do you do in the time you are idle?"

Jonathan laughed. "Oh, we're never idle. All the ladies in the family will be busy with preserving, canning, and making things for our store. We keep it open year-round. The men will be taking care of the trees in the orchard and the new ones to be planted. If you're interested in buying any trees, we sell those so you can plant a few of your own."

"That would be nice if I had a house or a farm, but I live in a flat in the city, so I wouldn't have a place for trees. Sounds like a nice idea, though." Nathan wrapped his woolen scarf about his neck and pulled on his gloves. "Thank you again for the hospitality. I must be on my way."

Outside, Nathan pulled his coat tighter. The sun had hidden behind a cloud, and the slight wind chilled him to the bone, but at least he had a warm meal inside. That bode well for the remainder of his trip and the pleasures awaiting in Briar Ridge.

CHAPTER
SEVEN

RACHEL SPENT FRIDAY planning the nourishment her mother required for the next week and deciding what was needed from the mercantile in town. Papa had given her the money to purchase whatever supplies were necessary, so she planned to go into town today. He had offered to go with her, but Fridays were reserved for studying and putting the finishing touches on his sermon for Sunday, so Rachel insisted she could do it alone.

The afternoon sun warmed her shoulders as she walked into the business area of Briar Ridge. The growth in just the years she and Abigail had been in Hartford was amazing. They now had a boutique that featured the latest in ladies' fashions, a new hotel, a bakery that sent tantalizing aromas out into the streets, and a new three-story brick building housing Daniel's law offices, Dr. Thornton's office, and a new dentist.

She entered the store and made her purchases for the week. When she stepped outside, someone called her name. She turned to find Daniel Monroe striding toward her from the bank.

"Rachel, I was planning to come out to see you later today, but now that you're here, I can ask you."

Rachel furrowed her brow. "Ask me what, Daniel?"

His cheeks looked flushed, and he ran his hand over his dark hair. "Well, hmm…well, Founder's Day is coming soon, and I would be honored if I could be your escort for the festivities."

Founder's Day? Rachel had forgotten all about the event. Now that she had responsibilities at home, she had to weigh her decision carefully. Someone must be there to take care of Mama and make sure she didn't try to overdo herself too soon. "I don't know, Daniel. I'll have to speak with Papa since Mama is not well."

Daniel's cheeks turned a deeper shade of red. "Pardon me, but I've already mentioned it to your father. He gave me permission to ask you."

How kind of Daniel. Fewer men these days sought a father's permission before courting a young woman or asking to escort her to a party. "If Papa said yes, then I must do the same. I'd be delighted to be your companion for the event."

Daniel's grin spoke of his pleasure at her answer. "Thank you, Rachel. I'll call upon you later and we can make firmer plans. Right now I must get back to my office."

He whirled around and ran like a man on a mission toward the building housing the law firm. Rachel wanted to laugh but glanced around to see others eyeing her with knowing smiles. Heat rose in her cheeks, and she swallowed her laugh then turned toward home.

A block from home she met Amy Hill. "Good afternoon, Rachel. How is your mother?"

"Still weak, but Doctor Thornton assures us she will be

better soon." Why in the world was Amy asking about Mama's health? Usually she only gave a hint of smile upon meeting and never spoke. Something else must be prompting her interest.

Amy pulled a gloved hand from a furry muff and leaned toward Rachel. "You know, Founder's Day is coming soon. I wrote to Nathan Reed and asked him to escort me to the gala. Perhaps we could all go together."

Rachel clutched the bags of groceries to her side. Nathan coming back for Founder's Day? Go together? "I don't understand."

"Oh, I've noticed the way Daniel looks at you. I'm sure he'll ask you to go with him, if he hasn't already. Since he and Nathan are such good friends, it would be fun to take in all the festivities together."

The idea didn't sit well with Rachel, but to say no would be rude. Then the idea that Amy simply wanted Rachel to see that Nathan preferred sunlight blonde over dark hair popped into her head. A bit of jealousy rolled in her stomach, but Rachel took a deep breath and pushed it aside. "I suppose it would be nice."

"Wonderful. We can talk again Sunday after church and make plans." Amy turned with a flounce of her skirt and crossed the street to where a buggy waited for her.

Rachel stood with narrowed eyes, watching as the vehicle pulled away. At church? The Hill family rarely, if ever, attended church. Now her anger became full blown. *The nerve of Amy.* She had deliberately waited for Rachel to tell her about Nathan. Then Rachel's anger stopped short. Nathan had no interest in courting Rachel, and Amy Hill had every right to be with him on Founder's Day.

Noah waved at her from the front walk of their home. "Rachel, do we have some of your baking waiting for us?" Miriam and Micah stood behind him, just back from school.

Where had the time gone? She had fully planned to be home before her siblings and have their afternoon refreshments ready for them. "I'll have it straightway. Go on inside and put away your belongings."

She hurried to follow her brothers and sister. No time to think about Nathan or Amy Hill. Rachel ran to the kitchen and opened up the tin holding the cookies she had made earlier that morning.

"Hmm, are those your oatmeal raisin cookies? I could eat a dozen." Noah grabbed one from the tin before she could stop him.

"Well, that's one less for you, brother," Rachel scolded. Noah simply grinned and plopped down in a chair. Rachel poured milk into three glasses and placed two cookies on plates for Miriam and Micah. True to her word, she gave Noah only one. He opened his mouth to complain but popped it closed again when she glared at him.

Miriam and Micah joined Noah at the table. Rachel put away the milk and the cookie tin and then the groceries but listened to Micah tell about his day at school. His dark blue eyes danced with mischief. A smile crossed her face. She didn't envy the teacher who had five little boys in her class of first- and second-graders who were all like Micah. When he finished, she'd take him up to see Mama.

Papa stepped into the room. "Rachel, I need to speak with you a moment. Will you come into my study?"

"Of course, Papa." Concern niggled at her heart. Surely

Mama was not worse. "Micah, stay right here, and I'll take you to see Mama when I return."

He nodded with his mouth full of cookie. Rachel blinked her eyes to thwart tears and hurried from the kitchen.

Ezra led the way into the study. "Close the door and have a seat, dear." He settled himself behind his desk. From the look on her face as she took a chair, his daughter expected bad news. He cleared his throat. "Rachel, with your mother's recent illness, I have neglected to tell you how much I appreciate your handling of the household. You are doing an outstanding job."

"Thank you, Papa. I've enjoyed doing it. Well…except when Micah and Miriam won't behave and do as they are asked. Other than that, it has not been a burden." She peered at her father with questions in her eyes. "What else is there? Is Mama worse?"

"Oh, no, my dear, but it may be several weeks before she is well enough to handle any chores." He stroked his short beard. "It's the church. Your mother has several commitments as pastor's wife that she can't fulfill at the moment. Several of the church ladies have approached me about finding someone to take over her duties while she's ill."

Rachel shook her head. "Why should you want to discuss that with me?"

Ezra considered all that his wife did at the church and realized Rachel didn't understand her mother's many duties. "Your mother helps with the altar guild in arranging the flowers and preparing the sanctuary for Sunday services. She also leads the women's missionary society that meets each Monday in the church parlor, and she heads up the visitation committee."

"Why does that concern me, Papa? Surely there are enough women in the church to help with those responsibilities."

Ezra reached over for his pipe. "Mrs. Lewis will lead the missionary society, but Mrs. Monroe has asked that you and Abigail help with the altar guild because you do so well with flowers." He tamped tobacco into the pipe bowl.

Rachel visibly gulped. "You mean take over some of Mother's church duties in addition to the responsibilities here at home? The household already takes all my time." She blinked and bit her lip.

He leaned closer and patted her hand. "My dear, perhaps this is God's way of helping you to become the young woman He wants you to be."

Rachel seemed to consider that for a moment then smiled. "After all you have done for me, I can't say no. If you think I'm capable, I'll do my best to keep Mama's good work going."

He leaned back and lit his pipe. "That is what I had hoped to hear. I'm extremely proud of how you've stepped in and taken charge. You are becoming a capable young woman, and it delights me to have you willing to take on church responsibilities too."

She stood to leave. "Is that all, Papa? I must see to dinner."

"Umm, no, there is one more thing." He puffed on the now-lit pipe, the cherry tobacco scent filling the room.

His stomach rumbled, reminding him of the pot roast cooking for dinner. He needed to let her get back to her duties. He'd also seen bread rising, and that required her attention, but this matter must not be put off. "Mr. Daniel Monroe called on me. He asked about escorting you to the Founder's Day celebration. I gave him my permission for not only that but also for courting you. Do you have a problem with that?"

A measure of doubt seemed to cross her face, but she smiled and came around the desk to hug him. "No, Papa, I don't mind, and I've already told Daniel I would accompany him to Founder's Day."

Papa hugged her in return. "Thank you, dear. I don't think you'll be disappointed in your choice. Now go on about your business for dinner. I've smelled that pot roast for the last hour and am anxious for a sampling."

When she had left the room, Ezra sat back and folded his hands together. Perhaps Daniel would be able to quench that spark of interest he'd seen in Rachel's eyes whenever Nathan Reed was mentioned. He might be an eligible young man with a secure financial future, but Ezra expected much more from a man interested in the daughter of a Winston.

Rachel rushed from the room and back to the kitchen. What an unusual day this had turned into. Wonder of wonders, Papa actually asked her opinion. She saw no need for objection to his telling Daniel that he could call on her. Besides the fact that he seemed more like a brother, Rachel could find no fault in Daniel. True, Nathan was more handsome than Daniel, but he had no serious interest in her as Daniel apparently did. And she owed it to him to give him a chance.

Micah sat at the kitchen table waiting for Rachel. Miriam had washed the glasses and plates, and they sat on the counter waiting for Rachel to dry them. She'd have to thank her younger sister for her thoughtfulness on doing the task without being asked.

"Can we go see Mama now?"

She reached for the cloth covering the bread dough. "Let me punch this down, and I'll take you right up."

A few moments later Rachel knocked on her mother's door. At the weak answer to come in, she opened the door and held Micah's hand as they entered.

"Micah is here to see you, Mama. Do you feel like company?"

"Of course I do. I'll never turn down a visit with my boy. Come here, baby."

Micah tiptoed to Mama's bedside. "I'm sorry you don't feel well, Mama."

"Ah, but your visit will make me feel better."

Rachel hid a smile and stepped from the room. She'd leave them alone and go back down to form her loaves, then come back up and check on them. Micah's visits did seem to make Mama feel better. Miriam and Noah would go in for a visit after dinner. Rachel's heart would be much lighter and filled with less concern on the day Mama could again join them for dinner every night.

Nathan rode into Briar Ridge and headed for the hotel. He would not impose upon the Monroe family this trip. He tethered his horse then entered the hotel to register. The clerk handed him a key to a room on the second floor. After a short climb, Nathan unlocked and entered the room.

He set his valise and satchel on a chair, then made his way to the window. A perfect view of Briar Ridge's main street lay before him. The offices of the real estate broker he needed to see were housed across the way. The light still shone through the window. Nathan picked up his satchel and hurried off to take care of his reason for being here before seeking the company of Amy Hill.

Fifteen minutes later he stood with the signed documents finalizing the sale of Mrs. Cargill's property in his bag. Now he had the whole evening stretching before him. Perhaps he should call upon Miss Hill and accept her invitation to the Founder's Day event tonight rather than tomorrow since the hour was still early.

He returned the satchel with the documents to his room, then tended to his grooming before calling on the Hill home. When he reached the lobby of the hotel, tempting aromas of coffee, pastries, and frying food wafted through to remind Nathan he hadn't eaten dinner. Rather than surprise Amy at the family dinner hour, he opted to eat in the hotel dining room.

After a hearty meal of fried steak, gravy, mashed potatoes, and hot rolls, he was ready to walk the eight blocks to the Hill home. When he arrived, the Hill housekeeper answered the door.

Her eyes opened wide with surprise. "Ah, Mister Reed. Come in. I'll tell Mr. Hill you are here."

He stepped into the entranceway, and the housekeeper disappeared behind one of the paneled doors. Nathan admired the elegant furnishings and the polished brass of the hardware in the lamps and doorknobs. A stairway directly in front of him led up to the second floor. Mr. Hill pushed open the double doors on Nathan's right.

"Nathan Reed. A pleasure to see you again. What brings you here tonight? Could it be my daughter?" The rotund man laughed and shook Nathan's hand.

At that moment Amy appeared in the doorway. When she saw Nathan, a smile lit up her face and eyes. She extended her hand in greeting. "Why, Nathan Reed, what a pleasant surprise to see you. To what do we owe this visit?"

Nathan accepted her hand and bowed his head toward her. "The invitation to attend the Founder's Day event with you. It gave me a desire to see you again and accept your offer in person."

Mr. Hill nodded. "Ah, yes, what a splendid idea." He gestured toward the parlor. "I'll leave you two to discuss your plans. I'll be in my study if you need me."

Amy turned and led Nathan into the parlor, where she sat on the deep maroon velvet sofa. He chose a chair nearby. At this point, propriety was in order. He'd have opportunity sometime in the future to sit closer to this young lady. A chaperone didn't seem to be in evidence until he spotted the figure of the housekeeper in a far corner in the shadows. A smile tweaked the corners of his mouth. Mr. Hill still adhered to the old ways.

He spoke to Amy. "Can you tell me a little about the event which we are to attend?"

"Of course. I've always thought we should wait and have the celebration in the spring after warm weather comes, but our town leaders believe it best to celebrate during the month the town was actually begun. February seems to be much too cold for it, don't you think?"

Nathan could agree with that. He remembered the great events held in his hometown when he was a child. All the booths, food, and music outdoors brought much joy and fun for everyone. He shoved the thoughts aside. His past was to be forgotten, even the good times.

"With the weather usually too cold for outdoor events, we start off with speeches in the city hall meeting room at two o'clock. Then everyone heads to the school, where booths for different games and crafts are set up in the gymnasium. Later, there is a huge buffet dinner back at the city hall, and then there is a dance across the street at the building they use for a theater." Amy folded her hands in her lap and tilted her head. Long eyelashes formed the perfect frame for her green eyes.

Nathan breathed deeply. This was a most beautiful young woman. Temptation loomed, but he must be careful not to pursue her or show too much interest in her until the proper time. "I see. They must plan for the event months in advance."

"Oh, yes. Mother and Father are on the committee, as is Mr. Monroe. It will be the best one so far according to my mother." She paused, then smiled broadly. "We are to go with Rachel Winston and Daniel Monroe. I thought it would be fun since you and Daniel are such good friends."

Nathan swallowed hard. "That would be most enjoyable." But would it? Could he spend an entire day with Rachel and not be attracted to her yet again?

After another half hour of conversation, he said, "I'll travel here on Friday as I did today. Daniel will let you know what time we will pick you up." He stood. "I've taken up enough of your time for one evening. I'll be in town until Sunday afternoon. Perhaps we can meet again tomorrow at your convenience."

She raised her hand to signal the housekeeper. "That would be lovely. If you'll come at noon, you can join us for our meal."

"Thank you, I'd like that." He turned toward the door to see the housekeeper standing there with his coat and hat. How had the woman acted so quickly and quietly?

"Thank you, Esma." Amy turned and smiled broadly.

Nathan grasped his coat and shrugged it on, then took his hat. "I look forward to seeing you tomorrow."

"I do wish you didn't have to leave so soon." She placed her hand in the crook of his arm, and they walked together to the entryway.

A few minutes later he stood on the sidewalk. The fresh air cooled his face after being indoors, and he breathed deeply. Not ready to retire to his room, Nathan decided to explore the town a bit before heading back to the hotel. He admired the homes in the area as he strolled. He knew the Monroe home would be over two streets to the north, but he decided against going that way.

Instead he turned south and shortly found himself standing in front of a neat two-story house with a sign on the post that read BRIAR RIDGE PARSONAGE. The Winston home. He stood and stared at the softly lit windows on the first floor. Lacy curtains hung between darker drapes so that he could see a little of the activity in the room.

Would he see Rachel if he stood here long enough? He compared her dark beauty to the fair hair of Amy's. No matter what he did or vowed to do, he could not rid his mind of Rachel's image. Her quick smile, soft voice, and peaceful eyes pulled him in like a whirlpool.

A chill filled the air and dark shadows gathered around, but he remained rooted to the spot. A movement behind the curtains revealed two figures. He stepped to the side behind a tree trunk and peeked around to glimpse Rachel talking with her brother. He couldn't see any facial expression, but from the body language, they were having fun.

A sigh escaped, creating a vapor cloud in the cold air. Envy filled his heart at the happy family scene. He clenched his hands into fists against his thighs. Why was he standing behind a tree in hopes of catching a glimpse of her? Why did he care so much about Rachel Winston? He swallowed hard and turned away to trudge back to the hotel and its warmth.

CHAPTER
EIGHT

ACHEL CHECKED THE calendar Mama kept in the kitchen
and smiled at the date and notation written there. Saturday,
February 25, Founder's Day. This day in February had become a
time for celebration. She had always enjoyed the festivities, and
this was the first year to participate again since she'd been off to
school. She actually looked forward to spending the day with
Daniel. The only flaw would be having to attend with Nathan
Reed and Amy Hill.

She made her way upstairs to finish dressing and remembered last Saturday when she had happened to see the couple.
On the morning of that day, Rachel had gone into town to pick
up pastries for Sunday breakfast.

After making her purchase, she gathered her bag and headed
outside. Just as she was about to push through the door, her
gaze shifted, and she spotted Amy and Nathan. They walked
arm in arm across the street. His attentive smile toward Amy
had pierced Rachel's heart. To be sure they wouldn't see her, she

waited in the bakery until they were half a block away before hurrying outside and turning toward home.

Rachel entered her room and strode to the looking glass there. Why did jealousy rear its ugly head whenever she thought of Nathan with Amy? Rachel prayed for God to remove such thoughts and help her focus on Daniel instead. She clenched her teeth as she fastened a brooch at her neckline. Today she would be put to the test, because the four of them would be together all through the celebration.

A knock sounded and Miriam's voice followed. "Rachel, Daniel is here."

"Thank you. I'll be right out." Rachel peered at her reflection in the mirror and pinched some color into her cheeks. Oh, to have naturally rosy cheeks like Miriam. Since Papa didn't approve of any type of cosmetics for his daughters, Rachel had to rely on pinching to bring color.

A few moments later Daniel helped with her coat. "Isn't it nice that the weather is cooperating today? The sun is shining, and the temperature is rather mild for this time of year."

Rachel buttoned her coat. "Yes, it will make walking from the town hall to the school and back a pleasure." She smiled, then hooked her hand on Daniel's arm. "I'm sure we'll have a delightful time today."

She turned to Miriam. "Remember that Papa wants us to keep a close eye on Mama. When he finishes saying the prayer at the beginning of the speeches, he will come back so you and Noah may go over to the school." She hated the idea of her sister and brother having to wait, but Papa insisted Rachel should have the whole afternoon and evening with Daniel.

"I remember. I don't mind missing all the speeches and

stuff as long I get to go over for the games." Miriam smiled and hugged Rachel. "Go on and have a good time."

A moment later, Daniel led her out into the sunshine, and they walked the six blocks to the town hall.

When they neared the steps where Amy and Nathan waited for them, Rachel's heartbeat took off like a horse at a derby. She had to get it under control, or she'd never make it through this day. She truly needed the Lord's help to curb her emotions.

Amy smiled, but it seemed to be only skin deep. "It's about time you two arrived. Nathan and I have been waiting for you."

Daniel bowed. "I'm so sorry. You should have gone on in without us." He stepped up toward the door. "I say we get out of this cold air right away."

Nathan shook Daniel's hand in greeting. "It's only been a few seconds actually. We spotted you coming down the walk." He opened the door and held it to let Rachel and Amy enter. Rachel carefully avoided meeting his gaze. Why did he have to be so handsome and polite? She gripped her purse to still her shaking hands.

The murmur of voices greeted them as Nathan led them to four vacant seats, gesturing that Amy should be seated first, then settling in beside her. Rachel hesitated. Should she enter the row to sit by Nathan or let Daniel go first? Stalling for time, she glanced around the room at all the familiar faces. "The room is filling up fast. I had no idea this many would be coming to hear the speeches."

Daniel nudged her forward, and she entered the row, sitting next to Nathan.

Daniel took his place beside her. "The speeches will

probably be boring, but as young adults, it's our duty to support our town."

Rachel nodded, trying to keep her focus on Daniel. "Of course it is, and I'm actually glad this many are interested."

All too aware of Nathan's nearness, Rachel clasped her hands in her lap and made sure her elbows stayed close to her body.

A hush fell over the room as the mayor stood at the podium. "Welcome to the two hundred twenty-sixth anniversary of the founding of Briar Ridge. The Reverend Winston will bring our invocation."

Papa stepped to the podium, and pride swelled in Rachel as he asked the blessings of the heavenly Father on the events of the day. When he stepped back, the mayor completed his welcome.

"Today is a reminder to us of the hardships borne by our forefathers. We have a rich heritage of courage and faith, and we celebrate today to commemorate those brave families who joined together to form what is now Briar Ridge."

Rachel had heard the same message many times and tuned out his words to remember the stories she'd heard and read about the hardships those first colonists had in forming the state. As early as 1633, men, women, and children traveled from the Bay and Plymouth colonies in Massachusetts to settle in what would become Connecticut. Cold weather, scarcity of food, and Indians threatened, but those brave men and women survived and formed the town of Briar Ridge in 1662.

Applause broke into her memories, and she turned to Daniel as they stood. "It's so humbling to think of all those early colonists had to endure to bring us to where we are today. If they had the conveniences we have, they wouldn't have suffered so."

Daniel grinned and placed his hand at her waist to guide her out of the building. "But they did survive, and we are here because of them. My great-great-grandparents were among those early settlers."

They stepped out into the sunlight, and Rachel blinked at the brightness. Beside her, Amy Hill pulled her coat collar tighter.

"Nathan, let's hurry down to the schoolhouse. It should be warmer there."

"Yes, it will be." Nathan turned to Daniel and Rachel. "You'll come with us, of course." He glanced at Rachel, but she averted her eyes and looked up at Daniel.

Daniel linked Rachel's arm with his. "We'll be right behind you."

Snippets of conversation between Amy and Nathan reached her ears as they walked. To drown them out, she commented to Daniel again about the history of Briar Ridge. "I'm glad we're here in 1888 and not in 1662."

He patted her hand resting on his arm. "So am I." His smile warmed her insides. He was such a good friend, and deep down she truly was proud to be on his arm this day.

When they reached the school yard, Rachel admired the new brick structure. "What a shame that only young men are allowed to attend the high school classes. Abigail and I could have finished here, then we could have gone on to the academy and not spent so much time away from home at that private school."

Daniel spoke beside her. "I believe that will change in the coming years."

The noise of the crowd greeted them when Daniel opened

the door. Squeals of delight came from the children's area, and shouts of victory resounded from the game booths. The warmth of heat from the school heating system and the presence of so many bodies caused Rachel to shed her coat almost immediately.

Daniel took it from her as Nathan did Amy's. The two men walked over to the coat check station, leaving the two young women together.

Amy tilted her head and peered at Rachel. "I can see Daniel has feelings for you. He's as attentive to you as Nathan is to me. This shall be quite a wonderful weekend with Nathan here until Sunday."

Rachel smiled but made no comment. The jealousy lurking in her heart might lead to embarrassment for both her and Amy. Those feelings must be controlled, or this day would be most miserable.

The men returned, and the four made their way through the crowd over to the booths. Although warm enough, a chill still surrounded her heart. "Could we get some of that hot cocoa over there?"

Both Daniel and Nathan headed for the stand. Amy looked sideways at Rachel. "Don't you think it was truly kind of Nathan to come all the way from Hartford yesterday so he could escort me to the celebration today?"

Rachel clenched her teeth and swallowed hard. She didn't want to hear how attentive Nathan was to Amy; she could see it well enough. She pasted a smile on her face and turned to Amy. "Yes, you are most fortunate to have such a man interested in you." Rachel disliked the smug expression that crossed Amy's face at her words.

The men returned with steaming cups of cocoa. As she

warmed her hands with the cup, Rachel caught Nathan gazing at her a few times, and it unnerved her. Why would he look at her like that with Amy Hill by his side? Especially when he'd already indicated he had no desire to court someone like her.

When they finished their drinks, they strolled around the large room, Nathan and Daniel both stopping several times to try their hands at some of the games. Nathan actually knocked down several wooden milk bottles with a ball and won Amy a little doll dressed in pioneer clothes. Daniel apologized for not winning anything for Rachel, but she didn't mind. In fact, she worried that the two men would make the games too much of a competition.

"That's all right, Daniel. Why don't we get our coats and walk to city hall and have our dinner?"

"Splendid idea." He turned to Nathan. "What do you say, old chum? Shall we head back to town and see what's going on there?"

Nathan agreed, and the two went to retrieve their coats. This time Amy said nothing, but the smirk had returned, and Rachel swallowed hard to tamp her jealousy.

When the men returned, Amy snuggled into her coat. "This weather is entirely too chilly for me. Nathan, run up to my house and ask Father for use of the brougham. Bentley can drive us to town. The carriage has blankets and will keep us warmer than if we walked."

Nathan glanced from Daniel to Rachel then back to Amy as if unsure as to what he should do. Since the vehicle had room for only two people, Rachel and Daniel would be left alone to walk the rest of the way. And that suited Rachel just fine. The less she saw of Nathan today, the better off she'd be.

She smiled at Nathan and grasped Daniel's arm. "I think another brisk walk to town is just what I need to work up an appetite for the good food I know is going to be served."

The look of embarrassment on Nathan's face tingled her insides. He was as uncomfortable as she had been a few moments ago. Somehow that filled her with renewed energy as she grasped Daniel's arm and prepared to walk to city hall.

Nathan didn't want to leave his friends in the cold, but Amy had the most insistent look on her face. Finally he nodded his head toward Daniel. "If you'll excuse me, I'll see to Miss Hill's request."

Daniel offered to procure transportation for Rachel. Nathan didn't hear her answer, but he admired Daniel for being a gentleman. Yes, his friend was a far better match for Miss Winston than he was. However, he couldn't help but notice the interest in her eyes when their gazes locked while drinking cocoa. Instead of the coquette spirit of others, he saw only sincerity, which intrigued him even more.

At Amy's house, Mr. Hill ordered the carriage to be brought around straightway. Nathan climbed into the vehicle for two, and Mr. Hill handed Nathan an extra blanket. "Watch out for my daughter, Mr. Reed. Make sure she stays warm and comfortable."

Nathan nodded. "I will, sir." Bentley snapped the reins and pulled away from the house.

Back at the school, Amy waited just inside the door. When he waved at her, she walked out to the brougham, and Nathan assisted her into the carriage box. When they were safely settled and covered with the blanket, Bentley proceeded forward.

"Did Rachel and Daniel walk on to town? Will we meet them there?" He truly wished there had been a way for the other couple to ride with them. He scanned the sidewalks as they passed.

"Oh, no, Daniel found a carriage for them right after you left. I heard him say he had a surprise for her. I wonder if it could be a token of his affection?"

"Perchance we'll see them at the dinner and you can ask her about it."

Amy's eyes opened wide. "Of course." She giggled. "I wonder if he is nearly ready to propose. He's quite smitten with her, you know."

A clamp went around Nathan's heart and threatened to squeeze it right out of his chest. What was wrong with him? He should be happy for his old friend.

With relief he found that they had arrived at city hall. He assisted Amy as she stepped from the box. The aroma of all types of delectable foods reached them, and Nathan inhaled deeply. "Ah, that smells like baking chicken, and I'm ready for a plate full." He offered his arm to Amy. "Shall we venture inside and see what the ladies have prepared?"

Nathan waved to Bentley. "We'll be back in an hour or so. You should have time to enjoy the meal yourself." The driver nodded and headed away toward an area where other carriages waited.

Beside him, Amy grasped his arm and let him guide her up the stairs to the entrance. The entire town participated in the event, with red, white, and blue buntings and flags everywhere, along with the state flag. It looked more like an Independence Day celebration to him, but then a Founder's Day would be considered patriotic since Connecticut had been one of the original colonies.

Inside, he scanned the room for a glimpse of Daniel and Rachel. He did not find them until he and Amy stood in the food serving line. Daniel hailed him and indicated two seats that had been saved.

Nathan waved back and nudged Amy. "Daniel and Rachel have seats for us." At the moment he wasn't sure if he wanted to be near Rachel and find out she was taken by another. He scolded himself to forget those thoughts and concentrate on Amy. Never would he pursue Rachel Winston. But he could no more keep from admiring her than he could keep the sun from shining.

When he and Amy joined the other couple, Rachel's eyes had lost some of their sparkle, and her smile seemed less sincere. He hoped nothing he had said had hurt her feelings in any way.

As Amy and Rachel conversed with each other, he observed Amy. She would make an excellent wife for an attorney. She had knowledge, a pleasant personality, and beauty, as well as being adept in social graces. Perhaps he should speak with Mr. Hill about courting Amy with the intent of marriage. But first he would have to reveal his past to the young woman.

Amy poked his arm. "Nathan, what do you think, being from the South?"

He blinked his eyes. "I'm sorry, what was your question?"

"Well, I was discussing the servant problem. We pay them quite well, but so few are willing to work hard except the immigrants. Thank goodness slavery is no longer legal. But my question concerned your feelings about having servants. Being from the South, did your family have slaves?"

Nathan swallowed hard. He had to be honest. "Before the war my family lived on a plantation in North Carolina. My father had a full retinue of slaves to work in the fields and in the house. I was born after the war ended, and by then, the Northern soldiers had all but destroyed everything my parents owned."

Amy's eyes opened wide, her mouth skewed as though she'd tasted something bitter. "You mean your parents actually owned people?"

Nathan cut his gaze to Rachel, who sat with her head down so he couldn't read her expression. "Yes, they did."

Rachel glanced up at him. "I've heard some harsh stories about how slaves were treated. It doesn't seem right to me that people should be owned."

"I don't know anything about that, although I've heard that my father was a good landowner and treated his people well, but it was all before my time. I wouldn't own slaves myself today, but I understand why it seemed necessary then. After the war, my father..." He swallowed hard. "My father had to leave our plantation, or what was left of it. I grew up in town in a place over the general store." With other people around, he didn't feel led to share the circumstances that caused them to leave the plantation. Thankfully his father had partnered with a brother and had turned the mercantile into a profitable business.

"I see. That is interesting." Amy smiled, but it didn't quite reach her eyes. The distaste for his revelation about his life in the South was clearly evident, while Rachel seemed to accept his explanation. "Let's don't talk about such things now. I'm ready to go across to the dance. It should be starting up soon."

"Yes, we'll be there shortly."

Nathan retrieved their coats. Second thoughts about Miss Hill entered his mind. If her attitude a few minutes ago was any indication of her feelings about the South, then perhaps he should tell her the whole story and get her reaction. That would tell him for certain whether he should pursue a relationship.

He glanced back at the table where Rachel and Daniel chatted. In truth, however, he was more interested in Rachel's feelings for Daniel. And that was one mystery he had no right to solve.

When Rachel and Daniel entered the theater, all the chairs had been pushed to the sides and the music ensemble played from the stage. Daniel took Rachel's coat, and she gazed about the room. The first couple to come into view was Nathan with Amy. What an attractive couple they made. They glided around the floor as if they'd been partners for a while. How could she ever compete with someone like Amy?

Daniel returned, and they joined the others in a waltz. Once again Rachel thanked her instructors at the academy for teaching ballroom dancing. Daniel swirled her about the floor with ease, and she relaxed, but then Daniel stepped back when the music ended.

Nathan had tapped him on the shoulder. "May I have this next dance with Miss Winston?"

Daniel grinned and turned to Amy. "Miss Hill, may I have the honor of this dance with you?"

Rachel's insides turned to mush as Daniel and Amy twirled away. Nathan placed his hand at Rachel's waist and grasped her right hand. The spot where his hand touched her burned like hot coals. She gulped and followed his first step.

"Briar Ridge certainly knows how to celebrate. The musicians are quite good."

Rachel swallowed and blinked. With her hand in his and his other at her waist, it was all she could do to concentrate on following his lead, much less talk. "Yes, and they are local." Heat flushed her face as her voice squeaked.

He merely grinned and spun her about in a step she hadn't done before. She stumbled and he caught her. "I'm sorry. That was my fault."

As much as she was attracted to Nathan, she'd never been more uncomfortable. The smile he gave her now sent a chill down her spine. Would this set never end?

"Where did your family live before you came to Briar Ridge?" he asked.

"We lived in Massachusetts about twenty miles west of Boston. Father was the minister of the church there. I was a child when we came here." How mundane an answer. She searched her mind for a more interesting line of conversation, but only a blank slate appeared.

When the music ended, Nathan's hand lingered at her waist a moment, and his smile sent rivers of delight flowing through her veins.

"Thank you, Miss Winston. Perhaps we can do this again."

"I'd...I think that will be possible." He released her hand and stepped away to rejoin Amy while Daniel stepped to her side.

"Are you all right, Rachel? You look rather pale."

"I...I'm fine, but I do think a cup of that punch would taste good." Maybe it would cool down her feelings too, because the imprint of Nathan's hand still burned at her waist.

CHAPTER
NINE

*R*ACHEL PUT AWAY her cleaning supplies, thankful for the week's end. In the week since the Founder's Day program, she had grown more accustomed to her daily routine and didn't mind the chores, especially since Miriam and Noah had become more diligent in taking care of theirs.

Still, she couldn't forget Nathan and the dance. She'd never experienced anything quite like it, and it colored her thoughts every free moment she had.

Then she remembered Daniel. He had been quite attentive in the week since Founder's Day and had surprised her with tickets to attend a performance by singer Maria Duvall tonight. Daniel understood about Mama's health and spent several evenings with the family rather than taking her away from home, but thankfully he hadn't proposed. It was too soon for that as far as she was concerned. However, Daniel may not think so since he'd known her for so long.

She prepared a tray to take up to Mama for her noon meal.

Each day brought more color to her cheeks, and Dr. Thornton had said she would be able to resume some of her duties in another week. Already Mama joined them for the evening meal and sat in the parlor with her embroidery or knitting for family devotions after dinner.

As attentive as Daniel had been, seeds of jealousy continued to sprout as Amy Hill never ceased to talk about Nathan Reed and his attentions every time she was around Rachel. It seemed as though the young woman wanted to flaunt her relationship with Nathan and arranged to be near wherever Rachel happened go.

Today, when Rachel entered Mama's room, the drapes were open to let in the sunlight of the early March afternoon. Soon it would be spring. Already the temperatures had begun to rise a little during the day, but that didn't fool her. Winter would have a few more freezing days before letting go.

Rachel set the tray on the bedside stand. Her mother sat up in bed with her Bible open on her lap.

"I've brought your meal to you. Papa ate then went over to the church to take care of some business there."

"Thank you, my dear. I think I may come downstairs tomorrow and dine with you and Papa at noon."

"Oh, that would be lovely. He will be so glad to have you at the table."

"Yes, we discussed it earlier when he came up to tell me he'd be out this afternoon. I've enjoyed having him join me here for a few meals, but I'm most anxious to again take care of my home."

Rachel made sure her mother was comfortable and that the tray was secure over her lap before she sat down close by. "Mama, I know you're anxious to become involved with everything again, but please don't rush into it. Take all the time Dr. Thornton wants you to so you'll be completely recovered when spring arrives."

"Don't worry, my dear, I will. I spoke with the good doctor, and he assured me that I should be strong enough in another week or so to take full responsibility again. Not that you haven't done an excellent job, but I love taking care of my home and family."

Rachel's heart filled with even more love for her mother, and she vowed that Mama wouldn't have to take sole responsibility for many of the chores Rachel had taken for granted. This past few weeks had opened her eyes to just how much her mother did in order to keep the home running smoothly.

Mama took a bite of stew and patted her lips with a napkin. "Now, tell me about Daniel. How is your relationship coming along?"

Rachel wanted to be enthusiastic about Daniel, but she couldn't. "It's doing nicely, but I just don't feel the excitement I should at the prospect of a marriage proposal. Although, if he does ask me, I shall have to consider it very carefully. He's a good man."

"Come here, my sweet girl." She moved the tray aside and made room for Rachel to sit beside her. She grasped Rachel's hands in hers. "Love doesn't always come easily in a relationship. Papa and I were fortunate that we were both attracted to one another from the beginning. Sometimes emotional relationships don't build until after a marriage."

"I suppose, but I see how you and Papa love each other so very much. He's always thinking of you and wanting what is best for you, and I see how you do so much for him. I want that kind of love." But how would she ever find it in Briar Ridge? Daniel was nice enough and attentive, and he'd make a wonderful husband. Still, Rachel felt there should be more. "Mama, am I being selfish in wanting that?"

"Oh, no, my dear, that's not being selfish. I've seen many an unhappy marriage because one didn't love the other with the love God meant for them." Mama furrowed her brow. "Of course, I have seen many other marriages last a long time without the passion you describe."

Rachel contemplated her mother's words, but as hard as she tried, Nathan's face would not leave her alone. She found herself thinking of him at the most inopportune moments. Why couldn't she get him out of her mind? She'd found him to be well mannered and considerate of those around him. Then whenever their eyes met or he spoke to her, her heart was drawn to him in a way she didn't quite understand.

She reached to pour more tea, but Mama's hand stopped her. "Are you still harboring thoughts of Nathan Reed?"

Rachel felt the blood rush to her face. Mama knew her too well. "I...I do think about him, but he and Amy Hill are very close. I wouldn't be surprised if they announce their engagement sometime in the near future."

"And how do you feel about that?"

Rachel set the teapot on the table and collapsed beside the bed. "Oh, Mama, it breaks my heart. I don't understand why I feel this way about him. He has never shown a bit of interest in me, except in the way our gazes somehow meet and there is a spark of something there that I don't quite know or understand. I feel so drawn to him." A shaft of sorrow burrowed deep into her soul as she confessed.

Mama's hand caressed Rachel's head. "My dear, he's out of reach, and like the forbidden fruit that tempted Eve in the garden, that is what draws you to him. It's simply infatuation. Concentrate on Daniel and all he could mean in your life. Eventually Nathan will be but a memory. I will be in prayer for you in regards to Mr. Reed."

And she would pray as well, but for Rachel, getting her own heart to cooperate with her good sense would not be an easy task. Tonight, however, she would bury the pangs of jealousy and give Daniel her complete attention and think only of his wonderful qualities as a suitor and a Christian young man. Perhaps her mother's prayers would be answered.

Once again Nathan prepared for an evening with Amy Hill. Daniel had procured tickets so the four of them could attend a concert tonight. Considering Amy's comments on Founder's Day, this night might prove to be the time to inquire further and determine if she could be the wife to suit his lifestyle.

The fact that he'd also see Rachel sent a ripple of pleasure through his soul. He had decided that his attraction to her lay in the fact that he had sworn never to pursue a girl who was as strong a Christian as she. Once again God had played a cruel trick on him. He'd led Nathan to the one girl he could never have.

Daniel greeted him in the foyer. "Our carriage waits, as do two lovely young women. This is going to be a wonderful evening." He slapped Nathan on the back and led the way to where a black, brass-trimmed coach sat at the curb.

As they neared Rachel's house, Nathan's stomach rumbled, but not from hunger. Perhaps it was what his sister once called "a butterfly feeling" that arose whenever she was nervous. Whatever the name, he wanted it to go away. He didn't want anything to deter him from his main goal this evening with Amy Hill.

When Daniel escorted Rachel to the carriage and assisted her into the cab, the surprised look in her eyes before she quickly turned her head told Nathan she had been unaware he would be present this evening.

Her words proved him correct. "Mr. Reed, this is a surprise. Is Miss Hill going to be with us also?"

"Yes, she is. It is a pleasure to see you again." And indeed it was.

Rachel lowered the hood of her cape, revealing her raven curls. She averted her gaze to Daniel. "Are our seats together at the concert?"

Daniel nodded. "Yes, and we'll let you two ladies sit next to each other. You will probably have much to discuss."

A quickly disguised look of displeasure on Rachel's face aroused Nathan's curiosity. It was better for her to sit by Amy, or he wouldn't be able to keep his mind on the concert. When they stopped for Amy and she joined them in the cab, neither woman engaged the other beyond the initial greeting. He sensed no friendship existed between these two. Apparently they were night and day in personality and interests as well as in appearance.

Despite Daniel's attempts at conversation, a pall fell over the group as they made their way to the auditorium. Every time Daniel tried to engage Rachel in discussion, he was met with silence. He finally gave up, and Amy began rambling on about some tea her mother planned with Mrs. Monroe. Never had a ride for such a short distance seemed so long.

When they arrived at the concert hall, Rachel clung to Daniel and gave him her undivided attention. Nathan observed the two of them as they entered the building ahead of him. Their heads inclined toward each other, and they appeared to be engaged in lively conversation.

Beside him Amy grasped his arm. "I'm so glad you were able to get tickets for this concert. Maria Duvall is supposed to be one of the most brilliant singers of our time."

"I have heard Miss Duvall, and she has a range for a soprano that is quite remarkable. I'm sure you'll be entertained."

They made their way to their seats, and just after they were settled, the lights dimmed and the program began. Maria Duvall did not disappoint. Her repertoire ranged in music from the opera *Aida* to the more popular songs of the day. Nathan sneaked a glance at Rachel several times, and her rapt attention on the coloratura soprano enchanted him.

Amy clapped with forced gusto at the end of each piece. "Oh, Nathan, she is marvelous. I'm so glad we came."

Nathan relaxed and enjoyed the music. At intermission he and Daniel bought cups of fruit punch for the ladies before the second half began. All during the second half, Nathan sneaked glances at Rachel, who never wavered from staring straight ahead.

After the concert, when Daniel suggested going for refreshment, Rachel declined and climbed into the carriage. Daniel shrugged. "Sorry, but I guess we'll go home."

Amy pouted. "Oh, but I hate for the evening to end."

Nathan grasped her hand and placed it on his arm. "It doesn't have to for us. Daniel, if you don't mind, I'll see Miss Hill gets home safely. We'll stop for coffee and pastries down the way."

A smile lit Amy's eyes. "That would be quite acceptable."

As the *clip-clop* of the horses leading the carriage away faded into the distance, a little bit of the light of the evening rolled away with it. No matter how hard he tried, Nathan could not get Rachel Winston out of his mind. She remained an intriguing mystery, one he didn't dare try to solve.

Daniel didn't mind a bit that Nathan wanted to take Amy home alone. Inviting him and Amy to share the concert had been a mistake. Evidently the two women did not get along well. Maybe he could salvage the remainder of the evening for Rachel.

Rachel once again became silent as they began the ride home. He couldn't understand her behavior. Usually she at least talked with him, but tonight she seemed to be far away in another world.

He reached to grasp her hand. "I'm so sorry about this evening. I know how much you looked forward to hearing Maria Duvall. I didn't realize having Amy and Nathan along would make such a difference."

Rachel turned her head to gaze at him. "It would have been nice had you told me first. Seeing them was quite a surprise. I thought we were going alone."

"I understand, and it won't happen again." Maybe she had wanted to be with just him, but at the Founder's Day events, he had thought they had a good time. Amy had been somewhat haughty, but then that was just Amy. He wouldn't make that mistake again. In the future all dates with Rachel would be just the two of them.

"I owe you an apology as well. I've been a complete bore all evening, but I truly did enjoy the concert. Miss Duvall has a beautiful voice, and her notes were clear as a bell. To sing like that is a blessing." Rachel blinked those stunning blue eyes and smiled.

That's what he wanted to see from her: pleasure. "Are you sure you don't want to stop somewhere for a late evening cup of tea or coffee?"

"No, thank you. It's best that I get home. Tomorrow is a busy day. I have to help with the cleaning of the sanctuary for the services on Sunday. Your mother and Abigail have some beautiful flowers to arrange for the altar tomorrow. Mama will be so pleased."

"Yes, and I do believe arranging the flowers gives my mother great pleasure also. That seems to be one skill that Abigail has picked up. She's so different from you. Here you are taking over all your mother's responsibilities at home and the church, and it seems to come natural to you. I'm not certain Abigail could do the same." Indeed, his sister had shown little interest in anything to do with domestic skills except entertaining.

"Don't underestimate her. She enjoyed our domestic science classes at Bainbridge as much as I did."

"Hmm, interesting." Daniel didn't plan on spending the evening discussing Abigail's ability around the home, but at least Rachel had started talking to him. Then the carriage stopped, and he realized they had arrived at her home. Oh, to live in a city where it took longer to get anywhere.

He stepped down, then assisted Rachel and walked her to the door. She turned to him before going inside. "Thank you for taking me to hear Miss Duvall. I shall never forget it."

The dim light from the lamp by the door accented her beauty, and Daniel hated to say good night. "Would you be so kind as to have dinner with me one night next week?"

Her eyes opened wide. "That would be lovely, but I must check with Papa. There is much to do until Mama is completely well."

"I understand, and I will wait for your answer." And he prayed it would be yes.

After she had gone inside, Daniel returned to the carriage. As much as he liked Rachel, there didn't appear to be the same spark of interest from her. He would give their relationship another month or so, and if nothing more developed, he'd have to accept it and move on. Despite what he'd said to Nathan, Daniel did want a wife who loved him and truly desired to spend the rest of her life with him.

Nathan followed Amy inside her home, where a butler took his coat. She led him to the parlor, where she sat again on the velvet sofa. He noticed the housekeeper's return to sit in a far corner. This time he sat closer to Amy in hopes his voice would not carry to the housekeeper's ears.

"Amy, you spoke of your feelings about the South last time we were together. I have the feeling you didn't approve of slavery."

"Of course I don't, Nathan. It's a sin to own another person outright like that. I have heard that the slaves were treated harshly, and—" She stopped abruptly. Pink tinged her cheeks. "Well, I can't speak of what the owners did to the young slave women."

"And where did you learn about such tales? You were just a baby." What she said had been true of many plantation owners, but not his father. Or at least that's what he'd been told as a child.

She smiled with her hand just below her throat. "Why, Mr. Reed, my father and uncles have told many tales about the war. My father was a Union army officer and served with Grant."

Nathan took a deep breath and plunged ahead. "My father served under Albert Johnston and fought at the battle of Shiloh, where Johnston was mortally wounded. After that he returned to North Carolina and served under Longstreet in our home state. My father even freed a number of his slaves during that time. He said he'd decided that he'd give them a choice. Many left, but others stayed to take care of Mother and my older sister."

"That's well and good, but why own them in the first place?"

"I'm not quite sure I ever understood that, especially since I didn't see it firsthand, and I don't believe I'd ever want to own others. But did your father ever tell you what their armies did to our land and our women?" He hated to ask such a question, but if she had heard only the North's side, she was sorely misinformed.

"Mr. Reed, that is something I do not care to discuss." Her voice dripped ice.

With her return to the use of his surname and her tone of

voice, he realized the subject must be quite distasteful to her. Still, he must know her true feelings.

Before he could speak again, she leaned forward. "I do know that your father owned one of the most successful stores in Fayetteville, North Carolina. My father made inquiries and learned that he became a quite wealthy man. Father also said your father died several years ago. I'm so sorry about that."

He didn't much like the idea of being investigated, but he'd probably have done the same thing if he'd been Amy's father. Still, the fact that his own father was wealthy had impacted her attitude toward him. Her facial expression when she learned he'd lived over a general store had clearly expressed her distaste.

"Thank you. He's the reason I came north to attend Yale." He paused a moment, unsure of how to go on. From things she'd said previously, she wouldn't understand what had happened to his family.

"I wondered how a man from the South managed to make it to New Haven. He must have wanted you to see how good our people really are. Is your mother still in Fayetteville?"

Nathan paused a moment before answering to allow the pain and bitterness of his past to ease. "Yes, she is. She lives with my older sister, Evelyn. My younger sister, Beth, lives in town with her husband. We never returned to the plantation after the Yankees destroyed it."

Amy's eyes opened wide. "They only did what they thought was right in order to achieve victory. After all, it was a war."

"That may be true in battle, but what they did off the battlefield was horrible and uncalled for. Ransacking homes and attacking the women is not my idea of how to wage war.

I haven't heard of any atrocities done by our troops here in the Northern states."

"Well, I never…never heard such nonsense." Her face paled, and her hand covered her throat. "I do think it is time for you leave, Mr. Reed."

"I will be going now, Miss Hill. Thank you for your honesty." He nodded toward the housekeeper. "If I could have my coat, I'll take leave. I don't know when I'll be back in Briar Ridge."

Amy's ashen face revealed her distaste for what he'd said. No matter what she thought, he held no remorse for his remarks. She gave him one last shake of her head, then practically ran from the room. Nathan took his coat from Mrs. Barron and stepped into the cold night air. At the moment the idea of not seeing Amy again did not bother him, and relief flooded his heart that he had chosen not to reveal the true reason for his coming north. It would have been the death of his reputation. No, some secrets were best kept as secrets.

He thrust his hands into his pockets and hunched his shoulders against the cold. Tonight only served to prove that God wasn't the kind, loving Father he'd heard about in his youth. He was a judge who meted out punishment to those who didn't do things His way. That kind of God he didn't need.

CHAPTER
TEN

*E*ZRA ENTERED THE kitchen where Rachel helped Felicity in packing a large basket for a picnic. The morning sun rays through the windows warmed the kitchen and created a halo of light about the two women.

Ezra peeked into the basket to find bread, cheese, apples, cookies, and milk. "Hmm, looks like we'll have a feast for lunch today."

"I'm so glad Doctor Thornton said some sunshine would be good for me, and the weather is certainly cooperating," Felicity said.

Ezra snitched a cookie from a plate on the counter. Sugar cookies with nuts and cinnamon were his favorite. "With the sun it feels like it's around fifty degrees out there, so it'll be a beautiful day for a trip to Anderson's apple orchards."

"Oh, Papa, are you planning to get some apple trees? I love their blossoms in the spring and the fruit in the fall." Rachel tucked napkins and forks into the basket.

"Yes, and this is the perfect time of year to get them ordered. If we can get them into the ground before the end of March, they should do quite well."

Felicity dried the last of the dishes she'd used for preparation and removed her apron. "Have you decided where you'll plant them?"

"Yes, up on the slope on the south side of the barn. They'll get plenty of sun there and be protected from harsh winds by the barn and tool shed. I'm already tasting the good apple pies and dumplings you'll be making." He reached around to hug his wife.

She swatted at his arm, her cheeks as rosy as the apples he hoped to harvest. "It'll be a while before we have that good a crop." Then she shooed him out of the way. "Get on with you now and call the boys to help load the wagon."

Ezra paused at the door and grinned at Rachel. "I can't begin to tell you how pleased we have been with the way you've handled the responsibility of the chores during Mama's illness. You'll make a fine wife."

Red bloomed on his daughter's cheeks. She ducked her head and finished tucking the checkered cloth around the food. "Thank you. I enjoyed doing it."

He nodded and headed out to finish hitching the team to the wagon. He called to Micah and Noah. "Boys, I think your mama would like to see you in the kitchen."

Micah ran past him, probably in hopes of getting a few cookies before leaving, but Noah stopped. "Papa, I finished hitching the team for you. I think we're all set to start loading and getting ready to leave."

Ezra patted his son's shoulder. "Thank you. I appreciate

your help." The boy grinned and loped into the house. Ezra shook his head. When had his second son grown so? At seventeen he stood an inch or so above Ezra, and his shoulders had broadened since last summer. This time next year he'd be off to school like his brother Seth.

He checked the hitch and reins. Noah had done a fine job. Pride swelled in his chest at the thought of his two older sons. Never had he dreamed that Seth would want to follow his father into the ministry, but that he had, and now Noah had mentioned maybe taking the same road.

If only a suitable young man could be found for Rachel. As much as he'd like to see Daniel become a member of his family, Ezra saw no spark of interest in his daughter where that young man was concerned, but the light in her eyes when he'd seen her around Nathan Reed at the Founder's Day celebration created a good deal of concern.

A nice enough young man, but not one Ezra particularly wanted as a son-in-law unless he changed his attitude and opinions toward God and the church. That matter would require much prayer in the days ahead.

Rachel handed her brothers the baskets she and Mama had prepared. "You boys be careful with those. We don't want to ruin our lunch with your carelessness."

The boys just grinned and grabbed the baskets before racing outside. Good thing she'd tucked the cloth snugly on each one or the contents might be spilling across the ground.

She hung her apron on a hook by the door as her mother

reentered the kitchen, fastening her cloak about her shoulders. "Best get your wrap, dear. Papa will be waiting for us."

Rachel hurried to the front hallway to grab her cloak and bonnet from their pegs. Papa had said she'd make a good wife, but for whom? Although Mama would like to see Daniel Monroe become her son-in-law, Rachel harbored no such ideas herself, especially after last evening and the concert.

Just a few more months until summer, and she'd be off to Boston with Abigail. Thinking about the trip brought on a smile. It'd be interesting to see what young men the city may have to offer. Brotherly love did not fit her definition of romantic love on which to build a marriage. She wanted what she had seen in her parents. Papa's tender care and concern these past few weeks had taught Rachel a great lesson about the kind of love a husband and wife should share. Perhaps she'd find it when summer arrived.

Papa opened the back door just as she stepped back into the kitchen. "Are you ladies ready? The horses are hitched and blankets are in the buggy." He glanced around the kitchen. "Where's Miriam?"

Rachel tied the ribbons of her bonnet. "She must still be in her room. I'll go up and get her."

Miriam rushed into the room. "Here I am. I couldn't find but one shoe until I looked under my bed."

"Good, good. Now let's go to the farms." Papa stepped over and grasped Mama's arm. "Let me assist you, Felicity. No need to tax yourself right away."

Rachel and Miriam followed their parents out to the waiting vehicle where Noah sat astride his own red bay. Papa climbed up to handle the reins.

Rachel settled the blanket around herself and Miriam with Micah on the seat between them in the back of the wagon. Her father guided the horses out to the Hartford road that would take them to the orchards. Rachel breathed deeply of the air fragrant with the hint of spring. It couldn't come soon enough for her. As much as she liked winter, spring held such promise for the summer to come, and her dreams with it.

Still, as nice as today might be, more snow could come any day. Winter wasn't over by any means. Sometimes she wished they lived in a place like Texas, where she had heard the winters were not as harsh. Her cousin Sarah had written several times about the weather there.

The low tones of her parents' voices carried to her ears. After all these years of marriage, they still had such a look in their eyes when talking with one another that Rachel felt she invaded their privacy. Oh, to find a love like that. Mama never spoke much of what married life was like, so Rachel only had her observations of her mother as an example of what it meant to be a wife and mother.

Color had returned to Mama's cheeks, and she gained more energy with each passing day. Once her mother took back full responsibility of the home, perhaps she would let Rachel help with the more difficult chores. No need for her to have a relapse.

Out of the corner of her eye, Rachel noticed a rider approaching from the side. As he drew closer, she recognized Nathan Reed. Gracious, what was he doing on this road? He'd only arrived in Briar Ridge yesterday afternoon. Her heart thudded with delight at seeing him again.

When he drew near, he tipped his hat in her direction.

Heat rose in her cheeks, and she ducked her head in hopes Papa didn't notice the bloom.

"Good day, Reverend Winston, Mrs. Winston. It's a lovely day to be out for a ride."

"Good day to you, Mr. Reed. We're headed for Anderson's orchards to look into purchasing trees."

"I know that place. I met young Jonathan Anderson on one of my trips between Hartford and Briar Ridge. I'm headed back to Hartford myself. Do you mind if I ride with you?"

Rachel bit her lip as her heart fluttered like the wings of a butterfly against her chest. She must keep herself under control.

Papa nodded to Nathan. "That will be fine. Noah would most likely enjoy the company."

The low murmur of Noah's and Nathan's conversation reached her ears, but strain as she might, not one clear word could be heard. She gripped her hands tightly in her lap, and Miriam cast a sideways glance at Rachel. The young girl's eyes sparkled with mischief.

A moment later Miriam teased, "I do believe Mr. Reed is attracted to you. His gaze keeps darting over to you."

At her sister's whispered words, a lump rose in Rachel's throat. She used all the willpower she could muster to keep from turning to see if that were true. Nathan and Amy had appeared quite close last evening at the concert, and he'd indicated he'd be in town until Sunday, so something must have happened. It was no business of hers, but it still aroused her curiosity.

Mama turned in her seat. "Rachel, if the store has apples left, I think we should buy enough to make some pies."

Papa laughed. "Now that's a fine idea. No one makes pastry quite as well as you do, my dear Mrs. Winston. I don't mean to offend, Rachel, as you are a very good cook yourself, but your mother has more experience."

Rachel smiled and shrugged her shoulders. Papa had not hurt her feelings; indeed, her own pastry had left much to be desired, but she was learning. "I think some of Anderson's apple butter would be quite tasty on our biscuits in the mornings."

Noah rode closer. "Did I hear someone mention apple butter?"

Mama laughed. "Yes, you did. I do believe you'd hear us mention food no matter how far away you might be."

"I can say one thing, much as I enjoyed some of Rachel's concoctions, I will be most happy when you are back in the kitchen, Mama."

Rachel's insides churned with her brother's comments. What must Nathan Reed think of her culinary skills? "Humph, I didn't see you leaving much, if anything, on your plate these past weeks, Noah Winston."

Noah's laughter rang out in the cool air. "When a man is hungry, he'll eat just about anything, dear sister."

Rachel turned to say something in return, but her gaze locked on Nathan, who had ridden closer with her brother. Her tongue became thick as the batting in her quilt. Despite his smile, she sensed sadness about him, especially in his eyes as he watched her and her siblings tease each other. He must be reminded of his own family, so far away.

His dark eyes bored into hers. "I think it would be a rare treat to dine on a meal prepared by your fair hands, Miss Winston."

If her cheeks had been pink before, they must be fire red

now. Rachel swallowed hard and turned back in her seat. Would this trip never end?

Nathan hadn't intended to embarrass Rachel. His only intent had been to compliment her. In addition to her beauty, she had other skills and talents that attracted him. Her camaraderie with her family told him more about her than talking with her had. The love among the Winston family members touched an aching hole in his heart. It had been many years since he'd talked in such a way with his sisters and mother.

Indeed, his departure had been in the most unfortunate of circumstances. The words he'd exchanged with Evelyn and Mother were branded on his heart, and he could no more remove them than he could stop the seasons from turning. The hurt he'd inflicted had left deep scars, and he couldn't go back and make them disappear.

He rode along in silence and listened to their playful exchanges. Even little Micah joined in with remarks that brought laughter from his siblings and a stern look from his mother. What would it be like to be a member of a family like that again? He remembered days when it had been such with his sisters, but the memory of the joys of such times dimmed as the years passed.

Miriam said something to Rachel, and her laughter rang out in the crisp winter air. He had noted how her eyes sparkled when she laughed. The wind had tinted her cheeks with an attractive red. Her demeanor was so unlike any of the women he had pursued. Perhaps that is what stirred his attraction to her.

Noah rode along beside him. He reminded Nathan of himself at that age—part of a loving family, the future stretching ahead with promise, and the only thing on his mind what he might eat at the next meal.

The young man leaned toward him now. "What was it like to go to Yale as someone from the South?"

Nathan raised his eyebrows. Such an unusual question, but he noted no guile in the boy's eyes, only sincere interest. Nathan pondered the question a moment before answering. "I suppose the most difficult part came from the deep accent I had at the time. I found none of the animosity toward southerners that I expected. Daniel and I became friends our first year there."

"The only thing I know about that war is what I've been told or have heard from those who are still around who served in the Union army. Were things really as bad as some say?"

Nathan furrowed his brow. How could he answer the boy's question without showing the prejudices that had popped up again yesterday after being buried for years? The truth as he knew it would be the best route to take.

"Noah, I'm sure there were atrocities on both sides. I was born after the war ended, so, like you, I don't know any more than what I heard about."

"I can't imagine losing one's home. We've lived in the same house all my life in Briar Ridge. I'm anxious to finish school here next year and attend a university."

How wonderful to be sixteen or seventeen again and thinking he could conquer the world. At that age Nathan had known nothing of the secrets his parents harbored. Life had been good, and he remembered how safe and secure he felt until the day his father lay dying.

He pushed the thoughts away and turned his attention back to Noah. "What is it you want to do with your life? I understand your brother is at the seminary studying to be a minister."

The boy nodded. "That's right. I thought of going that direction, and told Papa so, but lately my interests have turned elsewhere. I want to be a doctor who takes care of animals and plan on pursuing that when I graduate. I know it's a long, hard road, but I've liked taking care of animals since I was a little boy."

Miriam turned around in her seat. "Yes, he's always bringing home stray cats and dogs that need tending. One time he even brought home a skunk. That was awful."

The tips of Noah's ears reddened. "A skunk is one of God's creatures too. The poor thing just didn't know I wanted to help him."

Miriam then launched into a detailed account of trying to get the odors out of Noah's clothes. Mrs. Winston shook her head. "At least he didn't bring the creature into the house. We may have had to move out with that smell permeating everything. I finally buried Noah's clothes."

Once again their love for each other was evident, and it filled him with sadness for what his family had lost. If only he could go back and undo the things he'd done.

After another half hour of riding, the Anderson orchards came into view. When they neared the store, several other wagons and buggies filled the area. Reverend Winston pulled up the reins. "Looks like the fair weather has brought out a number of people on the same mission we are." He stepped down from the wagon.

Nathan and Noah dismounted and hurried to help the ladies down. Nathan's hands circled Rachel's waist, and her hands rested on his shoulders as she alit. Such a tiny waist. His hands went almost all the way around.

"Mr. Reed?"

Nathan started and realized he still held her. He dropped his hands from her waist as though she'd been a hot coal. He took a step backward. "I'm sorry."

Her brilliant blue eyes held a spark of amusement. "It's all right." She headed toward the store.

He followed and noted Jonathan Anderson near the building. "High-ho, Jonathan, 'tis a fine day for business."

"That it is, Mr. Reed, that it is." The young man offered his hand in greeting.

Reverend Winston joined Nathan. "I would like to inquire as to whether you will have young trees available for planting."

"I'm sure my father can help you with that. They're not ready for transporting as yet, but he can tell you more. If you'll follow me, I'll take you to him." Jonathan and the reverend walked away toward the orchards, with Noah following.

Nathan entered the store and found Mrs. Winston and Miriam examining the apples filling the baskets on the floor. Meanwhile, Rachel scanned the wares stocked on the shelves. Rachel's bonnet had slipped from her head and hung down her back. Dark curls shimmered in the light from the lanterns around the store. From her demeanor, he surmised Rachel had no idea how lovely she was. He had known many beautiful women, but Rachel's beauty came from deep inside her. Yet her graceful manners and attitude spoke of a gentility he didn't often see in women from small towns.

He approached her. "I've eaten here before, and everything

they served is quite tasty. Of course, the restaurant is closed now, but I'm sure these products on their shelves are just as good."

She turned, and her smile sent shock waves of warmth to his very soul. "We've shopped here before, and I've never found anything I didn't like. We brought a picnic lunch with us today. Perhaps you'll join us for that. I promise you, Mother's cooking is a great deal better than mine."

"I'm sure yours is quite tasty too. Daniel has spoken of your culinary expertise as well as your other talents." Now why did he have to go and mention Daniel?

Her cheeks bloomed pink again. "I'm afraid he might be exaggerating some." She turned back to the shelves to select a jar of apple jelly.

"He also told me how you took over many of your mother's responsibilities while she was ill." She must have a heart of service and love for her family to take on the tasks of being responsible for the care of the house as well as her siblings. Every time he was around this lovely young woman, he learned more about her spirit.

"I did, but it was what any daughter would do under the circumstances." She smiled and reached to the shelf for apple butter.

Instinctively he reached out to assist her, and their hands met. Neither of them moved for a moment. The fire from her touch flamed through his arm and to his heart. He jerked his hand away, but her gaze locked with his. Spellbound, he could only stare. Her eyes were such deep pools of blue that he could drown in them. The innocence he witnessed in them took his breath away.

Her gaze dropped, then swung back to him, politely veiled. "Tell me about your family, Mr. Reed."

Nathan gulped. What could he say about his family? "They're in North Carolina. I haven't seen them in four years."

Her eyes widened. "That must be terrible to be separated for so long. I missed my family terribly when I was away at school in Hartford. How are your parents?"

"My father passed away just before I came to Yale. My mother is fine."

She didn't seem to register the tepidness of his response and continued the questioning. "Do you have any brothers or sisters?"

"Yes, I do. An older sister, Evelyn, and a younger one, Beth."

"So you are the only boy," Rachel teased. "Spoiled and petted by your sisters, I'll bet."

Before he could control it, Nathan knew his expression filled with grief, because Rachel looked dismayed. "Sisters can be difficult," she said softly, patting him gently on the arm.

Just then Miriam came up and pulled on Rachel's sleeve. "We're ready for our picnic."

"What do you think, Mr. Reed? Would you like to join us?" Rachel looked at him inquiringly.

Reluctantly, Nathan shook his head. "Thank you, but much as I would like to, I should be getting back to Hartford. Please give my regards to your family."

And with that he hurried from the store and mounted his horse, relieved to be released from her questions. At least he wouldn't have to say more about his family. Even if her father were not a man of God, Nathan had reservations about courting her. Without a doubt, her reaction to the truth of his life would be like his own—shock and revulsion. Seeing those emotions on her face and encountering her rejection would be unbearable.

He prodded his horse into a trot. He had to put distance between him and Rachel, and he had to do it as soon as possible, or he might bring grief not only on her but on himself as well.

CHAPTER
ELEVEN

FOR THE NEXT week Rachel tried in vain to forget her encounter with Nathan at Anderson Orchards. Something in her yearned for his attention even though her father and mother would both frown on it. He'd been polite and circumspect in his behavior, but something in his eyes hinted at more than a passing interest.

At least the weather had been good this week. Perhaps she'd have time to walk to Abigail's home. It had been two weeks since they'd had a real chance to visit, and several questions tumbled around in Rachel's mind.

With the temperatures in the fifty-degree range, today would be a good time to start planning the garden she and Mama would plant soon. At least that would be a distraction to keep her mind away from a certain young lawyer.

Mama walked into the kitchen. "I see the teakettle is on. Some of the cookies you made this morning would be a nice treat to go with tea." She reached into the cabinet for two cups and plates and set them on the table.

Rachel poured the tea. "It's time to be thinking about your garden for this year. With this nice weather, we can get the ground all prepared and ready for planting after the last frost, but I'll take care of preparing the soil for our seeds. I don't want you to get too tired and end up back in bed." She set a tin filled with cookies on the table and sat across from her mother.

"Oh, dear child, I'm fine, and I love working the ground. I promise I won't do too much and will let you help. I have packets of seeds all ready for planting both flowers and vegetables."

Rachel frowned. "If I know you, you won't even notice if you do too much, but at least I'm here to help and keep an eye on you."

The front door bell rang, and Rachel rose from the table. "I'll get it. You stay here and enjoy your tea."

Rachel found Abigail waiting at the front door. "Oh, I'm so glad you've come. I was planning to come to your house because I've missed our visits. We haven't had a good talk in a while."

Abigail stepped into the entryway and removed her cloak and gloves. "I know. We're long overdue for a chat, and I couldn't wait any longer. Mother had nothing pressing for me to do the rest of the day, so I came here."

Rachel grasped her friend's arm and led her to the kitchen. "Look, Mama, Abigail's here."

"How nice to see you, my dear. Won't you join us for tea and cookies?"

"Yes, I will, thank you. I knew how busy Rachel would be with all her new responsibilities, and I didn't want to distract her." Abigail sat next to Mama.

"I'm getting stronger every day." Mama pushed back from the table. "You two have plenty to talk about, I'm sure. I'm going up and do a little mending before lunch. Give your mother my regards, Abigail."

"Yes, ma'am, I will." After Mama left, Abigail said, "I'm so glad your mother is better. Maybe we'll have more time to visit and do things again."

"I imagine we will, but let's go into the parlor where we can be comfortable." She placed the cups and cookies on a tray.

A few moments later she set the tray on the table near the sofa. Abigail picked up a cup of tea. "I understand you had a delightful time at Maria Duvall's concert. I really wish I could have gone too."

"It was quite lovely. You know Amy and Nathan Reed went with us." Rachel clutched her hands together in her lap. "I've wanted to ask you about something. When we went to Anderson Orchards to pick out apple trees, Nathan joined us on the trip. I was quite surprised that he returned to Hartford so soon. Do you have any idea why?"

Abigail sipped her tea. "Yes, I do. Daniel said Amy didn't want to see Nathan anymore. He told Papa she decided his past as a southerner didn't fit in with her background."

Rachel's mouth dropped open, and she fell back against the sofa. "I had no idea." How terrible for Nathan.

"Yes, it was rather sudden. I know you have feelings for him, but Rachel, you must forget about Nathan Reed. He isn't a churchgoer, and your father would never approve."

A chill passed through Rachel. "Oh, Abigail, I know, but I seem to be drawn to him no matter how hard I try not to be."

She had to find something else to occupy her mind and time until summer and her trip to Boston.

Abigail nibbled a cookie. "I do wish things could work out for you and Daniel. He speaks of you quite fondly."

"And I shall not refuse when he does ask me out. Perhaps he will succeed in changing my mind." Rachel leaned forward and grasped Abigail's arm. "I promise I will not do anything to hurt Daniel. If after a few more outings I feel the same as now, I will surely tell him. Otherwise it wouldn't be fair to him."

"That's all I can ask. But it would be fun to have you as a sister."

"We're almost like sisters anyway, and I do hope that won't change if I don't marry your brother." The mere idea of not having Abigail as her friend sent a shiver through Rachel.

"Nothing will change our relationship. We've been too close for too many years."

Those words brought some comfort. "Why does life have to be so complicated and uncertain? Sometimes I wish we were young again without thought for marriage."

Abigail shook her head. "I don't know the answer to your question, but I do know I wouldn't want to be young again." She stirred more sugar into her tea. "Sometimes I think it would be fun to have had younger brothers and sisters, but then I probably wouldn't have all the things that I do." Abigail fluttered her eyelashes and glanced down at her hands. "I suppose you must think that's rather selfish of me."

"Not really, because sometimes I wish I didn't have brothers and sisters, and I don't think of that as being selfish, just realistic. They can be a nuisance."

Abigail placed her cup and saucer on the tray and smiled. "I suppose they can." She stood and smoothed her skirt. "It's getting on towards noon, and I must get back home."

Rachel walked with her to the door and waited while Abigail tied on her cloak and pulled up the hood.

Abigail hugged Rachel. "I've enjoyed seeing you again. Maybe we'll have more time next week to do the same." She reached for the doorknob. "And I'll keep you informed if I learn anything new about Nathan Reed, although I can't see why you would still be interested."

"I don't understand it myself, but thank you." Rachel closed the door after her friend and leaned against it. This preoccupation with the affairs of Nathan Reed must stop. If Papa knew, he'd be disappointed in his eldest daughter. She pulled in a deep breath and exhaled before pushing away from the door. Time to begin preparation for the noon meal, and the aroma of the stew put on earlier now permeated the air. Rachel carried the tea dishes to the kitchen just as Mama came down the stairs.

"Did you and Abigail have a nice visit?"

Rachel tied on her apron. "Yes, we did." She arranged glasses and plates on the table. Papa would soon be home from the church and ready for his midday meal. "Mama, I learned why Nathan returned to Hartford last Saturday. It seems he will not be calling on Amy anymore. So I suppose we won't be seeing much of him in Briar Ridge now."

Her mother stirred the stew pot on the stove. "Oh, perhaps it is for the best. He has shown no interest in visiting the church on his previous visits."

There would be no chance of that now. She prayed the Lord would help her forget the young lawyer and concentrate on building a relationship with Daniel.

She observed the ease with which her mother performed her duties. "Mama, I have a much better appreciation for all you do to keep our home running smoothly. I truly learned a lot."

She smiled. "And I appreciate how well you handled the responsibilities while I was ill."

No matter what else happened in the weeks and months ahead, she would remember to thank the Lord for blessing her with the love of her family. He was in control of her life and knew what lay ahead for her. She simply must trust Him and be patient. But oh, how hard that could be.

Later in the evening Ezra sat in his study going over Bible verses to use in his Sunday sermon. He always enjoyed this time when the children had all retired to their rooms. He glanced at his pocket watch. In a few minutes Felicity would be in with a tray of coffee and a small slice of the pie left from supper. It had been her ritual to leave him alone to study until just before they retired for the evening. Then she would come in with a bit of refreshment.

He looked forward to these times together and had missed them in the past weeks of her illness. Rachel had done an exceptional job. Her cooking might not have been as expert as her mother's, but none of them had gone hungry.

A soft tap sounded on the door, and his wife stepped in with the tray. "I thought you'd be about ready for more of the apple pie from supper." She set the tray on a table near his desk.

"I'm always ready for a visit from you, with or without the pie." He moved some papers to the side, marked his place in the

Bible, and closed it. "The apple and cinnamon give the house a quite pleasant aroma."

Felicity set a plate and cup of coffee before him. "Yes, and I'm glad we went to the orchard and brought back those apples. They make the most delicious pies."

Ezra watched her with a keen eye. Her movements and tone of voice indicated she had something on her mind this evening. He'd be patient and let her tell him her concerns when she was ready. As it turned out, he didn't have long to wait.

Felicity sat across from him. "I'm somewhat worried about Rachel. Daniel is a fine young man and cares a great deal about her, but in my talks with Rachel, I haven't seen the same interest."

"What do you think the problem may be?" Even though he had his own suspicions, he did want to hear what his wife had to say.

"I fear she has become attracted to Nathan Reed. We've discussed him several times, and Rachel has expressed an interest in him."

Just as he had feared. However, knowing what he did about Nathan, Ezra could see nothing but trouble ahead for his daughter if she continued in that direction. He'd observed them together twice now, once at Founder's Day and once at Anderson Orchards. What he had seen did not sit well with him. "I thought that might be it."

Felicity closed her eyes and breathed deeply. "I fear so. All we can do is to pray for her to see that Daniel would be a good husband and that love will come if she will but let it." She kissed his cheek. "I'm going up to bed. I'm rather tired. Don't be long."

Ezra smiled and nodded. "I won't be, I promise."

Once again he sat in silence and contemplated his daughter and Nathan Reed. He had prayed for his daughter, but even as obedient as she had been in the past, when a girl was in love, she might be tempted to do things she wouldn't ordinarily consider doing. Perhaps he should let her go to Boston early. The recent mild weather would make traveling easy. He reached for pen and paper. He'd send a post off to his sister straightway and see what could be arranged.

On Monday, Nathan packed saddlebags and one valise to take with him to Briar Ridge. Mrs. Cargill had more business for him to attend to in regards to disposal of other property in Briar Ridge. The Cargill estate had turned into a rather profitable case for the firm. Mr. Fitzpatrick had told him just this morning how the widow had sung Nathan's praises at a dinner party recently. For that reason he was allowed to handle all her affairs.

At least he was doing something right. Everything else around him fell apart. First the relationship with Amy had gone sour. Then Alice Harrington had informed him that she had no sights on marriage now or for several years to come. Neither had broken his heart, but they had put a stall on his plans to marry.

He was unaccustomed to rejection from young women, and his ego stung. Usually he ended the relationships before any commitment on his part. That had been the way he wanted it these past few years, but now the game had lost its appeal. A touch of guilt touched his soul for the many young women he'd led to perhaps the wrong conclusion about their relationship with him.

Amy and Alice were not exactly what he would choose anyway. He chuckled to himself. Was it Amy's high-pitched giggle or Alice's sultry, throaty laugh that had annoyed him most? Not that it really mattered. Ever since he'd laid eyes on Rachel Winston, all others paled in comparison anyway. The opportunity to perhaps see her yet again fueled his anticipation for this trip to her town.

He mounted his horse and set out for Briar Ridge. The clear, mild temperatures of the day became cooler as his trip wore on. Although still late afternoon, shadows of darkness fell over the terrain, and rain fell as he approached the Anderson house.

When Nathan knocked on the door to the house, Jonathan answered. "Well now, Nathan Reed, how good to see you again. Come in out of this nasty weather."

"Thank you. I had hoped to be able to stop for a visit, but I had no idea it would be to seek shelter as well." Nathan welcomed the warmth of the home and removed his hat, coat, and gloves.

"Where are you headed?" Jonathan reached for Nathan's coat and gloves.

"Back to Briar Ridge for some business." He strode over to the fire and held his hands toward the flames there.

Mrs. Anderson greeted him. "I remember you from last week. Nathan Reed, isn't it?" She turned to her son. "Jon, where are your manners? Get Mr. Reed here something warm to drink."

The rain had chilled him, and he welcomed the offer of a hot drink. He dreaded the thought of continuing his journey and chided himself for not starting out earlier. He'd lived here long enough to know the fickleness of the weather.

Jonathan handed him a cup of steaming coffee. "Come on over and sit down."

Nathan followed the young man and sat on the sofa. Although not elegant like the Hill or Harrington homes, the Anderson house held warmth that far surpassed them. The sofa and one chair were the only upholstered pieces in the room. The wood of the other furniture gleamed in the light from the lamps set around.

Mrs. Anderson offered a plate of apple muffins. "Will you be able to stay and dine with us, and perhaps stay for the night too? The weather is much too harsh for travel this evening."

"Thank you, Mrs. Anderson. I hate to impose, but I accept your generous offer."

"Good. That's settled. Supper is almost complete. The others should be down shortly. You and Jon visit awhile."

Nathan smiled and nodded at the woman who was the true picture of what a farm wife should be. Her rosy cheeks gave her a healthy glow, and her bright eyes hinted at the love she shared with her family. She wore a green calico print dress under a white apron that encircled her ample body. Here was a lady he wouldn't mind having as a mother.

Mr. Anderson joined them by the fire. "Welcome, Nathan. I understand you'll stay with us tonight. That's good, because it's likely the weather will only grow worse."

"I think I can make it all right into Briar Ridge tomorrow morning. I have warm clothing, and the ride shouldn't be more than a few hours at the most considering this weather."

"That reminds me. I could use a favor from you."

"Anything, sir, as I'm truly thankful for your hospitality tonight."

"I have three young saplings that I need to deliver to Reverend Winston. I'll give you use of one of my wagons to tote them there. It will save Jonathan or me from making the trip. I told the reverend we'd bring them to him soon as we had them prepared for travel."

"Of course. I'd be happy to take the trees with me." What an excellent excuse to see Rachel again. He'd do anything for that chance, and carrying a few trees would be a small price to pay.

"Then we'll fix you up tomorrow morning." He stood. "Come, let's enjoy some of Mrs. Anderson's supper. I do believe I detected the aroma of chicken and dumplings when I came downstairs. That will fill you up and warm your insides too."

After the hearty meal, Nathan visited with the family. Again, pangs of remorse filled him as he watched the Andersons. They exhibited the same love and devotion he had seen in the Winston home. Would he ever experience this kind of family relationship again? Not unless he married a young woman like Rachel Winston, and that wasn't even in the realm of possibility.

CHAPTER
TWELVE

*T*HE NEXT MORNING the rain had changed to a threat of snow. Thick, dark clouds rolled across the landscape. Nathan eyed them as a seasoned traveler. If the temperature continued to drop, snow would be heavy by afternoon. He didn't mind the snow as long as he was dressed warmly.

Mr. Anderson hitched a horse to the wagon and covered the animal's broad back with a heavy blanket. "This will give him some protection from the cold. The trees are wrapped securely and should be safe enough. Do you have enough to keep you warm?"

"Yes, sir. Mrs. Anderson has wrapped hot bricks to put at my feet, and I have layers enough to protect me." Nathan secured his own horse to the back of the wagon.

"Good. You can bring my equipment by the next time you come through here." He stepped back. "God speed you on your journey. May He give you protection and safety."

"Thank you." Nathan clicked the reins and began the trip

toward Briar Ridge. He doubted Mr. Anderson's words would have much effect, but he sincerely appreciated them.

As he traveled, the skies became a strange mixture of black and gray. He'd never seen anything quite like it. The road, once a river of mud, was now iced over and made traveling the path slower than usual.

After an hour the rain became a snow like no other Nathan remembered. Thick flakes swirled and danced all around him. As the wind picked up, the flakes increased and blew from the side. The temperature dropped steadily, and even the heavy layers were no match for the icy air and wind gusts. He pulled his woolen scarf up to protect his face and secured his hat tighter on his head. Without the sun to guide him, Nathan had no real idea of how long he had driven the wagon.

His heart filled with guilt and remorse as his situation grew more dangerous. Again Nathan blamed God for everything that had gone wrong in his life. "I believe in You, God, but I sure don't believe You love everybody." The wind carried his words away, but if he continued to speak aloud, he'd have a better chance of staying awake.

"The preacher said You are a heavenly Father who loves us like our earthly father. That is not my idea of a loving God. In my life You have been as unloving and cruel as my father was to me."

The cold now penetrated deep into his bones. He had loved the man he called Father, but his love had never been returned, and on the day he died, Nathan had learned why. He closed his eyes against the stinging wind. The picture of that last day when Cyrus Reed, with his last breath, disowned Nathan as his son appeared as clearly as if it had happened yesterday.

The snow grew heavier and the air colder. He pulled the heavy blanket closer about his shoulders. His body grew stiff with cold. The snow flurries and wind had turned into a blizzard. If he didn't get to Briar Ridge soon, he'd die on this trail. If God loved him, He was the only one who could save Nathan now.

Rachel had watched the clouds all morning, and now the snow flew about in the wind. Never had she seen such a storm this time of year. The middle of March had brought bad weather before, but nothing like she witnessed through the kitchen window. The snowflakes dipped and whirled around in the wind gusts and fell in heavier and heavier amounts.

Mama looked up from writing her list of supplies. "I think we're all set for this storm if it lasts very long. We have plenty of food in the pantry, wood on the porch, and clean clothing for everyone." She rose and walked over to stand beside Rachel. "I'm sure they must have let school out by now. The children should be coming in any minute. Make some hot cocoa for them."

Rachel busied herself with the task. Papa burst through the door. "Looks like we're in for a big storm. Biggest one I've ever seen. Are we well stocked?"

Mama helped Papa with his coat. "Yes, Rachel and I baked bread and made stew this morning. We have the soup from yesterday and brought up dried fruits and canned foods from the cellar. Our hard work last summer will be well worth the effort for the next few days."

"I'm glad to hear it, although I should have known you

would take care of it all. The snow is falling faster than I've ever seen it." Papa stood by the stove to warm his hands.

Rachel poured her father a cup of cocoa and thought about snowstorms in the past. When more than a few feet fell, school let out for several days, and the whole family became homebound. Mentally she checked off games she could play with Miriam and Micah to help them pass the time.

Where could her brothers and sister be? Surely school had let out already. If it hadn't, the children would have a difficult time getting home with the heavy winds now blowing. Snow could be the most silent of killers if people were not properly prepared for the freezing air.

Papa grabbed for his coat. "I'm going out to check our wood for the fireplaces. The parlor, our bedroom upstairs, and the kitchen will most likely be the only rooms with heat in the next few days."

When he left to tend to that chore, Rachel went up to make sure adequate quilts covered each bed. The warm air from downstairs made the upstairs still bearable, but soon it would be very cold even in these rooms. Miriam would be sleeping with Rachel for the next few nights, as Micah would with Noah. Two bodies always provided more heat than one alone.

While she pulled covers from their storage chests and arranged them on the beds, she mentally calculated what would be needed for each room. Then she thought of Nathan. At least he was safe and secure in Hartford. The city had heat and electricity not available in a town such as Briar Ridge. She imagined him in his law offices discussing cases with his clients or his partners.

A noise arose from downstairs. Rachel jumped up and flew

down the stairway to see Noah and Miriam in the entryway. Miriam sobbed in Mama's arms. Rachel glanced around. "Mama, where is Micah?"

A worried frown spread over her mother's face. "He's not here. He ran away from Noah and Miriam when they walked home from school."

Rachel's hand went to her throat. Micah, lost? The little boy loved playing in the snow. But to be lost in a storm like this could be catastrophic.

Papa strode into the hallway. "Where's Micah?"

Mama ran to him. "He's out there lost in the snow. He's just a baby. He'll die."

"No, we'll find him." He tied another scarf around his neck. "Come, Noah, we can't waste time." He handed a rope to her brother. "Tie one end around your wrist, and I'll hold one end. Be sure your lantern stays lit so we can see each other's light. We don't want to lose each other."

Noah opened the door, and the howling wind shocked Rachel. It sounded so much worse now than it had even half an hour ago. She wrapped an arm around Miriam's shoulder. "Let's go into the kitchen for cocoa. We can wait there for Papa and Noah to come back."

Mama turned aside. "I'll be in the parlor praying. Rachel, you will need to make sure we have warm blankets for Micah when they return. Heat up some of that soup from yesterday, and keep it ready for them too."

"Yes, Mama, I'll take care of everything." Rachel led Miriam into the kitchen and poured her a cup of hot cocoa.

When she went to the sink, her throat tightened. She could no longer see across the street or even to the gate in the side fence. *O Lord, keep Micah safe. Help Papa and Noah to find him quickly and bring him home.*

The temperatures had steadily dropped and the winds became stronger, but Nathan sensed that Briar Ridge was near. The horses still plodded along. The bricks had long lost their heat, and snow mounded on the extra blankets. The shaking had not begun, but it wouldn't be long if they didn't find shelter. He hunched his shoulders and peered into the whirling whiteness. The fur lining of his gloves still protected his hands, and for that he was most grateful. Although he usually hated wearing long, woolen underwear, Jonathan Anderson insisted Nathan wear it today, and for that he was thankful as well.

For some reason he thought of his mother, and guilt filled his soul. He lifted his head toward the sky, the snow nearly blinding him. "God, I know You exist, and once I thought You loved me as Your own. If You love me, let me survive this, and I will go home and seek forgiveness from my mother. I have to tell her and my sisters that I love them. Please, God, I promise."

His head slumped against his chest. Why had he done that? God couldn't help him now. No one could. He lifted his eyes and peered ahead where a dark shape of a building loomed. The church was among the first buildings on this edge of town. If he could make it there, he could find shelter within its doors. For the first time in a long time, he'd be more than happy to see the inside of a house of God.

He made out the faint outline of the front entrance. Nathan climbed down from the wagon seat and led the horses to the walk leading up to the front doors. He stepped over a hump in the snow then jumped back when it moved.

Startled, Nathan bent down to see what it could be. He brushed away the snow and realized it was a child. He grabbed up the boy and stood, seeing with shock that it was Rachel's little brother Micah. He stumbled forward a few feet before a hand gripped his shoulder. A voice broke through the howling winds.

"You've found him. Thank God."

Nathan turned and recognized Reverend Winston. He relinquished his burden to the man.

"Noah, see to Mr. Reed's horses, but don't let go of your rope." He hugged the small body to his chest and said, "Let's get to the house. Grab hold of my arm, son. We'll have you inside in a few minutes." He handed Nathan a blanket, then wrapped one around the boy.

Nathan could only nod and pull the wrap around his shoulder. He gripped the man's arm and plodded beside him. It seemed that they must have walked forever, but in reality, it was only a few minutes. His eyes drooped, and he simply wanted to lie down and sleep, but he plunged ahead, holding firmly to Reverend Winston.

When he saw the outline of houses, relief filled him. He saw a light, and hands reached out to pull him into a warm place. Had he made it to heaven after all, or...

From that point everything faded to black.

CHAPTER
THIRTEEN

RACHEL GASPED AS her father stepped inside holding Micah. Another man fell into the entryway behind him. She reached down to remove his hat. "Nathan Reed! Oh my, Papa, what happened?"

Papa thrust his bundle toward Rachel. "Nathan found Micah, and we found them both. You take Micah and warm him up. Felicity, you see to Mr. Reed." He turned to Noah. "Son, take care of the horses. I'll be out to help after we get this boy into the parlor. Make sure they have plenty of feed and blankets. Tie the rope from the barn to the house. From the looks of this snow, we'll need it to find our way to take care of the animals later."

Rachel peered down at Micah's still face. She hugged him to her chest and hurried into the kitchen where the warmth of the stove would help revive him. Her parents carried Nathan's limp form into the parlor, where a fire blazed on the hearth. Rachel prayed for both the boy and the man.

Miriam joined her in the kitchen with fear in her eyes. "Is Micah dead? He's so white and still."

"He's alive. His heartbeat is slow, but I can feel it beating, and he's breathing. Heat up water in the kettle while I check him over." She carefully removed each piece of clothing. His toes were white and limp with frost nip, but she didn't think they had frostbite. His hands looked fine thanks to the thick woolen gloves Mama knit for him.

The first order of business was to get him warm inside and out. Miriam put a kettle of water to warm on the stove.

"Thank you," Rachel said. "Now run up to Micah's room and bring me down some heavy socks and dry clothing."

Her sister ran to do the task, and Rachel tended to Micah. She blew her warm breath over his feet and face, but concern for Nathan in the parlor filled her. How had he happened to be back in Briar Ridge, and how had he found Micah? The last time she had seen him at the Anderson farm, he left in such a hurry to get to Hartford, she feared never seeing him again. What reason would he have to come back, especially at this particular time?

Miriam's return interrupted her thinking about Nathan. "Here's everything you need. What else can I do?"

"Heat up a few bricks. I want to put them by his feet to keep them warm." She pulled dry socks over Micah's feet, which were no longer as white as they had been. The color returned to his face and hands as Rachel rubbed them and breathed on them. Each article of wet clothing was laid out to dry and replaced with a warm, dry, flannel nightshirt. She wrapped a blanket about him and held him close to the stove.

Everything in her wanted to jump and run into the parlor to

see how Nathan fared, but her mother's treatments would take care of him. Her responsibility lay with caring for her young brother.

She rocked back and forth with the child in her arms. "Oh, little Micah, I know how you love the snow, but this time your love almost killed you." She glanced over at Miriam, whose usual happy countenance now creased with worry and guilt.

Rachel wanted to ask how they had let Micah get away from them on the way home, but by doing so, she'd only add to her sister's misery. The reasons could wait until later.

When Micah coughed and moved in her arms, Rachel wanted to shout with joy. "Hey, little one, are you waking up?" His eyelids fluttered then opened to stare right at her. "Welcome back, Micah." She hugged the child to her.

"I want Mama. My throat hurts, and my feet hurt." He tried to wriggle from her grasp.

Rachel held him tight. "Mama's busy. I'll make some honey tea for your throat. You were lost in the snow and had a little frost nip in your toes. That's why they're tingling and hurting now."

She sat him down in a kitchen chair with the blanket still wrapped around him. "You sit here nice and still while I get you something warm to drink." She checked the water in the tea-kettle, then pulled the honey jar from a shelf and measured a spoonful into a cup. It would be soothing as well as healing.

Mama entered the room, and Micah held his arms out to her. "Mama, my throat hurts."

"I'm sure it does, my little one." She hugged the boy to her. "We'll get you up to bed right away." She glanced over at Rachel. "Are you making tea?"

"Yes, ma'am. I thought with a little honey it would be help his throat." She poured hot water over the tea leaves in the pot.

"Good. We'll need some for Mr. Reed later. That is, if he wakes up. I'm afraid he's in much worse shape than little Micah here. He's still unconscious."

Worry and fear squeezed Rachel's heart. "Mama, he has to get well."

"Dear, we'll pray for him and do all we can to make sure he does. He's young and strong, and a fighter. He'll wake up soon."

The words reassured Rachel, but worry and concern still plagued her. So many things she didn't know about him, but she wanted to. He had too much life still to live. Rachel closed her eyes. *Heavenly Father, please watch over Nathan and heal his body. He's one of Your children who needs to know You as his personal Savior. Help us to minister to him and to make him well.*

"Rachel, give Micah some of the tea, then take him to my bed. The fireplace is blazing, and the room should be warm enough. I'm going back to see about Mr. Reed."

"Yes, Mama, I will." She reached for Micah.

He jerked backward and clung to his mother. "No, stay, Mama, please."

Mama disentangled Micah's arms. "I must see about Mr. Reed, sweet one. He saved your life. He found you near the church gate, and then Papa and Noah found you both."

A tear trickled down Micah's cheek. "I was scared. I couldn't see where to go."

"I know, I know. It's all right now. You're safe and warm here." She placed the back of her hand on his forehead. "But I think you have a bit of a fever now, and with that sore throat, we don't want you to get sicker, so let your sister give you the tea and then put you to bed."

He held on for a few more seconds then peered up at Rachel. "Can I have a cookie too?"

Rachel smiled and winked at her mother over his head. "Of course, but if it hurts your throat, we'll save it for later." She knew the crumbs from the sugar cookie would scratch, but if she told him that, he'd only fuss. Better to let him find out for himself.

Rachel reached for the cookie tin. The wind howled louder, and the day grew dark. The back door burst open, and Papa and Noah practically fell into the room. Mama rushed over and helped them remove their damp coats.

Rachel dropped the tin and grabbed the teakettle from the stove. She poured steaming cups of hot liquid for both men. Papa spotted Micah and bent down to peer at him.

"Well, I see our little man is awake and looking his usual chipper self."

"Papa, I got lost in the snow. I'm sorry."

Papa wrapped his arms around Micah. "God took care of you this time. You must promise to never do anything like that again."

Micah sniffed. "I promise."

Rachel set the teakettle back on the stove. Papa and Mama conversed in low tones, but she caught Nathan's name and the worry in Mama's eyes. She leaned toward Noah. "Do you think this storm will stop anytime soon?"

Noah shook his head. "Doesn't look like it. I'd say it'll go on all night. What's for supper?"

She slapped at her brother's arm. "Is food all you can think about?"

"Hey, taking care of those horses was hard work. And you know what? Nathan was bringing us those apple trees we ordered from Mr. Anderson. Almost got himself killed for that good deed. How is he, anyway?"

"Mama says not too well. He hasn't woken yet." So that was why Nathan came to Briar Ridge, but then what had he been doing at the Anderson farm in the first place? She'd just have to wait until he was better to explain that. She bit her lip. He had to get well, he just had to.

Papa stood. "I'm going to see to putting that small wood stove we have in the barn upstairs so Micah and Nathan will have a warm room to sleep in. I'll have to vent it out the window, but it'll still provide some heat. I fear the rest of us may have to stay together in one room with the fireplace. Noah and I will take turns to make sure the fires are stoked. We don't want to freeze to death. I've never seen cold quite like this. The whole town is paralyzed." He kissed Mama's cheek, then went to see to his chore. She followed him into the other room.

Micah sat in his chair and sipped the tea. The cookie lay on the plate, untouched after the first bite. When the last drop drained from the cup, Micah sat back. "I'm sleepy. I'll save my cookie for later."

"All right. I'll put it away for another time." Rachel picked him up. "It's good you are sleepy. Rest is what you need now."

On the way up the stairs Micah began coughing. Mama stepped into the hall. "Rachel, that cough of his sounds bad. Give him a spoonful of that quinine tonic to help break up the mucus."

Rachel nodded and continued up the stairs. She'd settle Micah in her parent's bed then fetch the tonic. The congestion in his chest could lead to pneumonia, and that could be deadly in one so young.

"Rachel, can I have my bunny baby?" Micah's head lolled against her shoulder.

"Of course. I know just where it is." Her little brother really must be feeling ill. He had put away the little stuffed bunny two years ago when he declared he was no longer a baby and too big to sleep with his bunny. Mama had stored it away in her cedar chest.

Papa met her in the upper hall. "The stove is all set. It'll provide enough warmth with the quilts and hot bricks at their feet. Go ahead and put him in there. Noah and I will bring Nathan up to rest in the other bed. That way Mama can nurse both patients at the same time."

"Miriam and I will help take care of everything for supper. We made a big pot of stew, and we have fresh baked bread to go with it." She carried her brother into his bedroom and placed him on the bed. She pulled the covers up over him, thankful for the small stove that chased away the chill. "You get all nice and warm, and I'll go get bunny baby for you." She leaned over and kissed his forehead, which felt more feverish now than it had earlier.

A few minutes later she returned with the toy, hot bricks wrapped in flannel, and the quinine tonic. Micah tried to resist her efforts to get the medicine down, but with her persistence, he finally swallowed a small spoonful. A few minutes later his lids closed in healing sleep.

She sat watching the even up-and-down movement of his

small chest. Twice, coughing spells awakened him, but he fell right back to sleep. If only Nathan would fare as well as Micah. If he hadn't awakened yet, it may be a long time before he did. In this weather Dr. Thornton could not come and see either Nathan or Micah. They had to rely on Mama's skill and God's mercy and love.

Rachel's duties in the kitchen called for her to leave, but she hesitated in leaving the child alone. If he happened to wake up, he'd want somebody with him. In the hallway she met Noah and Papa carrying Nathan.

"We're going to put him in Noah's bed. Mama is bringing up warm bricks to put at his feet."

She stepped back and watched as the two men placed Nathan's deathly still form on the bed. His pale face spoke of experience in the freezing weather. Rachel's heart ached for him. How he must have suffered before Papa found him. Only God's grace had kept Nathan and Micah alive. Surely God meant for Nathan to live and grow strong again.

CHAPTER
FOURTEEN

*I*F RACHEL'S CALCULATIONS were correct, the storm raged for over thirty hours. By Wednesday evening, the winds subsided, and the snow now swirled and dipped in flurries as graceful as any ballerina. Papa measured over four feet so far on the gauge he set out in the yard, but drifts piled much higher than that between the house and the barn.

The night had been spent with Miriam and her in the big feather bed with Mama. Noah and Papa slept on the floor in front of the hearth. Rachel had heard them getting up during the night to check on the stove downstairs. Mama rose several times to take care of Micah and Nathan.

Rachel peeled potatoes to add to the pot roast and gazed out the kitchen window. Under overcast clouds, the snow covered everything with a blanket of white. In the places where the snow stood in drifts as high as most men's heads, neighbors' homes were hidden from view. Not a soul moved about the streets, and no signs of life could be seen anywhere. The quiet after the howling winds of last night gave an eerie feel to the world outside.

That morning Nathan still had not awakened, and Micah's fever had not abated. As soon as Papa could get out, he planned to go for Dr. Thornton. Rachel saw the worry for both patients etched in her father's face. Her mother stayed in the room with the two and bathed Micah's heat-filled body with a damp cloth.

Mama and Papa had decided that someone should be with the patients at all times. At first they had told Rachel she couldn't sit with them because it wasn't seemly to have her caring for Nathan, but later they had relented, seeing as how he remained unconscious. She added the potatoes to the simmering pot roast. As soon as she had the evening meal ready, she planned to go up and relieve Mama. Time almost stood still in her anticipation of sitting with Nathan.

Papa stamped into the kitchen. He shook snow off his hat into the sink. "I think the horses will be fine. They have plenty of feed and water and blankets."

Noah closed the door behind him. "Good thing we put that rope out there. I don't think I could have cleared the way to the barn without it as a guide."

Papa laughed. "The walls of that path are almost above your head. I've never seen the likes of it. This will be a March we won't soon forget."

Her father wrapped his arm around Noah's shoulders. "Let's go into the parlor. I'd like your opinion on Sunday's sermon subject."

Rachel shook her head and hid a smile. Papa didn't need anyone's opinion about his sermons, but it was one way to keep Noah occupied. Miriam was upstairs making sure the beds were ready for tonight. Rachel had promised to play a game with her and Noah later in the evening. Boredom could set in faster than that snowstorm had blown in if she didn't keep those two busy.

Mama appeared in the door. "Do you have any of that soup left from yesterday? I want to take some up to Micah. He's awake and hungry, a good sign."

"Yes, I'll heat it up right away. I have the roast cooking for supper." Rachel poured the soup into a pot and set it on the stove. "How is Na—I mean, Mr. Reed, coming along?"

Mama prepared a tray for the food. "It's all right, Rachel. In our home, you may call him Nathan. No need for formalities in times like this. It's been a good while, and he still hasn't awakened. I'm concerned."

Rachel checked the soup, then ladled up the broth into a bowl. Her mother placed it on the tray along with a chunk of bread. "After I feed Micah, I'll bring this back down, and you can go up to sit with him for a while and keep watch over Nathan. I'll finish up with supper."

"Everything will be ready when you come back."

"My dear, in just a few short months you have grown into a mature young lady ready to take on a great deal of responsibility. I'm very proud of you."

Mama's words of praise filled Rachel with great peace and satisfaction with her work. She wouldn't disappoint her parents now. Her mother left, and Rachel busied herself with putting out dinnerware for the evening meal. The stillness and quiet outdoors gave a sense of complete isolation even though neighbors were not that far away. The contrast between now and this time yesterday only served to prove that tragedy could strike at a moment's notice and change the lives of everyone. Every moment of every day was important.

She checked the roast again then adjusted the flame beneath it. What could have happened in Nathan's life that so turned him away from God? She had never known anyone who had denounced God as completely as Nathan had.

Nathan had been to church, yet he didn't want anything to do with religion. That bothered her more than anything else she had learned about him from Daniel and Abigail. And then there was the sadness she had again noted in his eyes that day at the Anderson farm when he'd talked of his family.

Because of his feelings about God, he would never be suitable for Rachel as a suitor. Besides, he had never shown any serious interest in her anyway. She must think of him only as a very sick young man who needed healing not only of the body but also of the heart and soul.

"I'm here to help. What can I do?" Miriam asked.

Rachel jumped. "Oh, I didn't hear you come in. You can finish the table."

Miriam grabbed a handful of cutlery and began placing it next to the plates. "I think it's fun not to have any school and to stay home and help you and Mama." Her brow furrowed. "But I do hope Micah gets well. And Mr. Reed too."

Mama walked through the door. "I think Micah will be fine in a day or two, but I'm worried about Nathan. I've taken care of the frostbite, but he's not waking up. We must pray for him diligently." She hugged Miriam. "It's wonderful to see my two girls working together like this. You two have certainly grown up this past year."

Miriam's face turned a bright red, and Rachel laughed.

"I don't mind having her around now nearly as much as I did before I went off to school." She reached over for her sister's hand. "I'm so glad we don't argue and fuss like we once did. This is much more fun."

"What's more fun?" Papa strode into the kitchen. "Umm, I smell something good cooking."

"The fun is in our not arguing and fussing about everything, and the thing that smells so good is supper." Rachel reached for the fork and knife to remove the roast from the pot.

Noah entered the room and rubbed his hands together. "I hope that was apple pie I smelled too."

"It was, and I made it plenty big just so you'd have enough. I've been sampling all afternoon, so I'm not hungry." Rachel untied her apron and hung it up.

Mama took over the kitchen duties to let Rachel take care of Micah and Nathan. When she entered the room, her brother peeked over the covers and wriggled his fingers at her.

"And how are you feeling this evening?"

"My throat hurts."

"Did you eat some of that soup Mama brought up?"

He nodded and pushed himself up on his pillow. "Tell me a story."

"All right, what do you want to hear?" She reached for the story and picture books at the end of his bed.

"David and Goliath. He killed that giant." Micah's dark blue eyes sparkled with anticipation of his favorite Bible story.

Rachel pulled the rocking chair close and began telling the tale of how David, the shepherd boy, slew the giant Goliath. As she talked, Micah's eyes drooped.

"And the stone from David's slingshot flew through the air

and landed square in the middle of Goliath's forehead. That great, big, huge giant of a man, Goliath, fell like a tree chopped down. God once again saved His people."

"He killed him dead, and God saved the people." Micah grinned, then flopped over on his side. Rachel arranged his covers and patted his head. His forehead felt only slightly warm tonight, much better than yesterday when his little body burned with fever.

She moved the chair to sit near Nathan's bed. His pale face showed no signs of awareness. Mama's Bible lay nearby, and Rachel picked it up. How she wished Nathan was awake so she could read to him of God's great love. She had heard that sometimes people in a deep sleep could hear and understand when someone spoke. Perhaps he could hear her. Watching his pale face, she kept her voice low to keep from disturbing Micah.

"Oh, Nathan, God's Book is full of great stories of how God loves His people and rescues them from their sins. I don't know what could have happened in your life to bring such sorrow and denial of God. I wish I could make it go away, but nobody can do that but God. If you'd only trust Him, you'd see how much better your life could be."

But then, who was she to say his life wasn't just like he wanted it?

Nathan heard a voice. So sweet and soft. His hands and feet stung with pain, and warmth filled the rest of his body. The last things he remembered were blinding snow, a numbing cold, and a child on the ground. He struggled to open his eyes to the light, but his lids remained shut.

The voice came again. He relaxed and listened to the words as soft as angel wings. Angel wings? Was he in heaven? That was unlikely, but the pleasantness of this place told him it couldn't be the hell to which he deserved to be sent.

He let the soothing sound wrap itself around him like a blanket. Then he heard the words *God* and *love*. His insides exploded with anger. God and love didn't mix.

The words continued.

"Nathan, no matter what has happened in your past, let God handle it. It doesn't make any difference what you have done. The important thing is what you do with the rest of your life. God led you to our Micah, and because you were standing there, Papa found you. God put you in that place for a reason, and He saved your life for a reason."

That was Rachel's voice! Where was he? Then he remembered holding a child and a hand grasping his arm and leading him to light and warmth. Why had God saved him? Oh, he'd made a promise in the blizzard. He had to go home to see his mother.

A hand caressed his forehead, and Rachel spoke again. "Oh, how I wish you would wake up. You have so much life still to live, and there's so much to tell you about our Savior."

He heard the sound of pages turning. "The Bible tells us that with God, all things work together for good. I believe He worked your being in the storm for good so you could find Micah, and so you could be here with our family.

"Daniel said that at one time you did believe in God and attended church. What turned you away? Don't you realize that in chapter eight of the book of Romans we read, 'Who shall separate us from the love of Christ? Shall tribulation, or distress, or persecution, or famine, or nakedness, or peril, or sword?' No, Nathan, we are conquerors over all these things through Jesus, who loved us and died for us. We're the ones to separate ourselves from God. He's always there waiting for us to come back. Jesus can take away all the pain and sorrow and give you new joy."

Joy? He hadn't felt much joy in the past few years. Could God truly restore him? Could he return to his mother and find her love again? He had to find out.

A low moan escaped his throat, and again he attempted to open his eyes. This time the light revealed the young woman standing by his side, his angel of mercy, Rachel Winston. She gasped, and her hand grabbed her throat.

"You're awake. Oh, thank You, Lord, thank You." She started to rise, but he grasped her hand.

"Wait, don't leave yet. Where am I?"

She glanced down at his hand but did not pull away. She sat back down. "You're in our house. Papa found you and brought you out of the storm. You've been unconscious a whole day. I must let Mama know you're awake. She's been so worried."

He continued to hold her hand. "Those words you spoke, tell me more." His heart yearned for more of the promise that God could take away his pain, not the physical, but the spiritual.

She leaned closer, squeezing his hand. "Oh, Nathan, God loves you and saved your life. He still has things for you to do in life. I don't know what made you turn away, but God is waiting for your return."

"Is it really that easy?" He searched her eyes, looking for truth. At the moment he couldn't see it, but his heart wanted something more than he'd been giving it the past four years.

"Yes, Nathan, it is. Just confess to Him the wrongs in your past, and He'll forgive them, no matter how bad they were, and joy will return."

"How did you get to be so wise? I've never met a girl with so much knowledge of God. It must be because your father is a man of God." Which easily explained the serenity and joy he had seen in her smile and demeanor.

"Yes, and he taught us early on that we could always rely on God to take care of us. Just like He's taken care of you."

God had taken care of him, and now the time had come for him to place his trust back in his Savior and right the wrongs from the past. "Thank you, Rachel. You've given me hope for the future that I never thought possible." And now he prayed that future would include this wonderful girl who had shown him the way to a new life.

That warm smile of hers filled her face. She patted his hand, then pulled away and raced for the door. "Mama, Papa, come quick. Nathan is waking up."

She returned to his side, and he savored the soft beauty of her face. Mrs. Winston rushed into the room, followed by the preacher. She lifted Nathan's wrist and felt for his pulse. A smile crossed her lips. "Your heartbeat is almost normal, and your fever has lessened. You gave us quite a scare, but we can never thank you enough for finding Micah for us."

Micah's voice sounded from across the room. "I was lost, and you found me."

Reverend Winston said nothing but stood at the end of the

bed with a serious look on his face. Nathan knew he must talk to him, but with the family all around that would have to wait. At the moment, he was simply grateful for the kindness and love they had shown him.

CHAPTER
FIFTEEN

*T*HE NEXT DAY Nathan's strength began to return, enough
that he was able to join the family for their evening meal. As
he ate, he mulled over the idea of telling Reverend Winston his
story. Perhaps he would understand and not judge him.

When the dishes were cleared, he spoke up. "Reverend
Winston, may I speak with you in private for a moment?"
Nathan gazed at the man sitting across the table. He didn't
want Rachel or Mrs. Winston to hear his story. At some point
he might tell them, but not now.

"Of course, son." Ezra turned to his wife. "We'll go into my
study for privacy."

Nathan followed Reverend Winston into the study and sat
across the desk from him. He searched for a way to reveal his
story to this man of God. If anyone could help him, it had to be
the preacher. With a deep breath to bolster his courage, Nathan
began his tale.

"Reverend, I once went to church with my mother. I loved

God, prayed, and believed He loved me enough to die for me."
He stopped, but the reverend said nothing, waiting for Nathan
to continue.

"I was born after the war ended, in late December of 1865.
My father served in the army of the Confederate states and had
to leave my mother and sister Evelyn alone on the plantation
with only the slaves to protect them.

"After Lee's surrender, Father came home, but most of the
slaves had been freed or killed in an attack on our place. He and
Mother stayed on our land as long as they could, but he didn't
have the money or manpower to work the plantation on his
own. Eventually, after I was born, my parents took what they
could load onto wagons and went into town. There my uncle,
who had a store, took my father in as a partner. Together they
built the business into a successful mercantile."

"I see, but none of that seems enough to cause you to have
bitterness toward God. You were just a baby."

Nathan nodded. Telling the complete story would be difficult, but would the minister understand how it had affected
Nathan's decisions in life? His insides groaned not only from his
recent ordeal but also because the memories of those years hurt
as much now as they had then.

"All my life I could never measure up to my father's expectations. Nothing I ever did seemed to gain his approval, and he
couldn't seem to love me as a father. Father loved my mother
and sisters, but he rarely showed any outward affection toward
me. They all blamed his attitude and actions on the war, but I
was hurt."

"It's difficult being a father under the most ideal of

circumstances, Nathan, but with what your father endured, I can see how troubled he was."

"But he still made a success of the store with Uncle Bert. The two of them spent more time building that store than they ever did with their families."

Reverend Winston furrowed his brow and stoked his chin. After a moment he spoke. "Why did you come up here and go to Yale? Why didn't you stay there and take over the store when your father passed on?"

The hard part, the humiliating part, the time when God abandoned him had to be told. Nathan breathed deeply. "Because I learned my father wasn't my father at all."

The reverend's eyes opened wide, but he sat in silence waiting for the full story.

Now that he had begun, Nathan rushed to the finish to get the sordid details into the open. "During Sherman's battle at Fayetteville in March of 1865, a group of Yankee soldiers ransacked our house, killed or set free most of the slaves, and burned the barns and outbuildings. They kept the house so they could headquarter there for a time."

"And when did you learn about all of this?"

"On my father's deathbed. That's when I found out that one of the Yankee soldiers assaulted my mother. I was the result of that attack."

Nathan peered at Reverend Winston with an anxious heart. Would he judge him as all others had done when they learned the truth?

The minister's eyes held only love and compassion. "And that is why you left your home."

"Yes, sir, as he lay dying, he told me the truth. I would not inherit his part of the store. He'd left his part of the store to his brother to manage for the support of my mother and sisters. I was given the money for a college education and told to go north to where the other half of my parentage lived."

"I see. And how old were you when this happened?"

"Just a few months shy of my eighteenth birthday. After the funeral, I had words with my mother. I denounced God, because if He loved me, He wouldn't have allowed my birth to happen.

"I blamed her for not fighting back. I even told her I hated her for letting it happen. And in my anger I even railed against my sister Evelyn, who was there through the whole awful scene. She probably hates me for what I said and what I put Mother through. I am still grateful that my sister Beth wasn't there. She would have been so hurt too."

"But you were young and upset. Your whole world had been turned upside down."

"Yes, but that is no excuse for what I said." In his heart he knew he had done wrong, but did he have the courage to leave his career and go back to face his mother and his sisters as he had promised?

"Son, all I can say is that God works things in our lives in mysterious ways. What you see as bad can be turned to good. God loves you and wants to help you make things right. You moved away from Him in your anger and feelings of betrayal, but He's waiting right where you left Him, ready to take you on the rest of your life's journey."

Nathan's chest tightened with the comprehension of the minister's words. Rachel had said the same thing. God was still here. The farther he had run, the less he felt God's tug to bring him back, but now God loomed so very near. The words "Come to me, all ye that labor and are heavy laden, and I will give you rest" filled his mind. The words from the Book of Matthew he'd learned as a boy now brought him comfort.

Reverend Winston reached over and covered Nathan's hands with his own. "My son, open your heart and let Him come back in. He loves you and will go with you wherever you travel. And I believe that's back to your home."

Nathan had promised God to do just that if he survived the storm. Now here he sat, ill, but living. "Yes, I know it is. As far as I know, my older sister Evelyn is still living with and taking care of Mother. She never wanted anything to do with suitors, and now I see she must have absorbed some of my mother's fears of men. Beth didn't, as she married a fine man. Mother suffered not only from that day in 1865 but also from my tirades against her and Evelyn before I left. Can God ever forgive me for that?"

"He already has. Soon as you voice it, He does it."

"But what about Mother? Can she forgive me?" Now that the decision was made, his fear of rejection by his mother played on his mind. No, despite that possibility, he had to make amends.

"Nathan, she's your mother. No matter what the circumstances, she gave birth to you and likely loves you with all her heart. Your leaving grieved her, I'm sure, and going home will be the best thing you can do for her."

The words spoke true, and a mantle of peace fell over Nathan as he remembered the woman who had cared for him all those years. Even if she didn't accept him now, he had to go back and tell her how much he loved her.

He pulled his hand from Reverend Winston's and grabbed the man's arm. "Please, sir, you mustn't tell Rachel about this. I don't want her to know. You can tell her I've changed my heart toward God, but nothing else."

Reverend Winston frowned but nodded. "I understand. What you told me is between you and me…and God."

Nathan relaxed against the chair, relief flooding his soul. He'd explain to Rachel sometime, but for now his secret was safe.

A knock on the door sounded, and Mrs. Winston called out. "I have apple dumplings for you, Nathan. May I come in?"

Reverend Winston told her to enter. Nathan turned to her and smiled. Now his heart was healed, and with Mrs. Winston's good care and good food, his body would be fine. His journey home couldn't come soon enough.

Rachel yearned to follow her mother into the study. What had taken Papa and Nathan so long to discuss? She prayed for Nathan's complete healing in the days ahead, not only of body but also of soul.

Micah leaned on the table, supported by his elbows. "Can I have a cookie now, Rachel? I ate all my supper."

"I think that can be arranged. Is your throat well enough to swallow it?" She removed two cookies from the tin and placed them before her little brother. "I'll get you some apple juice to go with it."

She poured the juice and watched as he took a big bite. He chewed a moment then swallowed hard. A huge grin lit up his face. "It don't hurt." He chomped down for another big piece.

"Be careful not to get too much in your mouth. I don't want

you to choke." Rachel set the glass beside his plate, then began picking up other plates and cups from the table.

Miriam shoved open the door. "I'm sorry, I meant to stay and help you." She grabbed an apron and tied it on. "I'll finish clearing and then dry the dishes after you wash."

"Thank you, I don't mind doing it all. I know you wanted to see the new pictures Noah has for his stereopticon, but I do appreciate your coming back to help."

"I can look at it later." Miriam tousled Micah's hair. "I'm so glad you're feeling better." Then she peered at Rachel. "Is Mr. Reed still with Papa?"

"Yes, but Mama just took them some of her dumplings." She wished she could be there now to see for herself how he fared. Now that he was stronger, she'd probably not have the opportunity to be alone with him again. Her curiosity about why he happened to be on the way to Briar Ridge when the storm hit rose as she washed dishes and handed them to Miriam. Surely bringing the trees had not been his only mission. Emotions swirled and dipped like the snow had done only yesterday, a lifetime ago.

Mama walked in with the tray of empty dishes. "Nathan and your father are about through with their discussion. I gave him a little of that quinine tonic. Don't want any phlegm or such forming in his chest, but he seems to be doing quite well."

Rachel placed the dishes in the sink. "Oh, I'm so relieved to hear it. I've been praying for him."

"I think all of our prayers did some good." She bent toward Micah. "I see you've had your treat, so I'm taking you back up to bed."

His lips formed a pout. "Do I hafta take med'cine again?"

Mama felt his forehead. "Well, you don't have a fever, and you haven't been coughing this evening, so maybe we'll skip this dose."

He threw his arms around his mother's neck and pulled himself toward her. "I don't like tonic. It tastes bad."

Mama stood holding him in her arms. "I know it does. Now let's get you back up to bed. A good night's sleep, and you should be good as new tomorrow."

Miriam hurried to the parlor to join Noah, but Rachel stood staring through the window into the dark night outside. The clouds parted for a moment and caused a diamond sparkle on the untouched snow there. How beautiful it looked tonight. So white and pristine, but in not too many days it would begin to melt and turn to slush and mud.

If the temperatures rose to usual levels for March, then the warm-up would allow people once again to go about their business and life would return to normal. But in her heart, Rachel knew her life would never be the same. No matter what common sense told her, she'd rather listen to her heart.

Then she remembered God's promise that all things were possible with Him. Her Lord was the only one who could change Nathan's heart and save his soul. A prayer escaped her lips. "O Father, I know Thy healing hands are on Nathan's health and his soul. If there is any chance for me in his future, please show me the way. If not, then take away my longings."

A tear trickled down her cheek.

CHAPTER
SIXTEEN

THE NEXT DAY the temperatures rose, and the snow finally began to melt. Noah and Miriam went off to school after breakfast while Mama cared for the patients and Rachel baked bread. Her heart had rejoiced when Papa told her of Nathan's change of heart toward God and how he wanted to make things right. She didn't know what "things" he meant, but at least Nathan accepted God's love for him.

After lunch Rachel prepared a mixture of milk and eggs to make custard. Feeling better, Micah came downstairs and sat at the kitchen table playing with his blocks. He'd go back to school soon, but for now he enjoyed being the center of attention. Rachel completed the custard filling and poured it into a pie shell, then pushed it into the oven to bake.

She headed for the parlor to check the fire there, but Micah called her back from the kitchen. She sighed.

"What can I do for you, Micah?" She sat down across from him.

"Don't go away. Stay here." His blue eyes pleaded with her.

Rachel laughed. "All right, baby brother. I'll stay here. How about a glass of milk and a piece of that bread I took out of the oven a little bit ago?"

"I'm not a baby. I'm seven. Can I have butter and jam on my bread?"

"Yes, you are a big boy. I'm sorry." She poured his milk and cut off a chunk of bread.

She heard the front door open and Papa's voice before he stepped into the kitchen. "Rachel, I'll be upstairs with Nathan and your mother. Here are most of the supplies she requested. Call us when dinner is ready." The next moment, he was gone.

Rachel stared at the closed door. What had happened? Papa wasn't usually that curt. Something must be wrong in town. She turned to the task of putting away the supplies he brought home.

Soon the children came in from school, hungry and wind-blown and full of stories about the storm and how it had affected their classmates. She fed them cookies and hot cocoa, then finished preparations for dinner.

Rubbing her hands on her apron, she called for her sister. "Miriam, run upstairs and tell Mama and Papa we're ready to eat. You might tell Noah on your way." After her sister left, Rachel removed her apron and smoothed back her hair but pulled a strand on each side to dangle in front of her ears. She had pulled the rest back and fastened it with a clip so it hung down her back. Putting it up in braids or curls took too long, and a bun made her feel like an old woman.

When Nathan entered the room with her parents, her heart pounded and her hands were as wet as though they'd been in the dishwater. She wiped them on her skirt. "Good evening, Nathan. It's good to see you downstairs again."

"And if the aroma I inhaled coming down is an indication of the meal ahead, I'm glad I'm here." He smiled and sat down.

When all were seated, Papa gave thanks for the meal. He finished and picked up a bowl of potatoes and handed them to Mama. From the look in his eyes, Rachel could see something troubled him. Noah and Nathan joked with one another, but for once, her attention stayed on her father.

Finally he put down his fork and gazed around the table. "I've already shared this with Nathan and your mother, but I think you children need to know also. While I was in town, I learned that this storm covered most of the states from New York up to Maine. Hundreds perished in the storm, and many cities and towns suffered damage to buildings and other structures."

Rachel gasped. She knew the storm had been bad, but for it to cover such a large number of states awed her. God had shown His power through the wind and snow. "What about Briar Ridge?"

"No lives were lost, and not much damage came from it, thank the Lord. The newspapers are calling it a 'White Hurricane.' I know I've never seen anything like it. Mr. Thompson at the general store says it may be a week or so before we're able to get some of the food and other supplies we need. We need to remember to pray for those whose lives have been devastated by this storm. I plan to mention it in my sermon on Sunday."

Mama nodded. "Yes, we will pray and in addition give thanks that God spared the lives of Micah and Nathan. We can also thank Him that we have a full cellar of vegetables and canned foods from last summer."

"And that is something else I wanted to discuss. Many of our people have been found short of some of the necessities. As the pastor of the church, I believe we must share our bounty and give to those in need." Papa gazed around at each one seated at the table.

Rachel's heart swelled with pride. Her father always thought of others' needs above his own, and not just because he was a minister. Caring for people was just his nature.

Mama rose from the table. "Rachel and I will go through what we have and pack baskets of foods to take to church Sunday. Perhaps you can make an appeal for members to share what they have also." Then she turned to the stove. "But right now, let's have some of that custard pie Rachel made this afternoon."

Heat rose in Rachel's cheeks, and she rushed to help her mother serve the dessert. When she set Nathan's plate on the table, he grinned up at her. "Hmm, it looks as good as it smelled earlier. You have no end to your talents, Miss Winston."

Now her cheeks flamed. This time when her gaze locked with his, she no longer saw sadness, but a joy and sparkle that only added to his charm and good looks. She blinked and turned away. "Thank you." Inwardly she groaned. Was that all she could say to his compliment? Where were the words she used to tease Noah and Micah?

Nathan cleared his throat. "As soon as I take care of the business I have in Briar Ridge, I'm planning to head back to Hartford. I think the roads should be clear enough by Monday or Tuesday. I'm most grateful for your hospitality and care while I was ill."

Rachel's spoon clattered to her plate. Her throat closed and she couldn't breathe. Leave? But how could he be well enough? She had hoped for him to be around for another week with thoughts of becoming better acquainted. Now he dashed her plans against the ground.

She swallowed hard to clear her throat and bit her lip. If he left, he'd have no need to ever return to Briar Ridge.

Nathan hated for Rachel to learn of his departure in this way, but it was best for all concerned. If he stayed much longer, he would not be able to hide his true feelings from either Rachel or her parents.

"Reverend Winston and I discussed it, and he helped with the arrangements. Your father has agreed to take the wagon back to the Anderson farm, and Mr. Monroe has offered his carriage and Daniel to take me to Hartford. That way I will not have to exert myself during the trip."

Rachel's gaze cut to her father's. Hurt and confusion were written across her face. The more he saw of her, the more he wanted to stay, but he had to leave...for both their sakes.

Reverend Winston reached for Rachel's hand. "Nathan has much to do upon his return to Hartford. After all, he's been away from his work for a week."

"That's right. I wouldn't want them to find they can get along without me for any length of time." Nathan swallowed the last bite of pie and followed it with the few drops of coffee left in his cup. "I thank you again for your hospitality. You have been most generous in your care for me." He turned to Mrs.

Winston. "Especially yours, for I'm sure it was your tonic and other treatments that have renewed my strength."

She smiled kindly. "And I know the Lord had as much to do with it as I did."

"Yes, He did." Then he gazed at Rachel. "And I thank you, Rachel, because you knew what I needed for my heart and soul."

When she simply stared without response, Nathan drew a deep breath. "Reverend Winston, will you allow Rachel and me to have a few moments together in the parlor?"

After a moment and a nod from Mrs. Winston, he said, "Yes, I believe that will be fine."

A few moments later, Rachel seated herself on the sofa, and Nathan sat across from her. He clasped his hands between his knees as he searched for the words he needed to say. "Rachel, I cannot leave without telling you how much these last few days with you have meant to me. I see things more clearly now than I ever have in my lifetime. I have some issues back home with my family that I must go and clear up. I'll be leaving for North Carolina within the next week or so."

Her hands gripped one another, and her knuckles turned white. "Does that mean you won't return to Briar Ridge?"

"I don't know. Quite possibly. It all depends on what happens while I'm there. Please know that I appreciate all you've done for me. With my faith restored, I believe I'm ready to face whatever lies ahead."

Rachel frowned. "What do you mean by that?"

"If you care for me, you will pray for me and whatever God has in store with my family. You know so little about me, and if the circumstances were different, I would probably ask your father permission to court you. As it stands, I can't do that.

Rachel, you have a wonderful life here and a great future, so don't waste your thoughts on the likes of me."

Rachel said nothing, but the questions in her eyes that he could not answer gripped his heart with a pain like none he'd ever experienced, even when his father revealed the truth.

After a moment or two of silence, he excused himself and went up to his room and prepared his belongings for his departure.

Reverend Winston knocked on the door frame. "May I come in for a moment?"

Nathan nodded, and the minister came in and sat down. "How long will you be gone, son?"

"I don't know, sir." And he honestly didn't know. Any hopes of Rachel waiting for him had to be weighed against what he found at home. If they didn't accept his apology and welcome him home, he would stay until they did, or he'd never have true peace. If they did, then he may have to remain there for a period of time to make sure everything was as it should be with them.

Nathan picked up the Bible lying on the table beside the bed. "This book is full of promises as well as instruction on how we are to live. I want to honor my mother by asking her forgiveness and restoring our relationship."

Reverend Winston gripped Nathan's shoulder. "I'm proud of you. You have taken a giant step toward being the son your mother deserves and the man God wants you to be."

"Thank you. I told Rachel that family matters call me back to North Carolina."

The minister narrowed his eyes. "Have you declared your feelings for her?"

Pain gripped Nathan's heart in a vise, but he couldn't

promise Rachel anything for the future until he took care of the mistakes of his past. "I've never felt this way about a young woman before," he admitted. "But I cannot pursue a relationship with her when my family relationships are in tatters. She needs a good man like Daniel Monroe who can love her and take care of her without any ties or hindrances to things of the past." As much as the words hurt, he'd rather that she be with Daniel than to wait for what may never be with him.

Nathan turned away, filling his satchel with the few belongings he had brought with him. "It's best for her to forget me," he declared. This one thing he would do for her, and if the Lord had other plans, He would work it out.

The reverend looked at him searchingly but said only, "Our prayers will be with you." With those words he left the room, closing the door behind him.

Nathan slumped onto the bed and swallowed hard. How could he ever prove worthy of Rachel's love? And even if he did, would she be available when he returned?

CHAPTER
SEVENTEEN

Rachel went about her chores with a heavy heart. Nathan had given his life back to the Lord, but he had walked out of hers. When the carriage with Daniel and Nathan left Monday morning, her dream of Nathan's loving her had melted like the snow dripping from the eaves. Why had she even considered that he would be attracted to her?

Since Papa had already given his consent for Daniel to call on her, she would honor that. As nice as Daniel was, Rachel still couldn't get past the fact that she had known him most of her life and he was like a brother to her. Now, with Nathan gone, she must give Daniel the proper chance to court her, despite her own feelings.

Mama had gone upstairs to see to Micah, and Miriam and Noah had just returned from school and gone to their rooms. Rachel wandered into the parlor. Her cross-stitch lay in the sewing basket where she had left it last night. Perhaps a bit of sewing would remove Nathan from her mind. She sorted through the thread and picked one to use.

No matter how hard she tried to concentrate, Nathan's words continued to fill her thoughts. His eyes now held a peace that could come only from his reconciliation with the Lord, but his dark past still lurked in their depths.

After taking out three mistakes, she dropped the hoop to her lap. Her focus did not include embroidery this afternoon. She picked up the sewing basket and stowed her materials in it. Still not satisfied, Rachel searched for something else to occupy her idle hands.

Finally she marched to her father's study, then hesitated just before she knocked on his door. He was studying and shouldn't be disturbed. Rachel bit her lip, took a deep breath, and knocked.

At his bidding to come in, she opened the door and poked her head around it. "Papa, I know you're busy, but I do need to talk to you."

He removed his glasses and waved his hand. "I'm never too busy for any of my children. The sermon can wait a little longer."

"Thank you." She sat down in the fine leather chair opposite his desk and clasped her hands together in her lap. The words she wanted wouldn't come to her mind, and her tongue stalled.

He leaned forward and peered at her. "I believe I know the topic you feel a need to discuss. It has to do with the young man who left our home this morning. Am I right?"

Rachel nodded, still not sure just what she wanted to say. "He seemed to be much more at peace and even happier than times I've seen him in the past." She groaned inwardly. Although true, that's not what she really meant to say.

"Yes, he did. Restoring a relation with God will do that for people. He's quite an interesting young man."

"I know. He's always been a pleasure to be around whenever we happened to be together. Abigail told me that he avoided me in the beginning because I was a minister's daughter, but should that make any difference now?"

"Dear child, there's much you do not know, and I'm not at liberty to tell you. Nathan has a hard past, and he must deal with it before he can get on with his future."

Rachel sighed. So many questions ran through her thoughts, but one remained dominant. "Do you think he'll ever come back to Briar Ridge?"

Papa tapped his fingers on his desk for a moment before answering. "He is friends with Daniel, so I would assume he perchance would return for a visit with the Monroe family. Once he clears up a situation with his family, he may very well return."

He leaned back in his chair and clasped his hands together. "I realize you might have more than a passing interest in Nathan Reed, but I have given my consent for Daniel Monroe to call upon you. Is that going to be problem?"

She hesitated, then said dutifully, "No, Papa. Daniel is a wonderful man, and I'd be honored to be courted by him." Even as she said the words, Rachel wrestled with the doubts surrounding both Daniel and Nathan. One was right here ready to become a suitor for her hand. The other was so far away and not likely to return anytime soon. At the moment she couldn't imagine being a wife to Daniel while still harboring feelings for Nathan. Common sense told her to forget Nathan and focus on her relationship with Daniel, but her heart kept getting in the way.

Papa stood and came around the desk to put his arm around her shoulders. "My precious daughter, you have shown much courage and patience in the past weeks as you have been called upon to take on more than your share of responsibility. As your mother and I have said, we are very proud of you. Keep praying for Mr. Reed, for he will need it in the days ahead. If you are faithful to God, He will honor your dreams. Perhaps not in the way you desire, but in the way which is best for you."

"Thank you." Rachel's heart swelled with respect for her father. His love for her far outweighed his stubbornness, and she must always remember that.

"Now, I just asked Noah to go into town on an errand for me. Why don't you go with him? It would do you good to be out on such a beautiful day."

"Yes, it would. Thank you again for taking time to talk with me." He hadn't really solved her dilemma, but he had made her feel loved and valued.

She grabbed her coat from the hallway rack and ran out to find Noah with the wagon, ready to leave for town. "Wait up, I want to go with you."

Noah only nodded and grinned, but he stopped long enough for her to climb up beside him. "Any special reason for this trip today?"

"No, Papa just thought it might be a good idea." Rachel breathed deeply of the air now filled with the promise of spring even with piles of snow still banked around. The icy, frigid weather had given way to just-above-freezing temperatures and scattered sunshine. Although cold, spring was coming with summer not far behind. To her, spring meant a time of hope, new beginnings, and dreams fulfilled.

When they passed the street where the Monroes lived, Abigail flew out the door, waving an envelope in her hands. "Rachel, I was just preparing to come to see you. I have a note for you from Nathan. He gave it to me just before he left with Daniel."

Rachel grasped the envelope and tore it open to find a single sheet of paper.

> Dear Rachel,
>
> Words cannot express my appreciation for the love and care your family gave me. Thank you for sitting by my bedside and reading God's Word to me. I now understand His great love and forgiveness. There is much in my past you do not know, and until I resolve all the issues, I won't be back to Briar Ridge. If the Lord is willing, and things work out as I hope, I may return sometime in the future. I shall never forget the kindness you showed me.
>
> Nathan

She clutched the note to her chest. "Thank you, Abigail." It wasn't exactly the letter she'd hoped for, but it still held a promise based on what God would do. She didn't know what lay in Nathan's past that required resolution, but she could trust God to work things out in a plan best for both of them.

Nathan's heart hung heavy in his chest as he rode away from Briar Ridge with Daniel. His friend handled the reins in silence for the first few miles, and Nathan thanked the Lord for his friend's silence. Too many thoughts and feelings had to be sorted through.

Loyalty to Daniel and their friendship weighed against the love he had developed for Rachel Winston. For the first time in his adult life, Nathan wanted to pursue a girl because of her character and her love of God, not just because of her beauty and what she could do for him. Every woman he'd known to this point had been carefully wooed and then dropped when no longer of use to him.

Still, peace had come amid the turmoil because God had forgiven that past. All of his sins had been wiped away, and now it was Nathan's turn to seek forgiveness from those whom he had hurt. He especially needed to hear his mother's and Evelyn's words that would set him free from the guilt plaguing him.

Nathan gazed at the scene surrounding the carriage as they rode. Spring had come to Connecticut on the calendar, but lingering snow from the great storm still covered much of the ground. Soon flowers of various hues and green sprigs of grass would poke their way through the ground and declare the handiwork of God. Spring always held the promise of summer to come, and he prayed to claim that promise this year.

A verse he remembered from Ecclesiastes came to mind. God had a plan and a time for everything under heaven, from a time to be born, to a time to die, to a time to be silent, and a time to speak. Now was Nathan's time to speak, not only to Daniel but also to his mother and sister.

Although the air still held a chill, the glow of the sun lent its warmth to his shoulders. How different from the journey when the snow had blinded him and frozen him nearly to death. He raised his face to the heavens. "This is much more pleasant than my last journey."

Daniel laughed. "I would imagine it is. Never have I seen such winds and snow as that of last week. Soon warmer weather will make short life of the drifts and patches left. But I say the best thing to come out of this storm is your return to the Lord. You can't know how much that thrilled my family, as we have been praying for you for several years."

Heat rose in Nathan's cheeks. The idea of people praying for him would have infuriated him weeks ago, but now the gesture from the Monroe family and their love for him filled him with awe. "I owe so much to your parents and the Winston family. Reverend Winston and Rachel both showed me the love of God like I knew it as a child. Satan blinded my heart and eyes from seeing Him all these years."

"I can tell you're a changed man. I've always known you as someone who chased the ladies and scorned God, but no more."

Nathan grimaced. "I hate to admit you're right about my past." The question foremost in his mind had to be asked. If Daniel had feelings for Rachel, then she would be off limits, and Nathan would depend on God to bring someone else to fill his life.

"Daniel, I count you as a longtime friend. You've seen me through many disastrous antics, yet you've remained loyal and defended my cause more times than I care to think about."

"Nothing more than you would do for me."

"That is true, but what I need to know now is exactly what your intentions are toward Rachel. Do you love her?" Daniel's expression changed, and Nathan held his breath waiting.

A sly smile turned up a corner of Daniel's mouth. "She's a very comely young woman, and I've known her almost all my life. I have asked her father's permission to call upon her, but simply because she is the most available young woman in Briar Ridge, and we get along so well."

"So you are not in love with her?" Nathan asked.

"Our relationship has not progressed to that, no," Daniel replied.

Nathan's breath escaped in a whoosh of air that brought a laugh from his friend. "I say, old boy, have you set your heart on wooing Miss Winston?" Daniel nudged him in the ribs.

Heat again flushed Nathan's cheeks. "I think I've been in love with her from the first moment I glimpsed her in church. She had something about her that spoke of more than having beauty. I saw that quality on more than one occasion. I now realize her loveliness comes not only from her facial features but also from the love of God in her heart."

Daniel nodded. "Now that's quite a statement coming from you, dear friend."

Nathan chuckled. "I guess you're right. I've never thought of any woman in that light before."

"Now, as her friend, I have a few concerns. Not that I feel you're not good enough for her, but she must have all the facts concerning your past." Daniel shot him a glance.

Nathan had as not yet shared his secret with his friend, but he knew his words were true. Rachel must know the whole story, but he had to make sure everything that could be done to repair his broken family would be done.

"Yes, but not until I make amends with my family. If reconciliation happens and all else goes well, I will return and then tell her the entire story and hope she understands." He paused for a moment before continuing. "That's one of the reasons for our friendship, Daniel. You never judged me or thought me not worthy as a friend because of my Southern background."

"Man doesn't choose when, where, or to whom he is born. Only God does that. What we have to do is live out that life in His will and be obedient to His teachings. I can see you're ready to accept what happened because you're starting out on that path of obedience."

Nathan appreciated his friend's support more than he could ever have imagined. He had never sought Daniel's approval, only his friendship, and Daniel had offered both. "I am, Daniel, I am. My first step after settling things in Hartford will be to take a train back to North Carolina."

"And what about Rachel Winston? Surely she deserves an explanation of why you're leaving."

"I left a note with Abigail to give her. I didn't actually promise my return, but I did explain I had unfinished business to resolve at home."

"If you truly care for her, you will make plans to return to Briar Ridge and declare yourself to her and her father."

"I can't make any plans until I know the outcome of my journey home. I don't know how long that will take. I have no right to ask her to wait that long. And what if things don't work out? What if I make a bigger mess of my life than it already has been? No, what I've done will be the best for Rachel."

Love filled Nathan's heart, but so many conflicting emotions lay in confusion in his soul. Only this morning before they had left, he had resisted the urge to go to Rachel and reveal every-thing, but after time in prayer, common sense prevailed and he'd left only the note, giving it to Abigail so that only Rachel would see it. God would take care of his future whether it included Rachel or not. He had to believe that or go crazy with doubt and fear.

Daniel rode in silence for the next few minutes. Nathan could read nothing in the man's expression. Finally, he narrowed his eyes and turned to gaze directly at Nathan. "I have a propo-sition to make. I shall keep Rachel company as a close friend. She thinks of me more like her brother anyway, so that should not be a problem. But you must promise me that you will return no matter what the outcome of your visit to your family."

Nathan could trust Daniel to watch over Rachel. He envi-sioned Rachel as his bride and the mother of his children. All doubt and uncertainty fell aside. God had given the answer, and he'd come back no matter what. New confidence filled him. "I don't know how long it will take me, but I will come." He thrust his hand toward Daniel, who grasped it in a firm handshake to seal their agreement.

"One thing, you still mustn't tell Rachel why I've gone to North Carolina. I need to tell her that myself. If all goes well with my family, then I will have good news to share with her. If not, I will still try to return and tell her, because she needs to know, and then let her decide what our fate may be." Besides, he had no inkling of what Rachel's feelings might be toward him.

What if something happened and he couldn't return? Then Rachel would have her hopes dashed, and she may miss other opportunities for her life if he'd told her he'd come back for her. "Daniel, whatever the future holds, watch over Rachel and protect her, but don't let her get her hopes up too much about my return in case…" His voice trailed off. Daniel would understand.

"I will do that, and all of us will pray for you." Daniel snapped the reins on the horse to increase their speed.

Prayer. Yes, that's what Nathan needed. God was in control, and only He knew what lay ahead in the mountains of his home state.

CHAPTER
EIGHTEEN

*R*ACHEL SMOOTHED BACK her hair, then teased the spiraled tendrils in front of her ears. Daniel would arrive momentarily to escort her to dinner and then to a play at the new theater opening this weekend. She had only seen him for a few minutes at a time since his return from Hartford four days ago. Tonight would be the first chance she'd have to inquire about his trip with Nathan.

A stab of guilt pierced her heart. The last thing she wanted was to hurt Daniel's feelings, but she feared that would happen if she kept up the charade and continued to let him court her. She'd tell him tonight and then think about her plans to go to Boston and spend several weeks with her aunt—although at the moment she doubted any young man in Boston could begin to take Nathan's place in her heart.

Mama appeared in the door. "Dear, Daniel is here." She tilted her head. "You look so beautiful. Daniel will be proud to have you on his arm tonight."

"Mama, am I being deceitful by spending time with Daniel when my thoughts are on Nathan?"

"No, my dear. If you spend enough time with Daniel, you'll become better acquainted, and you'll find enough in common that you will grow to care for him. Not all marriages begin on the kind of relationship that comes from romantic love. Sometimes romance comes after marrying and living together as husband and wife."

"How did you feel about Papa?"

Mama smiled. "Like my life would end, my heart would break, and I would never love again if Ezra Winston didn't ask me to be his bride."

Rachel hugged her mother. "That's the kind of love I want."

"Then if you pray about it, God will show you what to do. Let Him be in control of this relationship. He won't let it happen if it's not the right one for you. Now, hurry. You don't want to keep the young man waiting." With another quick hug, Mama hurried back to her guest.

Rachel stared at her own reflection. Mama's wisdom never ceased to amaze her. So many times she had seen her mother's faith at work. Now Rachel's faith called for her to completely rely on God for the answers to all dilemmas. That had not been difficult in the past, but she wanted the solution now, not later.

She grabbed up the filmy scarf that would cover her hair and headed downstairs. At the end of the staircase Daniel gazed up at her.

"You look even lovelier than usual tonight. I will be the envy of every other man in the theater." He lifted his hand to grasp hers as she stepped down into the foyer.

"Thank you, Daniel. You are quite handsome yourself." And

indeed he was with dark trousers, a cutaway coat, and a gray striped cravat. Any other woman would be clamoring for the opportunity to be escorted by him. For her, it only made the words she had to say to him more difficult.

Papa reached out to shake Daniel's hand. "Take care of our girl, and enjoy your evening."

"We will, sir." He grasped the cape Mama handed him and slipped it around Rachel's shoulders. "Good evening, Reverend and Mrs. Winston. I'll have her home at the proper time."

A few moments later he held her hand to assist her up onto the carriage seat. Once snugly settled, Rachel bit her tongue to hold back the questions that flooded her mind. But eventually she had to allow herself just one comment. "I trust you and Mr. Reed had a pleasant trip to Hartford. It was most kind of you to take care of him."

A smile crept across Daniel's face. "We had a pleasant and enlightening ride, but the care in the Winston home far out-weighed mine. You are responsible for saving his life in more ways than one."

Rachel blushed and looked away. "It was God at work, not I."

"Then God certainly used you as His hands and voice," Daniel said. He covered her hands with his. "Rachel, I can't tell you what Nathan and I talked about, but one thing I can tell you is that he does care for you. He just can't make any prom-ises for the future."

Rachel's hopes rose like the sun coming out of a fog. Clouds of doubt drifted away, and she let the warmth of Daniel's words wrap around her heart. "Thank you, Daniel. I couldn't ask for better news." She squeezed his hands. "And I couldn't ask for a better friend than you."

"And that's what I'll be. Nathan's been like a brother to me. Even though I had to rescue him from serious scrapes from time to time, he's still my friend. I've known that you care about him for some time now, and that's all right with me. You and I have always been friends, and nothing will change that."

Rachel said nothing but let his words sink into her heart and soul. God had taken care of her relationship with Daniel, and what a friend he proved to be. The evening ahead now looked far brighter than it had only minutes earlier. For the next few months she would occupy her hands and her mind with the things of God, and He would take care of Nathan.

That evening Ezra laid aside his Bible and prepared his desk for the tray Felicity would bring shortly. During Felicity's illness he had missed this daily ritual of coffee and dessert together after the children were occupied elsewhere. With a full house, their time alone was limited, and he welcomed the minutes they found at the end of the day.

He pulled an envelope from his desk drawer and removed the contents. A letter from his sister Mabel had arrived in answer to his request for a spring visit for Rachel and Abigail. Mabel had wholeheartedly agreed to have the girls come in April rather than wait for summer. She had even sent train tickets for them both.

Doubt crept into his heart that he had been wrong in asking Mabel to invite the girls now instead of summer. Still, with all that had happened in the past weeks, the trip would go far in giving Rachel something to occupy her thoughts and pass the time.

Felicity rapped on his door, then entered with the tray bearing two mugs of hot coffee and two plates with slices of warm apple cake. She smiled at him and set the tray on the cleared space on his desk.

"I noticed that something troubled you at dinner. Is there a problem?" She eased into the chair across from him.

"No problem. My sermon notes are ready for me to organize tomorrow, but there is a matter I wish to discuss with you." He picked up the letter and handed it to her. "I received this letter from Mabel today."

She held the sheet of paper before her and read. Her eyes grew round with surprise. "I had forgotten you wrote to her before the storm. This is a wonderful opportunity for Rachel and Abigail."

"I'm glad you think so too, although we may have to persuade Rachel to go now that she's so taken with Nathan Reed."

"We had a discussion about that before she left with Daniel this evening. She's afraid she's deceiving Daniel by continuing to see him when her heart is with Nathan. I had to remind her that he is gone, and God will take care of the relationships in His own way and time." She glanced again at the letter. "This says Mabel sent the tickets for them, so that should be some incentive for our Rachel. She does have a practical side and wouldn't want her aunt to waste money on a trip not accepted."

"Yes, I have the train tickets, and if the girls are going to leave in two weeks, we must tell them now and help them get ready for the journey."

Felicity nodded then frowned. "I don't understand why Nathan left. I thought I saw a spark of interest for Rachel in his eyes."

The promise made to Nathan rose in Ezra's mind, but since he never kept secrets from his wife, now would be the perfect time to explain the reasons for the young man's abrupt departure. "My dear, there is a long story behind Nathan's attitude toward God and his reasons for leaving Connecticut. He told me about it when we had that long discussion after he had awakened."

Ezra then related the same information to Felicity that Nathan had given him. At the end of his discourse, he noticed the tears glistening on Felicity's cheeks.

"That poor boy. No wonder he turned so completely away from God. And his dear, sweet mother suffered so much more than Nathan can imagine both when he was born and when he left. Oh, Ezra, we need to pray extra hard for him and for his mother. As a mother myself, I know she will welcome him with open arms."

Ezra stood and came around the desk to wrap his arms about his wife's shoulders. "I knew you would understand, and with your prayers being lifted up, we can be assured that all will end well." He kissed her forehead. "You are a very precious lady, and I'm so thankful you are my wife and mother to our children."

She gazed up into his eyes. "I believe God sent this trip as a blessing for Rachel at this time in her life. Surely she will see that."

"I pray she will, but you must remember not to say anything to her about Nathan's background or the true purpose of his visit to his family." She wouldn't, but he still had to issue the warning as part of his promise to Nathan.

"I'll remember." She gathered up the coffee mugs and the two plates with the half-eaten dessert. "Do you want the rest of this, or shall I take it to the kitchen?"

"Leave it. I want to compose a letter to Mabel, so I'll eat it while I write." He'd get the letter written tonight, then fill in the dates as soon as they were decided.

On Saturday Rachel finished her morning chores and headed upstairs to her room for a spell of reading before preparations for the noon meal. Before she reached the second step, her father's voice halted her.

"Rachel, will you come into my study for a moment? There is something I want to discuss with you."

"Yes, Papa." She followed him down the hallway. His face wore no stern look, so she couldn't be in trouble. Her curiosity blossomed even more at the sight of her mother sitting primly in one of the side chairs in the room. This must be serious for both of them to be there. Her breath caught in her throat. Something had happened to Nathan.

"Oh, Papa, is it bad news? Please tell me quick." Her heart hammered in her chest. God wouldn't have let something happen to him so soon after his recovery.

Papa smiled, slowing the awful pace of her heart. "No, it isn't bad news but rather good news instead. Sit down, child."

Rachel winced at his calling her a child, but she always would be one to him, no matter how grown up she may be. She eased into the chair and clasped her hands in her lap. Once again her pulse pounded in anticipation of her father's words.

"Several weeks ago I sent a letter to your aunt Mabel telling her that we would allow you and Abigail to come to Boston this spring. Her response arrived yesterday, and she has agreed to a visit by you and Abigail within the next few weeks. She even sent the tickets for both of you. Your mother and I discussed the matter last night while you were out, and we agreed that you should accept her invitation."

Mama leaned over and grasped Rachel's hand. "Isn't this wonderful news, my dear?"

Rachel's throat constricted with dismay before she remembered her recent resolve to look forward to her trip to Boston in Nathan's absence. If she went now, she would be back by the end of April. At the moment, uncertainty about going at all reared its head, but Aunt Mabel had already sent the tickets for her and for Abigail. How ungrateful Rachel would appear if she refused the offer now.

Papa raised his eyebrows. "Have you no comment one way or the other? We thought you would be pleased at the invitation."

"I...I am, but I'm also surprised. I thought you wanted us to wait until summertime."

Papa exchanged a glance with Mama. "Your mother and I feel that this would be a good diversion for you and a reward for the extra work you took on while she was ill. A trip like this would be educational as well."

"Yes, you are right. Tell her I gladly accept the invitation. May I go right now to tell Abigail about it?"

Papa nodded and Mama smiled, looking pleased at her excitement. As Rachel ran down the stairs and out the door to Abigail's home, she reflected on her good fortune. Summer was but a few months away, and the trip would help it come sooner. She would go and enjoy her aunt's hospitality and look forward to returning home to await news of Nathan. Excitement grew in her heart. With Abigail accompanying her, they most certainly would have a grand time.

CHAPTER
NINETEEN

*N*ATHAN SPENT NEARLY a week in Hartford settling his office affairs and preparing for his journey. When he had explained the purpose of his journey, Mr. Fitzpatrick had been most understanding. He helped Nathan arrange for other members of the firm to assume Nathan's cases with easy transition. He'd been told his position would be held with the understanding that he would return as soon as he was able.

Now on the long journey south, the scenery outside Nathan's window on the train steadily changed from the barren fields of winter in the northeast to the budding green in Virginia and on to the burst of color in springtime North Carolina. When he spotted the dogwood trees and then the purple-pink azaleas, the beauty of the South once again gripped his heart.

The closer Nathan came to his home, hurt and humiliation began to loosen their hold on his soul. Anxiety mixed with anticipation at seeing his family replaced the near-hatred that had filled his heart on the day he left Fayetteville.

From townspeople he had learned of the battle put up by Fayetteville to defend their town against the Yankees. In fact, one of the last cavalry battles of the war had been fought at Monroe's crossing in March, when Major General Kilpatrick had held off Union forces and delayed the inevitable defeat that would come with Sherman's capture of the town. That same march had devastated the plantation homes in their path. If only his father had been at home, perhaps he could have fought for his wife and daughter. Nathan shook his head. He'd played out that scenario more times than he liked to count, and it never gave him anything but misery. His very existence was dependent on a vile and unspeakable act, and he shivered at the pain he'd given his mother not only in his birth but also in his rejection of her.

However, he refused to let pain take away the joy he had found in his Lord and Savior. The dogwood now blooming in the fields and woods along the tracks gave him hope. The beautiful blossoms spoke of the great love of God who loved him and died for him. That love overrode any evil circumstances of his birth. Now that he had experienced love for Rachel, he understood the anger his father held against the man who had violated his wife. The accusations Nathan had thrown at his mother during that last fateful encounter now weighed heavy on his conscience.

Reverend Winston had told him that a mother's love would forgive all those words and welcome him with open arms. He prayed that would be true.

On Wednesday evening, when the train pulled into the station, his first stop after retrieving his baggage was the hotel. He decided to check in first, then find out more about his family.

They had written him numerous times while he was at Yale. Beth wrote to tell him of her marriage to Theo Barnes and how Uncle Bert had invited Theo to help manage the store. But because he hadn't written one letter home, Nathan had no idea what had happened since he'd left law school and moved without leaving a forwarding address.

The sun set in the west as he explored his hometown. In the years since he had left, the town had grown considerably. Although not the place of his birth, Fayetteville was a resilient town, and he had loved living there. After fire almost destroyed the city in 1831, it rose from the ashes even stronger and greater than before. The same had happened after the damage left when Sherman marched through.

He shook himself. That was history he couldn't change. His mission on coming here concerned the history he could make right. And the first place he needed to visit was his old home. There he could bury all the pain of learning the truth in the dirt where it all began.

The livery beckoned from across the street. Nathan crossed over to find the owner just about to close for the day. "Excuse me, would it be possible to make arrangements right now to rent a horse in the morning?"

The scrawny man scratched his whiskered chin and peered at Nathan through the narrowed slits of his eyes. "I think that can be arranged. If you'll step inside, you can pick your mount and let me know what time you will want it ready tomorrow."

After making the arrangements, Nathan sauntered down the main street of the town. A sign on a storefront up ahead stopped him in his tracks. REED AND REED MERCANTILE AND DRY GOODS was painted in bright red and yellow letters.

The store still stood in the same spot but occupied much more space. The business now included the old bank building that had moved to a new, larger building he could see down the street beyond the store.

A man appeared in the doorway and proceeded to close the doors and hang a "CLOSED" sign in the glass-paned window. Nathan didn't recognize him. Of course, it could be one of his cousins who had worked with Uncle Bert. Beth's husband was taller and heavier than the man he saw. Perhaps when he returned from his errand tomorrow, he would stop in for a visit and discover what changes had been made since he'd worked there as a clerk in his teen years.

He turned and hurried back to his hotel. Hunger drew him to the dining room, where he ordered a dinner of steak and potatoes along with a slice of lemon pie. After the server filled his water glass and left, Nathan planned what must be done the next day. After a visit to the old homestead, he'd return to look for Mother and Evelyn as well as his younger sister, Beth.

Then his thoughts turned to Rachel. She was about Beth's age. If he could come back here with all wounds healed and Rachel as his bride, she and Beth would most likely become good friends.

He paid for his dinner then headed up to the second floor and his room, wishing that tomorrow had already come.

Nathan ate his breakfast in the hotel dining room. Just a little over twenty-three years since the battle that lost Fayetteville, he would return to the place of his conception. What would be left after all these years? Would he even know where to look? How stupid he'd been not to have found out more about the land around Fayetteville before setting out. However, he did know the name of the town not far from Reed Hall.

He finished his meal and headed for the livery. True to his word, the stable owner had a horse saddled and ready. He paid the man and swung up across the dark brown horse's back. He headed northwest toward his childhood home.

When he neared the edge of the small town, the streets teemed with horses and wagons and men. A few women and children scurried about their business. One of the first buildings he spotted was a land assayer's office. Nathan stopped and dismounted. This was the place to start if he wanted to get information to help him find his old home.

A tall man behind a plain oak desk stood and greeted Nathan. "Good afternoon; what can I do for you?"

Nathan shook the man's hand. "My name is Nathan Reed. My folks once owned a plantation around here. I wanted to inspect the property and see what condition it is in."

The man furrowed his brow. "Reed property? Could that be Captain Cyrus Reed and Reed Hall?"

"Why, yes, yes it is. He was my father." Nathan almost choked on the words. How did this man know his family?

The man beamed and his eyes lit up. "My name is Townsend. Your father was quite the hero around these parts after the war. People admired him, myself included, for his part in defending our state against Sherman's forces. I was just a lad, not old enough to join the Confederate Army, but I sure wanted to follow your daddy and Hampton's cavalry."

His dad a hero? No one ever mentioned that, but of course

no one in his family even talked about those days. Everything he'd learned about the war had come from books, letters, and men like Mr. Townsend. "I wasn't born until after the war was over, so I knew none of that."

"Cyrus Reed's son. My, my. People will be mighty glad to know you're back."

Nathan shook his head. "No, no, I don't want to anyone to know I'm here. I came because I wanted to visit the property one last time, but I'm not even sure where it is or what happened to it."

Mr. Townsend frowned and strode over to a filing cabinet. "I should have that information for you. Just a moment." He flipped through some papers in a drawer. "I know it's here somewhere." His hand stopped and pulled out a few documents. "Yes, here we are."

He handed the papers to Nathan. "You'll see that your father came back and sold the land. My father is the one who went out and surveyed it to determine the boundaries. It was divided into three smaller plats, and farms occupy it today."

Nathan examined the deeds and bills of sale for the land. "Can you tell me exactly where these farms are?" He had to see the land for himself.

"Of course." He pulled out a map and pointed to a section. "Here is where the property lies. The creek is one boundary along the western edge. It's about an hour's ride from town to the west."

Nathan examined the route from town and made note of a few landmarks. "Who owns the land now?"

"The Calhoun, Jenkins, and Henderson families. I believe..." He bent over the map. "Yes, the Jenkins farm is the first one you'll see. Herman Jenkins planted cotton on his, but the other two have tobacco fields."

At least some good had come from the land. "Thank you, Mr. Townsend. I'll ride on out that way. With these directions, I shouldn't have any trouble finding it." He had only vague memories of visiting the plantation home as a child, but sorrow filled him to know that it had been torn down and the land divided.

Mr. Townsend followed him to the door. "I still wish you'd let me tell the mayor you're visiting. He's sure to want to meet you."

Nathan stepped outside then turned to shake the man's hand. "It will be better not to do that on this trip. Perhaps I'll come back at a later date. Thank you for your help. I appreciate it."

A few minutes later Nathan found the road leading west from town and headed toward his father's land. He lifted his eyes toward heaven, thankful for the blue skies overhead and the mild temperatures to warm his back.

As he rode out of town and to the west, he admired the beauty of the lavender-pink azaleas that bloomed in the yards of the homes. Signs of spring burst forth from everywhere. Along the road toward Reed Hall, the bright spots of color in the wildflowers growing in profusion along the roadsides added to God's palette and painted a magnificent picture. How could he have looked at the wonders and beauty of the earth and ever doubted the love of God? But then, he'd never paid much attention to those things before.

A gentle breeze wafted across his cheek like the gentle caress of a mother's hand. A tear sprang into his eye. His mother had loved him despite the circumstances of his birth. She had sat by his bed during illness and prayed with him to receive Jesus in his heart. How cruel he had been to her.

"Father, please let her forgive me. I know I sinned against her and Evelyn with my anger and cruel words. I know You have forgiven me, but I know Your Word tells me I must seek forgiveness from those whom I have wronged. Give me the courage to do what I must do."

Speaking the words aloud filled him with hope that the future would bring better times. He sat taller in the saddle and urged his horse on.

The gate to the first farm bore the name of Jenkins and told him he was in the right place. Several hundred feet ahead sat a two-story farmhouse. Sturdy and homey, this house had been built with great care.

Nathan dismounted and walked through the gate. He paused a moment and gazed around at the fields newly planted with this year's crop. A man hurried toward him.

"Good afternoon, young fellow. I'm Herman Jenkins. Can I help you?"

Nathan shoved his hat back on his head. "Nathan Reed. My family once owned this land."

"Reed, you say. That's a well-known name around these parts. Was Cyrus Reed your pa?" Mr. Jenkins wiped his forehead with a kerchief.

"Yes, sir, he was."

"Come on up to the house with me. The missus and my boys will be glad to see you."

Nathan hesitated. "Thank you, but I'd appreciate it if I could just walk out toward your fields and be alone for a spell."

"Of course, I understand." Mr. Jenkins stepped back and allowed Nathan to pass.

Nathan tethered his horse, then walked to the edge of the field nearest the house, then turned to amble along the edge until the house was some distance behind him. There he knelt to the ground and reached for a handful of dirt.

On this soil his family had lived and worked. His father, yes, his father, for no man could take the place of the one who had brought him up. Even though his life had been without as much love and approval as Nathan had wanted, this is where his family had grown cotton.

He bowed his head and rested his elbow on his knee. "Heavenly Father, You've opened my eyes on this trip. Cyrus Reed may not have sired me, but he kept me in the family. He loved my mother enough to accept me. I can see now how difficult that was for him. I forgive him for what he couldn't give me freely. Lord, I don't understand how slavery could have been so important that it caused a war between brothers in this country, and I may never understand it, but I pray I will never treat other men as anything except children of a loving God. You have given me a new heart, and I can thank Cyrus Reed for his provision for me. I have an education and career because of that. Thank You for loving me and not giving up on me when I gave up on You."

Nathan used his hands to scoop out a small cavity in the earth. He raised his left hand toward heaven and placed his right hand over his heart. "Lord, I take all the hatred, anger, and fear I harbored for so many years and bury them on this land where they all began. Father, I forgive you for the hard times and the harsh reality you had to reveal. You were a strong man, a good man, and I loved you."

He made a throwing motion toward the hole with his left hand; then he bent over and filled the hole with dirt. He swiped his hands together to rid them of the dust and then stood. A soft mantle of peace fell over him. At last he was free of the pain of his father's rejection.

Nathan turned back toward the farmhouse. A new courage and new strength filled him. Tomorrow he'd begin his journey into the future. Maybe Easter would bring not only a celebration of the resurrection of his Lord but also a renewal of cherished family ties.

Late Saturday afternoon, Rachel gathered in the laundry. She loved the fresh smell of sunshine on clean clothes. Even though patches of snow still filled places hidden from the sun, spring had begun to make an appearance in Briar Ridge. The crocuses had just begun to poke their colorful heads through the snow, and the daffodils wouldn't be far behind. Thoughts about the trip to Boston, her feelings for Nathan, and the uncertainty of the future tumbled through Rachel's mind like rocks down a hillside, each one chasing the other until they all fell in a heap at the bottom of her heart.

She picked up the basket of clean clothes and headed into the house. No time to sort through things now. Soon as she could put away the folded pieces, she had to hurry over to the church to help Mama and her friends with preparing the altar for Easter Sunday services, which fell on the first day of April this year. The ladies had liked her work with the altar guild so much that they had invited her to continue even after her mother resumed her duties.

Silence filled the house, as Rachel was the only one at home. At times like this she could imagine having her own home and taking care of a husband and family. Whenever those images came to mind, Nathan's face always appeared as her husband. What wonderful dreams she had of him. She folded the last of the towels and sighed. Only God knew if those dreams would be fulfilled.

Almost two weeks had passed since Nathan had left, and no one had heard from him. Surely he would write if he intended to come home, but she refused to worry about it. She'd turned all that over to God.

After storing away the last of the clothes, Rachel hurried to the church. The altar guild had just finished their meeting and trooped into the sanctuary like soldiers on a mission. Rachel stifled a giggle at the sight of the women with their heads held high and their backs stiff as starch marching to the altar with their arms full of greenery and early spring flowers.

Mrs. Bivens held an armful of Easter lilies. "Oh, Rachel, we're so glad you're here. You have such a way with arrangements." She thrust the bouquet toward Rachel. "I just know these will be beautiful for services Sunday."

Rachel grasped the array of pure white lilies. "Oh, these are lovely. Mrs. Bivens, you surely know how to find beautiful flowers. They smell absolutely heavenly."

The plump little lady handed Rachel a crystal container. "Thank goodness the roads are cleared and the trains are running again so we could order these flowers. I cannot imagine celebrating Easter without lilies."

Abigail came to join her as Rachel laid the blooms on a piece of paper spread over the table. She found a pair of shears and began her work. God's handiwork was so perfect. Each blossom held its own beauty in the perfect shape of the petals and the enchanting scent.

The fragrance of lemon oil filled the room as the ladies wiped dust from pews and altar tables. One amazing thing Rachel had learned about this group: they worked in silence. When she had asked about that, her mother had said they used the time to pray for the people who would be filling the pews and the pulpit. What a wonderful thing to do. Now Rachel did the same as she worked side by side with Abigail.

Abigail grinned, as full of anticipation for the refreshment time as Rachel. Then they'd be able to talk. Now she remained silent as the other ladies and prayed for her father and others who would assist in worship on Sunday.

After finishing in the sanctuary, the ladies gathered in the church parlor for tea and cookies. That was when the conversation flowed like a mountain stream in spring after a thaw. Rachel enjoyed listening and discovered many new tidbits of information about the women.

Rachel found a seat, and Abigail sat beside her. "I never knew how much work our mothers and the other ladies did to make our church so pretty on Sunday mornings," Abigail said.

Rachel nodded in agreement. "And what is so wonderful is that they love doing it."

Abigail nibbled on a cookie and said, "I'm excited about our trip. I can't believe it's actually going to take place."

"I'm excited too. Now that Daniel and I have established the friendship between us, I think even more about Nathan. I pray he will resolve the issues at home and return soon. This trip will help make the time between now and then seem shorter."

"I'm glad you have hope for Nathan's return. I just wish there was some other girl in Briar Ridge for Daniel. He's glad we're going to Boston too. He says it'll be good for us both, as if he really knows what's good for us." She giggled and bit into a pastry.

Rachel laughed. Yes, going with Abigail to Boston would be fun, and Aunt Mabel would make sure that both girls had an enjoyable visit. "Mama has already begun packing for me."

"Mother ordered two new dresses for me, and Mrs. Fitzsimmons said they'd be ready by the time we were ready to leave. And I can't believe we're leaving in just over a week."

"Yes, I was surprised Papa let us go so soon, but April should be wonderful in Boston." Easter celebrated resurrection and new life, and this year it also signified new hope for Rachel and her future.

*A*FTER A WEEKEND of prayer and reflection, Nathan finally stood on the sidewalk outside his sister's house. He had made inquiries at the hotel to discover the address. He had decided against disturbing his family on the holy weekend, choosing instead to attend services outside town and spend further time preparing his heart and mind for the upcoming reunion. Part of him wished he'd come earlier, but if Beth rejected him, he would have no hope with his mother and Evelyn. He wanted nothing to mar the first Easter of his return to his faith.

From the looks of the house before him, Beth's husband, Theo Barnes, was doing well for himself. A dark blue door beckoned him, and shutters of the same color graced each window. The touch of Beth's hand was seen in the large containers of red tulips standing guard on either side of the front door. He knew Theo, having attended school with him, and approved of his sister's choice for her husband. He regretted now having missed their wedding two years ago.

He strode to the door and lifted the brass knocker. A moment later an attractive young woman answered the knock. Her eyes opened wide for a moment, and her hand covered her mouth.

Then she smiled and opened her arms wide. "Oh, my, Nathan, it is you!"

He stepped into her embrace. "Yes, I've come home."

Beth hugged him hard, then called over her shoulder. "Theo, we have a visitor."

A tall, broad-shouldered man appeared in the entranceway. When he spotted Nathan, he grinned broadly and extended his hand. "Welcome home. It's so good to see you, Nathan." He glanced at his wife, then said, "I'll leave you two to catch up while I do some work in my office." He nodded and smiled at Nathan, then headed to the back of the house.

Beth turned to Nathan. "Come in here and tell me where you've been and what you've been doing these past four years. I've really missed you." She nudged at his arm. "You never even sent us a note telling us where you were."

"I'm sorry about that, Beth." He looked down awkwardly.

Beth hooked her arm through his. "Mother hasn't said a word about your being back in Fayetteville." Then she furrowed her brow. "You have been to see her, haven't you?"

Guilt again flooded Nathan, and heat rose in his cheeks. "I...I haven't been to see her yet."

"Oh, Nathan, you must go. We've been so worried about her the past few months."

"Is something wrong?" Had he returned only to find her too ill to accept his love and forgive him?

Beth led him into the parlor. The brightly colored furnishings reflected Beth's sunny personality. He picked up one of the yellow pillows from a chair and sat down.

Beth chose to settle on the sofa across from him. She tilted her head at an angle. "You look none the worse for the years you've been away. Life must be good for you. But why haven't you been to see Mother? She has missed you terribly all these years."

"Yes, life has been good to me, the most important part being that I've recently returned to the Lord. He forgave me for what I did, and now I've come back to make amends with Mama. I just haven't had the courage to see her yet." He didn't want to talk about himself, but Beth would take her time before revealing what he wanted to hear about their mother's condition. She'd always dragged things out until he was ready to hit her. He fought the urge to scold her now and force the information from her.

Beth bit her lip. "You should go see her right away." She sighed and gazed out the window nearby, avoiding looking directly at him.

Nathan clenched his teeth and held his tongue. Why didn't she just say what was wrong? Were things that serious?

At last Beth turned her gaze straight to his. "Mother's been quite ill the past few years, and she seems to have become worse in the past two months. She and Evelyn rarely go out. We see them in church on Sundays, and that's about it. Mother says she's too weak, and Evelyn says she has no use for the general public. Sudie is still with them, and she takes care of the house and preparing meals for them."

Sudie, the one slave who'd stayed with the family in the

move to town, loved Mother and would make sure both Mother and Evelyn had everything they needed.

Beth leaned forward and shook her head. "Sudie and Evelyn do everything for Mother. But there's one thing they can't do, and that is fill the empty spot you left when you took off north."

He sensed Beth's disappointment, and the set of her jaw indicated some anger. A bitter taste rose in Nathan's throat. He'd hurt Mother much more deeply than he imagined. How could he undo the damage of these past years? He had to try, or he'd never be at peace.

"Beth, what I did was horribly wrong. I took out all my anger, bitterness, and resentment toward our father on the one person who deserved none of the blame. The words I said can't be taken back, but God has shown me that without her forgiveness, I can never rest."

"Oh, Nathan, she loves you so much despite the circumstances of your conception. Every time I see her she asks if I've heard from you. I know she'll be so happy to see you, but Evelyn will be a different matter."

Yes, she too had borne the brunt of his angry words and their consequences, and he must ask her to forgive him too. "I didn't go there first because I was afraid of the reception I would receive. You weren't there that awful day to hear how terrible I was. And you and I always got along, so I came here to test the waters first."

Beth moved to his side and hugged him. "Oh, my dear brother, we never stopped loving you. Theo has always said you'd come to your senses and see what a mistake you'd made."

"How...how are things at the store?"

"Very well. You may have noticed they expanded. Theo now

works with Uncle Bert as an equal partner. Our cousins work there too."

Nathan nodded, pleased that Theo did what he loved, leaving Nathan free to practice the law he loved. Perhaps his father had sensed that managing the store wasn't right for him.

"We're going to see Mother right now, and you can't say no. It's past time for reconciliation."

"All right, I'll go with you." Better to go with her now and get it over with. He didn't want to waste more time fearing what may happen.

Beth tilted her head. "Oh, I didn't even think. Have you eaten?"

Nathan nodded. "At the hotel where I'm staying."

"Hotel? No, Nathan. You'll either stay here with us or at Mother's."

"I don't want to put you out, and she may not want me in her house." The hotel offered safety from scorn and rejection, and he'd stay there as long as necessary.

"Nathan, you do exasperate me." Beth pulled on his hand. "Come on, this is a visit I can't wait to have happen." She called out to Theo to let him know where they were going.

His sister certainly had more confidence in the situation than he did, but then she'd been here all along. Perhaps the reunion would turn out to be all he hoped for. He had placed this trip in God's hands. Now he was about to see exactly what God had in store for him.

When Nathan approached the house where he had grown up, the muscles of his stomach tightened with fear and threatened to make him ill. Then a verse from the Psalms came to mind. *The Lord is my light and my salvation; whom shall I fear: The Lord is the strength of my life; of whom shall I be afraid?*

He had nothing and no one to fear. God was in control. With renewed courage he followed Beth up to the porch. She didn't knock but opened the door and walked straight in.

"Hello, it's Beth, and I've brought a visitor."

Sudie scurried from the parlor. "Land sakes, Miss Beth, we weren't expecting you." Then her eyes grew into white saucers in her dark face when she spotted Nathan. Her hands flew to her cheeks. "Mr. Nathan." She stepped back and clutched the door handle. "I don't believe my eyes. You've come home."

"Yes, Sudie, I'm home." He heard a noise in the parlor, then his mother's voice.

"Who is it, Sudie? Beth, is it you? Come in here."

The weak voice sent shivers down his spine. He should never have waited this long to see her. He stepped around Sudie and into the room where his mother sat by the window looking out over the side garden.

She peered up at him for a moment with a blank stare before recognition dawned. Her mouth dropped open and her eyes glistened with tears. She placed a finger on her trembling lips. "Nathan? Is it really you?"

He rushed to her side and knelt on the floor at her knee. "Yes, Mother, I'm here." He clasped her hands into his and gazed into the face of the woman who had suffered so many hardships for him. The tears flowed from his eyes. "I love you, and I've come home to beg your forgiveness for all the horrible things I said to you before I left. God has shown me the truth and the mistakes I made. Oh, Mama, please forgive me." Reverting to his childhood name for her came as natural as breathing, and he longed for an embrace like she had given him so often in those days.

She pulled her hands from his and leaned over to wrap her arms around his shoulders. Once again he became that child of long ago, and the comfort he had known then filled him to the very core of his soul. She rested her head against his, and her tears dampened his face.

When she sat back, she placed her hands on his cheeks. "Oh, my son, I've waited so long for you to come home. You're my child, and I love you no matter what. I knew you'd find your way back to God eventually, and when you did, you'd come home."

Nathan blinked back tears. "Thank you, Mother. God did bring me home." He pulled up a chair to talk further when he noticed someone come into the room. Evelyn. He smiled at her, hoping she'd welcome him too.

Instead her mouth drew in a tight line and her jaw clenched. Animosity streamed from her eyes. She picked up the hems of her skirt and dashed from the room. Nathan stood to follow her.

"No, son, let her be for a few minutes." Mother turned to Beth. "You go after her. She might listen to you."

Beth hurried after her sister. Mother patted his hand. "Now tell me what you've done since you left."

Nathan sat at her side with love spilling over his heart like water over a dam. The years seemed to have disappeared, and he could have just returned from a short trip. He began by telling her of his years at Yale and his friend Daniel. She laughed with him and nodded in approval. Then he explained his distance from God and the turmoil in his life. She continued to pat his hand and his arm. The love flowed through her hands to his, and the peace that had been so long in coming coursed through his veins.

Then he remembered Rachel. "Mama, I met a young woman in Connecticut. She's the daughter of the minister and his wife who saved my life in the snowstorm. You'd love her because she loves God and serves Him with her life. And she's pretty as well."

Mother smiled and gripped his hands. "I can hear the affection for her in your voice. Perhaps you can bring her here so I can meet her."

"I plan to do just that if it all works out. I want to ask her to marry me, but I couldn't until I had come home to make things right with you."

Sudie cleared her throat to announce her presence and entered with a tray set with tea and pastries. "I thought you might like a little refreshment."

"Thank you. That was most thoughtful. Did you hear Nathan say he's planning to ask a young woman to be his bride?"

"Yes'm, I did. That's a fine thing, Mister Nathan. You sure turned into a handsome young man." Then her cheeks flushed, and she scurried from the room.

Nathan laughed. "I'm glad you have her." Sudie had scolded him often as a child whenever his mischievousness aggravated his mother. He must remember to thank her for staying with Mother all these years.

He frowned as Mother poured a cup of tea and handed it to him. Beth hadn't returned with Evelyn. No matter what else happened, without her forgiveness, his mission would be incomplete.

As if in answer to his thoughts, Beth walked into the room without Evelyn. She shrugged her shoulders and set about to pour a cup of tea.

"I'm sorry, Nathan, but she's not ready to see you just yet. These years have been hard on her." She lifted the cup to her mouth and sipped.

Nathan picked at a tart with his fork. "I don't blame her."

Mother shook her head. "If Evelyn lets her bitterness take root, it will grow up and defile this family by keeping it apart."

Nathan grimaced. That's exactly what he had been doing for four years, but now that root had been dug up and a new plant grew in its place. If only the same could happen with Evelyn.

Beth clapped her hands. "I know just what we need to do." She called to Sudie. When the woman appeared, Beth said, "I have an errand for you. Well, actually two. First, go over to Uncle Bert's house and tell Aunt Maggie that they're all invited to a special dinner at my house tomorrow night, but don't tell them why. Then I need for you to go to the mercantile with me tomorrow and pick up a few items."

"Yes'm, Miss Beth. You can make me a list, and I'll fetch them for you."

"No, I'll go, but I need your help in making sure I have everything I need."

Beth and Sudie left the room to tend to the food

arrangements. Nathan sat in stunned silence. Trust his sister to come up with some plan to get the family together. "You don't mind, do you? About going to dinner at Beth's?"

"No, I'll enjoy it. Why, just having you here makes me feel stronger already. Why don't you stay here with me tonight?" She put up her hand when he started to protest. "No, I insist. Your old room is there ready and waiting."

The offer was what he would like, but he couldn't as long as Evelyn felt the way she did. It wouldn't be fair to her. Surely his mother understood that. "What about Evelyn?"

"Son, Evelyn just needs some time to adjust. The longer you are here, the more she will see that you are sorry for that terrible scene before you left."

"I still think it best if I spent a few more nights at the hotel. I'll consider coming, but not before the weekend."

Disappointment filled his mother's eyes, but he didn't let it sway him. One thing he did note was that she looked better. Her color had improved immensely, and the old sparkle had returned to her smile. Now he must make an attempt to bring the same glow of happiness to Evelyn.

The dinner Tuesday night passed without Evelyn in attendance, and the family gathered at Beth and Theo's home once again on Friday night. All but Evelyn sat around the table, and Nathan had to swallow his disappointment. He'd tried twice since the first visit to see her, but she had refused. He gazed around at his family now gathered. Along with his aunt and uncle, his cousin and her husband joined them with their two children. A great love and gratitude for them all filled his heart.

Although the last four years had been painful, he didn't think of them as wasted years because he had learned so much that made him a better man. He had gained a good friend in Daniel, a law degree, and some understanding of how to make his way in the world. The last year had even brought Rachel into his life, and his only goal after reconciling with Evelyn would be to return to Connecticut and ask Rachel to be his wife. His earnest prayer was that she would love him in return.

Daniel had written to tell him that Rachel and Abigail would be traveling to Boston to visit Rachel's aunt. Although he felt a bit jealous of the young men Rachel might meet in Boston, he had to be glad that she had the trip to fill her days. No matter how much he wanted to be back in Briar Ridge, he couldn't leave here until things changed with Evelyn.

Uncle Bert spoke from across the table. "It's good to have you here, son. We could use a good legal mind like yours for the expansion we plan. Do you have any idea how long you plan to stay?"

"I don't really know. I do want to spend time with Mother, and I don't want to leave until I've made things right with Evelyn, either. What type of help do you need?"

Theo leaned forward. "We want to buy some property and need legal advice in order to get it at the best price, and then some help with bidding for contractors and work on the expansion."

"Couldn't your own lawyer here in town take care of that?" Nathan would be glad to help, but not at the expense of taking business away from the man who usually handled the family affairs.

Theo and Uncle Bert both shook their heads. Uncle Bert said, "Our solicitor, Clyde Farnsworth, recently passed away, and we haven't replaced him."

That put a new light on the situation, but as much as he'd like to help his family, he didn't want to delay so long that he didn't get back to Connecticut by summer. "How long do you think this business of buying more land might take?"

Theo grinned. "Not more than a few weeks. We had hoped to have everything signed and sealed by the middle of May."

Nathan calculated the time. He could give them four to five weeks. If he settled things with Evelyn in that time, he could still get back to Briar Ridge in June. "If that's the case, I believe I can stay and help you."

Uncle Bert grinned. "I promise to not keep you too long. I understand there's a young lady waiting for your return."

The laughter that followed reminded Nathan of the Winston and Monroe families and how much he had envied them. Now he had his own family to remember and cherish. God had been good to him. Now if only Evelyn could forgive him, his joy would be complete.

CHAPTER
TWENTY-ONE

*T*EN DAYS AFTER Easter, Rachel and Abigail stepped off the train at the Boston station to find Aunt Mabel calling their names and waving. Rachel waved back and nudged Abigail forward. "There she is, the woman with the large feather on her hat."

Aunt Mabel rushed forward to greet them. She hugged Rachel first, then Abigail. "Oh, I'm so excited to have you two girls visiting me. Last month was horrible with the snowstorm and everything being shut up and immobile for so long. Boston is just now really getting back to life."

"We're excited to be here, Auntie." Rachel returned her aunt's hug and stepped back for the older woman to embrace Abigail. Just stepping onto the Boston platform had created more anticipation of the days ahead than she'd experienced in all the days of preparation.

"The first thing we must do is find a redcap to bring your luggage to my carriage." Aunt Mabel hooked her arms into theirs and headed toward the stacks of baggage being unloaded from the train.

Rachel had no trouble spotting hers, and Abigail found her own almost as quickly. Aunt Mabel signaled for a man in uniform and wearing a red hat to pick up the bags. He followed along behind them as Aunt Mabel again grasped Rachel's arm.

"I have a number of things planned for you, and they will all start tomorrow. Tonight will be for resting from your journey and settling into your rooms. You'll each have your own bedroom so you can unpack and stow things more quickly."

Rachel glanced at Abigail, who shrugged and raised her eyebrows. They had hoped to share a room, but apparently that wasn't to be. But they'd be able to spend time each evening going over the day's activities before bedtime.

When they arrived at Aunt Mabel's home, Abigail gasped, and Rachel smiled at her reaction. She had to admit, the beautiful brownstone home before them now was even grander than what she remembered. The last time she'd been here, she was only thirteen years old. After Micah's birth, Mama had decided traveling with five children was too difficult, so the visits had stopped.

The coachman jumped down from his perch and opened the carriage doors for the ladies.

Aunt Mabel stepped down first, followed by Rachel, then Abigail. The front door with leaded glass panels opened, and a man in a black suit stood there waiting as they came up the steps to the porch.

"Good evening, Mr. Lewis. This is my niece Rachel and her friend, Abigail. Would you help Jimson with their luggage?"

The man bowed slightly. "Yes, ma'am, we'll take care of it.

Mrs. Lewis has their rooms ready. Molly will be up to see to their needs."

Rachel gazed around the entryway at the rich, polished wood panels of the walls, the gaslit chandelier shedding its light on them, the shiny banister along the stairway to the second floor, and the round table with a magnificent floral arrangement in a crystal vase. The vase brought back a memory of nearly breaking it one day when she had run through the entryway and had bumped into the table. Only Mrs. Lewis's quick hands had saved it. Since then the only other home she'd seen with such elegance had been the Monroe home in Briar Ridge.

Abigail grasped her arm. "This is much larger than I expected."

"Wait until you see the remainder of it." Through double doors on her right she spotted the dining room with its cherry table and upholstered chairs, just as she remembered. Another crystal container held more flowers, and another chandelier hung from the ceiling there.

Aunt Mabel started up the stairway. "Come, girls, your rooms are on the third floor. Mine is on the second. I trust you will be comfortable as your beds both have new feather mattresses."

Neither Rachel nor Abigail commented as they made their way to the third level. Thick carpet runners on the stairs muffled the sound of their footsteps as they climbed. On the last floor, Aunt Mabel swept her arm about the hall. "There are three bedrooms here. Rachel, yours is the one you've always had on the left, and yours, Abigail, is to the right. Both rooms have closets with dressing areas for your personal needs." She headed for Abigail's first and opened the door.

A squeal of delight escaped Abigail. Rachel peeked inside and found it decorated in all shades and hues of purple, from lavender to a deep violet as well as splashes of dark green and cream.

"This is beautiful. I love it. These are my favorite colors." Abigail turned and hugged Aunt Mabel. "I just know this will be a wonderful visit. Thank you."

"They happened to be my daughter Mary's favorite colors too. I've kept the room the same for when she visits with her family. I'm so very happy my brother decided he'd like for you to come earlier. It will be such a pleasure having young people in my home again." She stepped back. "Now, come, Rachel. We'll go to your room."

After seeing Abigail's, Rachel hurried to hers and opened the door. Sunshine yellow filled the room from the comforter on the bed to the drapes on the windows. Even the dressing table stool had a yellow seat. Cream, gold, and blue flowers bloomed from the bed covering to match the fabric at the windows. The deep cherry of the bed, dressing table, armoire, and desk complemented the color scheme.

"Oh, Auntie, it's just like I remembered it. It's perfect." She embraced her aunt. "Thank you for all of this. I'm so glad we decided to come now." The room she'd shared with her cousin Sarah on visits as a young girl held many special memories. How sweet of Aunt Mabel to remember how much Rachel loved being with Sarah.

Mr. Lewis and Jimson entered with her travel trunk and set it at the end of the bed. After the two men departed, Aunt Mabel stepped to the door. She glanced back at Rachel. "Dinner will be at seven sharp. That will give you time to rest and tend to your personal care."

Rachel nodded and, after the door had closed, plopped down on the bed. It was as soft as she remembered. She and Sarah had shared many secrets snuggled up in this very bed, and although she had been two years older than Rachel, her cousin had been a good friend. Two weeks in her room and enjoying the sights of Boston would lift Rachel's spirits and certainly speed summer on its way.

Nathan's image played about in her mind. She had prayed for his safety and success in whatever it was he had to do in North Carolina. No letter had come as yet, but if he had only just arrived, he'd be too busy for that now.

She slipped off her shoes and leaned against the pillows. Weariness overtook her as her body went limp and sleep crept in. A whisper rose toward heaven. "Oh, Nathan, wherever you are and whatever is happening, I pray God will bless you in a mighty way."

Spring had arrived in Boston with all its glory. Daffodils had burst forth into blooms of sunny yellow. Rachel smoothed the sides of her pale green dress and sighed. These past few days with her aunt had been delightful. They had attended two luncheons where friends of Aunt Mabel had welcomed Abigail and her with open arms. Tonight was to be one of the first of several dinner dances for young people that she and Abigail would attend.

However, at the moment, Aunt Mabel expected the girls to

have tea with her to go over the activities for the weekend. She stepped into the hallway just as Abigail closed her door. "You look lovely in that blue. Are you excited about tonight?"

"Yes, I truly am. It will be wonderful to see young men like we did at the academy and have an opportunity to visit with them." She hooked her hand in Rachel's bent elbow. "Thank you so much for inviting me to come along with you."

"You're welcome. I don't think I would have come without you." To be truthful, she would have stayed at home and moped around the house waiting for summer to come.

They made their way downstairs and into the parlor. Molly entered with a tray bearing a tea set and frosted tea cakes. She set them in front of Aunt Mabel, curtsied, and left the room.

Rachel chose one of the rosewood chairs and sat down. Abigail sat in a matching one next to her. Both of them clasped their hands in their laps, waiting for Aunt Mabel to serve and to begin the conversation.

"You both look lovely this evening. I'm sure more than a few heads will be turned by your presence. The Wentworths are known for their entertaining, and their sons are two of the most eligible young men in Boston. She was delighted when I told her about your coming and planned this dinner in honor of the two of you." She poured a cup of tea and handed it to Rachel.

"I'm sure we'll have a grand time, Auntie. Two of the girls we met at the luncheon yesterday said they'd be in attendance, so not everyone will be a complete stranger." The girls they had met were not the friendliest, but Rachel figured they looked upon her as well as Abigail as competition for the two Wentworth men.

Aunt Mabel handed Abigail her cup and offered them both

a tea cake. Dinner would not be served until after eight, so this was to carry them over until that time. She had told Rachel that she didn't want them to faint from hunger before the late meal. With all the food they'd consumed in the past few days, however, hunger would not be a problem for quite a while.

More than excitement about this evening's activities filled Aunt Mabel's face. She picked up an envelope from the table beside her. "I received the most wonderful news today. Sarah and her husband are coming for a visit in July. They're bringing baby Jeremy, so it'll be the first time to see my grandson."

"Oh, Auntie, how wonderful their visit will be for you. I remember when Jeremy was born last fall. It will be a long trip from Texas for them, so how long will they stay?" Rachel's mind raced ahead to summer. Perhaps there would be time for another short visit. Seth would be home, and if Mary and her family came from Philadelphia, everyone could be together again, just like when they were children.

"She says for several weeks. They'll come by train, so it will take some time. I can't wait to see that baby. It's hard to imagine my little Sarah having a child of her own now."

"I can't believe it either. I can't imagine what it would be like to live so far away from family and friends. Of course, knowing Sarah, she has a lot of friends already."

"Oh, she does. Donavan's Aunt Mae runs a boardinghouse in town." She narrowed her eyes and peered at Rachel. "I would much prefer that you find a suitable young man here in Boston or Briar Ridge, but if not, then you should consider going to Texas with Sarah and Donnie when they return. She says men are four or five to one for the women."

Rachel's mouth dropped open. Go to Texas? What a wild idea.

Before she had the chance to respond, Aunt Mabel shook her head at her own idea. "Of course, that's out of the question. Ezra would never allow it."

Aunt Mabel was right about Papa, but the idea lodged itself in the back of her mind. Of course, if she married Nathan, she'd be going to North Carolina with him, and that would be far from her family. Since Nathan hadn't even contacted her since his departure, she shouldn't even be entertaining such thoughts. Perhaps a letter would be waiting when she returned home. A shudder passed through her. If she didn't get her thoughts in order and stop rambling, she'd never get anywhere. Best to pay attention to Aunt Mabel at the moment.

"Now let me go over tomorrow and Sunday with you. Tomorrow I want to show you some of the more historic areas of Boston. It's only been a little over one hundred years since our forefathers won independence for this nation, and so much of it happened right here."

History had been one of Rachel's favorite subjects in school, and she'd reviewed all she could about Revolutionary times before making this trip. Tomorrow would be a most interesting day, and one to which she could look forward. Sunday would be church with Aunt Mabel at the famed Old North Church.

As her aunt went into more detail, Rachel's thoughts turned to Nathan. How she wished he could be here to enjoy the sights and sounds of this city, the heart of independence for the thirteen colonies. Perhaps someday she'd be able to return with him and show him all the beauty of this city. Her heart longed to know what he had to do in his home state that kept him away for so long a time.

Rachel and Abigail arrived at the Wentworth estate on the outskirts of Boston. Uniformed men waited on the driveway to assist the ladies from each carriage as it arrived. The red brick structure stood on a curved, graveled drive to let guests alight at the front steps. Double polished wood doors with beveled glass stood open to welcome each one. Another man in black attire waited at the entrance to accept any cloaks or hats from guests.

Aunt Mabel led the girls into the grand entrance hall with a curved staircase to the second floor dominating the space. Crystal chandeliers, even more elegant than those at her aunt's, hung from the center of the hall as well as in each room on the sides.

Mrs. Wentworth greeted them and beckoned to someone behind them. "Edward and Charles, come. I'd like you to meet Miss Rachel Winston and Miss Abigail Monroe."

The two young men ambled over to the women. "Miss Winston and Miss Monroe, these are my sons, Edward and Charles."

Rachel swallowed a giggle as the young men's smiles widened as they acknowledged her and Abigail. The one named Edward bowed his head slightly. "It's my pleasure to make your acquaintance, Miss Winston. I believe I am to be your escort for the evening." He offered his arm to her.

"Thank you." She placed her fingers on his forearm and walked with him into the main salon. She couldn't help but compare his countenance with that of Nathan. Edward was handsome with his dark hair, strong chin, and dark eyes, but he lacked the warmth she had known with Nathan.

Charles and Abigail followed them into the room, and both men began introductions to others who had formed small groups. Edward stopped in front of a distinguished-looking gray-haired man. "Alderman Thornberry, Mrs. Thornberry, may I introduce one of our guests of honor this evening. This is Rachel Winston from Connecticut and Mrs. Newton's niece." He turned to Rachel. "This is Alderman Thornberry and his wife."

The older woman smiled broadly. "Oh, my dear, I've heard so much about you from your aunt. And I must say you are as lovely as she claimed you to be. It's a pleasure to meet you."

Heat rose in Rachel's face. "Thank you, Mrs. Thornberry. It's a pleasure to meet you too."

After a few moments Edward led her across the room to another group, this time of guests closer to her age. When introductions were made, the two young men smiled and greeted her, but the two young women narrowed their eyes and barely acknowledged Rachel's greeting. She swallowed a laugh. If they harbored any jealousy about her being with Edward, they were wasting their energy. No matter how sophisticated Edward may be, she had no real interest in him as a suitor.

Later, after the dinner, the guests returned to the main drawing room that had been turned into a ballroom. At one end a group of musicians took their places. Chairs and tables formed small groups against the wall. Tables at the opposite end of the room held punch and an array of pastries and cakes that were far more elaborate than any Rachel had ever seen at social events in Hartford.

How different this social gathering was from the last one she had attended in Briar Ridge. The dress of the men and woman, though as formal, was much more elegant, as was the table service. The Wentworth household employed many more servants than did Abigail's parents, and many more guests attended tonight. Still, she enjoyed the friendlier atmosphere of the Monroe household compared to the stiff formality found here in Boston.

Here she was a stranger, an intruder into their society. If not all, most heads turned in her direction when Edward escorted her into the ballroom. No matter how much information Aunt Mabel may have shared with her friends beforehand, they were sure to have many more questions about her as well as Abigail. Although Rachel was blood kin to Aunt Mabel, who was a prominent member of Boston's social elite, she was still a minister's daughter. Abigail was much more suited to their expectations.

Edward handed Rachel a card. "This is your dance card for the evening. As you can see, my name is on there several times. Mother said I must dance with you for the first and last one, but it was my pleasure to add it a few more times. Indeed, now that I see how charming and lovely you are, I'd take great delight in filling all the spaces, but that would be rude of me as host."

Rachel eyed the card filled with the names of several young men whose names meant nothing to her at the moment. She couldn't even remember the ones she'd met briefly before dinner. "Thank you, Edward. I'm sure I'll enjoy my times with you."

Abigail and Charles joined them. Her face glowed with

happiness. "Isn't this the most exciting evening?" She tapped her fan against her chin. "Oh, look, I do believe the musicians are about to begin."

Across the room the leader of the group bowed and then led the stringed group in a waltz. Edward grasped Rachel's hand. "Allow me, Miss Winston. I believe this dance is mine." He smiled, and the creases around his eyes deepened.

"Yes, it is." She followed him to the floor, thankful now for the hours she and Abigail had spent learning all the dance steps for parties such as this. The waltz was Rachel's favorite, not only because of the beauty of the movement but also because it allowed for decent conversation.

"Miss Winston, do you have any idea how long the stay with your aunt will be?" One hand held hers lightly and the other hand skimmed her waist to steady her.

"We planned on two weeks, but Aunt Mabel is talking about longer. However, I think two weeks should be quite sufficient for us."

"Then I must show you some of Boston's finer sights. Would you do me the honor of allowing me to take you on a carriage ride tomorrow afternoon? The weather is supposed to be lovely."

The prospect of riding about Boston with Edward appealed to her much more than taking the same trip with Aunt Mabel. Surely she wouldn't object to the invitation. Knowing Aunt Mabel, she'd probably swoon over the idea and start thinking up more things for Edward to do with Rachel. However, she couldn't forget Abigail. "Could Charles and Abigail come with us?"

"Of course, because I do believe my brother will be extending the same invitation this evening." His brown eyes twinkled with amusement, and his smile warmed her heart.

She swallowed hard. Any other time Edward's handsome looks and polite demeanor would have charmed her right off her feet. If she hadn't met Nathan first, Mr. Wentworth would most definitely catch more than a passing interest. Tomorrow looked to be an interesting day.

CHAPTER
TWENTY-TWO

As they rode through the city Saturday afternoon, the historic sights fascinated Rachel. She drank in the narrow cobblestone streets, the red brick buildings, graveyards, and churches. A new appreciation for the spirit and determination of the early colonists filled her. They rounded a corner to find an unusual gray house with a second story that was larger than the first and formed eaves above the windows on the first floor. She leaned forward. "That's a rather different way to design a two-level house."

Edward laughed. "It is, and it's the home of Paul Revere. At least he lived there during the Revolutionary times. I'm not sure who lives there now. Many immigrants have moved into Boston and taken over this section of town."

Shortly afterward, the carriage stopped in front of the North Church where the lights had been lit to signal how the British would arrive. Abigail peered up at the tall steeple. "Doesn't the saying go, 'one if by land and two if by sea'?"

Charles nodded, then grinned at Abigail. "That's right, and the bells are some of the oldest in America. It is said that Paul Revere rang them on occasion. It's still an Episcopal church and holds services on Sunday."

Rachel stared upward where the white steeple soared into the perfect blue sky. "Yes, I know. We are to attend services there on the morrow. I think it's one of the most beautiful churches I've ever seen." Nothing that tall existed in Briar Ridge, and none of the churches in Hartford were quite like it either. She stared hard to imprint the image in her memory.

Edward pulled a pocket watch from his vest. "I say, it's time we return to your Aunt Mabel's. We did tell her we'd be back in time for late afternoon tea."

He turned the carriage back toward the area where Rachel's aunt lived. In all the times she'd previously visited her aunt, she'd seen nothing of the city except the route between the church and Aunt Mabel's home. From what she'd seen and heard today, Boston had many more attractions that would be worthy of further exploration.

She had to admit that Edward and Charles were perfect gentlemen. Abigail's face fairly glowed with the attention Charles paid her. To see her friend happy made the trip even more enjoyable.

When they were seated around the tea set in the parlor, Aunt Mabel wanted to know all about their excursion through the city. Rachel sat back and let Abigail relate the events and what they had seen. Conversation faded to the background as once again Nathan invaded her heart.

There just had to be a letter waiting for her at home. If he cared about her, he'd write and let her know when he expected to return. No matter what Daniel said, until she heard the words from Nathan himself, she wouldn't be able to believe he truly cared about her. Of course, Daniel wouldn't lie, but he might color things in such a way as to make her feel better.

To be practical, she must think about her future without Nathan until she had a guarantee of his love for her. With Edward seated across from her, she contemplated spending more time with him. His courtesy and attention to details impressed her. He had turned the afternoon into a most delightful excursion.

Aunt Mabel's voice interrupted her train of thought. "Rachel, I do believe your attention has left us."

Rachel blinked her eyes. "I'm sorry, Auntie. I was thinking of the history I saw this afternoon. I'm truly grateful we came for a visit now and not in the winter when you first invited us."

"Yes, the city is much prettier this time of year. I don't know what I was thinking when I suggested February."

Edward nodded and smiled as he set his plate of tea cakes back on the table. "Indeed, this is a lovely time of year in our city, and your presence has made it even more so."

Heat flooded Rachel's cheeks, and she dropped her gaze to the floor.

Charles said, "Yes, you and Miss Monroe have added a great deal to our city. It has been a pleasure to be with you today."

This time Abigail turned pink, but she batted her eyelashes and smiled. "The pleasure was all ours. You and Edward were such knowledgeable escorts."

Conversation then turned to other topics of interest, but Rachel's mind strayed away once again. If Edward asked to visit her in Briar Ridge, she most probably would give her consent.

She hadn't had such attention since she'd been at Bainbridge, and it was a most enjoyable feeling.

On Monday evening Nathan looked over the papers Theo had brought home. Today Nathan had inspected the property in question and decided it would indeed be a good investment for his family. Uncle Bert's enthusiasm for the expansion of the store added to Nathan's decision. The one-room general merchandise store of his childhood years had grown into a prosperous mercantile featuring everything from produce to pillows.

He read over his uncle's plans for the expansion. Since he'd built a new home for his family, the second floor of the building now was used for storage of new merchandise. The property next door was three floors and would a little more than double the space of the two floors and half again as much on the third in the new building.

Theo leaned over his shoulder. "Uncle Bert knows exactly what he wants and where he wants it. I've never seen a man with such a head for mercantile as he has. The bank is ready to loan the money for the expansion, so all that's holding us back is coming to an agreement over the price of the new building."

"I walked through it today, and it appears that not a lot of restructuring or remodeling will need to be done for what Uncle Bert wants to do. I'd say it's a very good investment for the right price. I do agree that what Mr. Denison is asking now is rather steep, but it may be that he wants to be sure you two are making a firm but fair offer before he relents and comes down in his price. I say offer several thousand less than you're willing to pay.

Then when you counter offer, you can come up to what you can afford."

Theo thought for a moment before nodding. "That sounds like a good plan. I'd probably have gone over there and told him right off our bottom line and not left any room for negotiation."

In handling Mrs. Cargill's affairs, Nathan had learned the art of bargaining and could now use the same skills to help his own family. To think that only weeks ago he'd feared their rejection. Now he fit in as though he'd never been away. If only Evelyn would accept him, his joy in the reunion with his family would be complete.

Beth stepped into the room. "Supper is ready if you two can pull yourselves away from business long enough to eat."

Theo reached over to encircle his wife's waist. "Business can always wait when it comes to one of your meals." He kissed her cheek before they turned and headed to the dining room. He tossed a few words toward Nathan. "You coming? I smell roast pork."

Nathan laughed and stacked the papers in a neat pile, then put them back into a folder. Tomorrow he'd go with Theo and Uncle Bert to see Mr. Denison about the building. Tonight, however, he planned to enjoy the meal his sister had prepared.

After Theo said grace, Nathan helped himself to the sweet potatoes. His sister had covered the top of them with pecans, and they looked scrumptious. "You've certainly become one fine cook. If I don't watch myself, I'll be returning to Connecticut with a few unwanted pounds."

Beth's cheeks glowed pink as she ducked her head. "Sudie taught me most of what I know about cooking, and you know how good she was." Then she raised her eyes to his. "I just wish you'd leave the hotel and stay with us. I can understand why you don't want to be at Mama's just yet, but we have room here and would love to have you stay."

Nathan had considered it, but he didn't like the idea of the inconvenience to his sister. Now he could see that she truly offered her home out of her love for him. After two weeks the hotel bed was getting rather uncomfortable, and living out of a valise was not exactly as pleasing or convenient as being in Beth's home would be. "I think I will have to take you up on your offer, my dear sister. Living in a hotel room isn't as comfortable as one might be led to believe. A nice feather bed sounds more than tempting."

Beth's face beamed with pleasure. "Then you'll check out of that place as soon as possible and bring your things here."

He was glad to be home, but the amount of time he spent here would soon become a concern. He would not leave Fayetteville until Evelyn gave her forgiveness, but that seemed to become harder for her with each passing day. What if his presence just made things worse for her? What then? He could not bear to leave without reconciling with her, but he also could not stay on if he knew his presence caused her pain. Torn inside, he did not know what course to take. Even the letters he'd sent Daniel and Reverend Winston had been vague and uncertain as to future plans.

Beth's arm went around his shoulder. "Something seems to be troubling you. Is there anything I can do?"

"No, this I must do myself. I've said I cannot leave until Evelyn forgives me and speaks to me, but that hope is getting fainter with each day she won't see me."

"Oh, how I pray for her every day. Mama says Evelyn won't

even talk with her or Sudie much and wants meals brought to her room. That can't be good for her." She wrapped her arms around him and laid her head against his. "Let's pray for Evelyn to open her heart to forgive you."

Nathan's heart filled to overflowing with love for his sister. How much he'd missed by letting his bitterness and anger control his life these years. He vowed to never again let such feelings dominate his life.

He reached for Beth's hand. "Thank you. I'm sure Jesus will hear us, and I pray He will answer us soon."

And the sooner it happened, the sooner he could make his way back to Connecticut.

Ezra sat at his desk and tapped a sheet of paper against his fingers. The letter from Nathan had arrived in the Saturday morning post, and it troubled him. Almost five weeks had passed since he left their home, and according to his letter, he had been with his family since the beginning of April. But the letter was postmarked April 16, and so far the boy had made no progress in finding forgiveness from his sister Evelyn. Until then, Nathan declared he couldn't return to Briar Ridge.

Rachel had another week left in Boston before her return home. He wouldn't spoil her visit there with this news. However, when she came back, he'd have to tell her that Nathan might not make it back. Somehow he'd have to help Rachel understand she couldn't wait around forever for what may never be.

Then he smiled. He'd have waited for Felicity forever if it had taken that long for her to decide to marry him. The course of true love can run as smoothly as satin sheets on a bed or as roughly as the white waters on a raging river. The relationship between Nathan and Rachel would take the latter for sure.

He placed the letter in a drawer and picked up his sermon notes for the next morning. No matter what verses he used or what words he spoke, they must all arrive at the same conclusion. Without the Lord Jesus Christ as Savior, man could not hope to spend eternity in heaven. Tomorrow's message would be based on a verse from Philippians that promised God would supply all our needs from His glorious riches in Jesus Christ.

Ezra believed the promise because the Lord had taken care of him and his family since the beginning of his marriage to Felicity. His task here on this earth was to convince others of the security of that promise when they put their trust in the Lord.

A light rap at the door sounded, and Felicity opened it a crack. "Are you still working on your sermon?"

"Yes and no, but do come in, my dear. I always welcome your presence." He shuffled the papers of his sermon notes and stacked them in a neat pile to the side. The message stood ready to deliver to his congregation on the morrow.

Felicity sat down across from him with hands clasped in her lap. "I read Aunt Mabel's post, and I'm so glad Rachel and Abigail are having a good visit. Have you heard anything at all from Nathan Reed?"

"Yes, I have." He retrieved the letter from the desk drawer. "One came today. I'm concerned because he hasn't resolved all the issues with his family as yet. He's had a delightful reunion with his mother, but thus far his sister is still angry with him and won't forgive him. He says he can't return to Briar Ridge until it's resolved."

"Oh, dear, that isn't exactly encouraging news. We must pray harder for his dear sister to see that Nathan has changed and has true remorse for his behavior. As a mother, I understand how quickly Mrs. Reed forgave him and welcomed him with open arms. A sister is a very different matter. She feels betrayed, and it will take a while for him to rebuild the trust she once had in him."

Ezra pressed his lips together. His wife saw the heart of the matter immediately. He leaned forward with his forearms resting on his desktop. "This is a matter for our prayers indeed. In the meantime, we must decide how much we can tell Rachel. We can't break our pledge to Nathan to let him reveal the circumstances of his life, but our precious daughter needs to understand why he is delayed."

Felicity twisted her hands together. "I know, and that will be very difficult. I will keep her very busy when she returns at the end of next week. May is almost here, and Seth will be home from seminary. If we keep her distracted or whet her interest in other matters, the time will go much more quickly. Perhaps everything will go well, and Nathan will be able to return in June."

"That's a good idea, my love. In the meantime, we have a week to help us decide what we need to tell her without getting her hopes too aroused. I'd sorely dislike having her hopes dashed." Until he had better news to share with his daughter, he'd give her only the information she needed to know that Nathan may not return to Briar Ridge as soon as he had hoped.

CHAPTER
TWENTY-THREE

*R*ACHEL PLOPPED ON her bed clad only in her camisole and knickers with lace trimmings. Although the outside air had warmed, it still held a slight chill. She grabbed a pillow and hugged it to her chest for warmth.

One more dinner party tonight before their departure for home tomorrow, and she would say good-bye to Edward. Exhaustion from so many activities in the two weeks they'd been at Aunt Mabel's caused her to yawn now and wish for a nap. Auntie wanted both her and Abigail to be at their best for tonight's farewell dinner.

Rachel sighed and rolled over on her stomach with her chin now propped on the pillow. Edward had been quite attentive and had managed to garner all of her time and escort her to the social events of the past week, and to her surprise, she had enjoyed every minute of it. Abigail, on the other hand, had attracted a number of suitors with her golden-brown hair and hazel eyes. Charles had tried to keep her to himself but had failed. Even tonight Abigail's escort was someone by the name of Adam.

None of that really mattered now. Tomorrow they'd be on the train headed back to Hartford. It would be an all-day ride, but they would be home late in the evening, and she was so ready to go to church the following day and hear one of father's informal sermons. The two Sundays she'd been to church here with her aunt, everyone and everything had been so formal, even to the assigned pew boxes for families.

Someone tapped on the door, and she glanced up to find Abigail standing there. She had tied a wrapper about her and at Rachel's invitation joined her on the bed. "It doesn't seem possible that we'll be leaving tomorrow. I've had such fun and can't thank you enough for allowing me to come with you."

"You can thank Aunt Mabel for that. She didn't think it proper for me to travel alone, so she wanted to be sure I had a companion. But if she hadn't invited you, I planned on asking Papa if you could. It's so much more fun when you have a friend to do things with."

Abigail twisted a lock of hair around her finger. "Are you anxious to get home? I know things will seem quite dull for me."

Rachel bit her lip. She'd enjoyed the time here and all the sights and sounds of Boston in the springtime, but home beckoned. "Without knowing Nathan's whereabouts or when or if he might return to Briar Ridge, I'm ready to be at home and make plans for the summer."

"It will be here before we know it." A sigh escaped from Abigail. "I am going to miss all the attention from the young men. Are you sorry Edward took up all of your time?"

Laughter rang out from Rachel. "Oh no, I much preferred

it that way. I didn't have to worry about learning new topics of conversation or the interests of my escorts. I just let Edward do most of the talking."

"He is rather handsome and so very polite and gracious to everyone."

"Yes, and I must say his attention was most pleasurable. He mentioned coming to Briar Ridge to visit, and I told him that would be nice." Nathan still filled a place in her heart, but there was no assurance there would be a life with him. She should be planning what to do with her life back home instead of daydreaming about something most likely not to happen.

An idea popped into her head, and she sat up, her brow furrowed with thought. "I just had the most intriguing idea. If for some reason Nathan doesn't come back, I think I'd like to go with my cousin Sarah and Donny back to Texas after their visit here in July."

"Go to Texas! Whatever in the world for? I know there are supposed to be a lot of eligible men there, but I'm not sure I'd go there for that."

Again Rachel laughed. "Oh, it's not for the men. I just think it would be a great adventure. I could go for a visit like we have here, but if I like it, I could stay there." Of course, that would mean leaving Mama and Papa, but the experience would be worth it. After all, she didn't have to stay in Texas forever. She leaned forward, still hugging her pillow. "You could go with us. Think what an adventure that would be for both of us."

Abigail's eyes opened wide and her mouth gaped. "Rachel Winston, you are the most exasperating person I know. I've never seen you flit from one distraction to another like you have the past few months. First it was all Nathan, and then Edward took your attention, and now you're talking about Texas." She planted her hands on her hips. "I think it's time you decided just exactly what it is you want out of life and quit this back-and-forth nonsense."

Rachel cringed a bit at her friend's accusations. Mama would probably say the same thing. "Do you really think I'm being too flighty? What if something happens, and Nathan doesn't come? I must have alternate plans for my future."

"I can see you having a life with Edward, but going to Texas is really outlandish, and what if you go and Nathan returns?"

Before Rachel could reply, Aunt Mabel called from the hallway. "I hear your chatting and hope you are getting ready for this evening." She popped her head through the opening. "Oh, dear, neither one of you is near being ready. I'll send Molly up to help you. We don't have time to dawdle."

Her skirts swished as she turned and hurried back to the stairs. Rachel bit her lip. "I do suppose we'd better hurry. It wouldn't do for us to be late to our own farewell party."

Abigail scampered from the room, calling over her shoulder, "I bet I'm ready before you are."

Not if Rachel could help it. She pulled her dress from the wardrobe and stepped into it dreamily. Abigail's earlier words had stung, but right now her future was wide open. She day-dreamed about Texas. Such delightful tales she'd heard about cowboys and ranches and horses. The more she considered the idea of a trip there, the more intrigued she became with the notion of visiting that illustrious state. She'd send a post off to Sarah as soon as she could discuss the idea with Papa. Of course, if Nathan came home, she'd drop all her plans in a heartbeat to be with him.

She bit her lip. There she was—flitting from one idea to another again. But how could she help it? She could not see into the future. Only God could.

Daniel read the letter from Nathan and sat back in his chair. His friend's journey had been successful except for the reunion with his older sister. Nathan's skills as a lawyer would be a great help to his uncle. It was just like God to have Nathan at home at exactly the right time to make sure his family would get the best counsel possible.

Perhaps the time had come to make plans for his future away from Briar Ridge. With three lawyers now in town, Daniel's client list had not grown as much as he had hoped. If he wanted a wife and a more successful career, it would have to be somewhere else. He'd enjoyed Hartford the times he'd been there, and that would be a nice place to marry and settle down to live with a family.

He picked up the Hartford paper he subscribed to in order to keep up with the news elsewhere. Briar Ridge's paper still circulated only three days a week, and the news was usually old by the time it made it into print.

As he turned the pages, an advertisement caught his eye. Experienced lawyers, teachers, and clergy were needed in the western states. The more the country expanded westward, the more people were needed to provide the services already provided in the eastern states. He tapped his pen on the desk. Yes, the opportunities offered in the expanding country would be an excellent way to start a new life.

He made note of the information, copied it onto a tablet, and then stored it in the top drawer of his desk. It wasn't something he wanted to do right away, but at some later date he may want to investigate those opportunities. If business didn't pick up considerably by the end of summer, he'd give great consideration to moving West.

In the meantime, he had another will to write for a couple from church. Writing wills wouldn't bring in much money, but it was business, and he'd take whatever came his way. If he could have his dream, he'd be in court arguing cases that had great importance, like prosecuting criminals or defending clients in civil suits. He imagined there would be more of those types of affairs in the untamed West. In the meantime, he'd write wills, settle disputes, and find missing heirs.

Nathan sat in the wingback chair Beth had provided in her spare bedroom. This certainly offered more comfort than the hotel room, and the warm welcome from his sister and brother-in-law only added to the enjoyment of being in their home. But he had been back in town a month now, and still his sister Evelyn showed no sign of relenting toward him.

However, Beth had commented just this morning about how much happier and healthier their mother looked since his return. She did have much more energy and more color in her cheeks than the first day he'd seen her. God had been good thus far, and Nathan had to trust that He would soften Evelyn's heart eventually.

A knock sounded on the door, and then Beth's voice called, "Nathan, dinner is ready."

Nathan called, "I'll be right there."

He washed his hands in the ewer on a table near the chair then headed down to dinner. After Theo returned thanks, Nathan sampled the fried chicken. He turned to Beth. "This is as good as what I remember from when we were children. Sudie has taught you well."

"Yes," Beth laughed, "and even though she's getting on in years, she still manages to cook delicious meals for Mama and Evelyn."

At the mention of Evelyn's name, remorse mixed with the love he held for his family squeezed his heart. He had to make another attempt at apologizing to his sister. He couldn't be happy until her forgiveness freed him.

As soon as politely possible after dinner, he excused himself from the table then bent low to whisper to Beth. "I'm going to see Evelyn. If I'm successful, I'll bring her and Mama back here. If not, I'll come alone. Pray for me."

Beth smiled and squeezed his hand. "I will."

With long, determined strides he walked the few blocks back to his childhood home. Evelyn had been so deeply hurt that he may never be able to reach her, but his love for her demanded he keep trying.

When he reached the home, Nathan stopped at the front walk and gazed at the house. He lifted his face and breathed in the fresh spring air.

Lord, give me the words to say to my sister. I know she loves You and reads Your Word. May You use Your Word to speak to her and to bring healing. Amen.

He strode up to the door and entered the hallway. Sudie saw him and motioned toward the library. Nathan nodded and entered the room quietly. Evelyn sat in a wingback chair, head back and eyes closed. A Bible lay open on her lap.

The rug on the floor silenced his steps, and he stood beside her chair. Even in repose, her face didn't hold peace. How he wanted to change that. He touched her arm. "Evelyn, it's Nathan. I have to speak with you."

Her eyes flew open and she jerked upright. "You're supposed to be at Beth's." She attempted to draw away, but Nathan held her arm.

"I know, but I can't go any longer without your forgiveness, Evelyn. You were so good to me as a child. You always took care of me and played with me. I had no right to say those horrible things to you or Mother, and I am deeply sorry for hurting both of you."

She turned her face away and stared off to the side. A slight tremor crossed her lips, and he prayed for her not to go back to that awful scene in this very room when he cursed her and stomped out of the house. He had been a different man then. Somehow she had to see that.

Nathan knelt beside her and loosened his grip on her arm. "I hurt so much that day myself that I wanted to inflict pain on whoever was in my way. You and Mother didn't deserve my anger." He moved slightly to be more in her line of vision. "Look at me, Evelyn, really look at me. I'm not the same man I was that day. I have come back to God and sought His forgiveness. Now I seek yours."

They sat in silence a few moments before Evelyn's soft voice reached his ears, quoting Scripture. "'For if ye forgive men their trespasses, your heavenly Father will also forgive you, but if ye forgive not men their trespasses, neither will Father forgive your trespasses.'"

Nathan remained silent. Those verses had been etched in his heart when he stood on the old plantation and buried his anger toward his father. He saw a tear on her cheek and reached out to cover her hand with his. "I'm so sorry. I love you. Please know that."

She touched his cheek with the fingers of her free hand. "You were such a precious little boy, so we couldn't help but love you. Beth and I were as shocked by the truth as you, but my shock and pain turned to anger at you, and I was angry so long that my heart turned to stone." Evelyn opened the Bible on her lap.

"God spoke to me through some verses in Ezekiel, and I was thinking about them when you startled me." She picked up the Bible and pointed to a verse. "Ezekiel is telling the people how God is going to deliver them from exile and bring them home. Verse twenty-six in the thirty-sixth chapter really spoke to me. It says, 'A new heart also will I give you, and a new spirit will I put within you; and I will take away the stony heart out of your flesh, and I will give you an heart of flesh.' That's what I prayed for...a softened heart to replace the one of stone I've had for so long."

The tears now flooded her eyes. "I...I forgive you, Nathan. You are my brother, and I love you just as I did when you were a child."

Nathan swallowed back his own tears before bending forward to hug her. "Those are the words I've waited these many weeks to hear. My joy is now complete."

She returned the embrace. "God has been good to us, little brother. He's given us a second chance."

A second chance he wouldn't take for granted. God had answered his prayers and given him back his family. He reached for Evelyn's hand. "Come, let's find Mama and join the rest of the family at Beth's." What a night of rejoicing this would be, as their family would once again be complete.

CHAPTER
TWENTY-FOUR

$\mathcal{M}$AMA LAID ASIDE her shopping list and peered at Rachel. "My dear, your mind is not with me today. You've been home several weeks now, but ever since your return, you've been distracted. I thought since Seth was now out of school, you'd be busy with him."

Rachel slumped in her chair. "I'm sorry. I guess I have been letting my mind wander. The visit with Aunt Mabel was wonderful. Now that I'm home again, everything is so different. Summer is almost here, and I have decisions to make. I can't mope around home waiting for something that may never happen. Nathan hasn't written one word of encouragement in all the time he's been gone."

Nathan had been gone two months. Surely he would have returned by now if he was going to come. Now she doubted if she had really loved *him* or just loved the idea of someone different who was a challenge. She really knew so very little about him.

Mama reached across the table and grasped Rachel's hands. "Papa and I told you that there were special circumstances surrounding his return to North Carolina. Until he can get those issues resolved, he won't leave his family."

"But why hasn't he written me? And why can't you tell me what the problem is?"

"First, I imagine he didn't want to get your hopes up for his return and then be disappointed and hurt if he couldn't come back. As for the second question, we both explained we could not break the confidence Nathan put in us. It is up to him to tell you what happened that made his return to his home so important."

The season may not be official, but she'd always looked at June as the beginning of summer. She had put off thinking about her plans for the trip to Texas in hopes she'd hear from Nathan. Sarah and her family would be in Boston soon. If she hadn't heard anything by their arrival, she planned to ask Sarah about going to Texas with them. If nothing else, she could be nanny to her nephew. Of course she had to discuss it with Mama and Papa first.

Mama folded her list and tucked it into her pocket. "Right now I need your help with the church anniversary celebration. You can either help me with the food or Mrs. Bivens with the decorations and flowers."

Better to help Mama and get her mind off Nathan. Sitting around worrying and thinking about him would not bring him back any quicker. "Where do you need me? You know I'll do either one. Although I do have a leaning toward the decorating." Working with Mrs. Bivens would be fun and provide an opportunity to learn more about the flowers grown in the Bivenses' garden.

"Then I'll tell Minnie you'll be working with her. I think everything is covered now. It's exciting to think about celebrating eighty-five years for our church."

Just then Seth burst into the room waving a piece of paper above his head. "I got it! I got it! The church I wrote wants me to come as soon as possible to be their full-time preacher since their present one is retiring in June. Isn't it great? And it's in Texas, where our cousin lives." Her twenty-two-year-old brother, just graduated from seminary, rocked on his heels and beamed. "I want to be here for the church anniversary celebration on May 19, of course, but I think I will leave just after, on May 21. How does that sound?"

Rachel jumped up from the table and grabbed the letter. "Texas? I don't believe it. I've been thinking about going there with Sarah and Donavan after their visit with Aunt Mabel in July."

Mama gasped and clasped her hands to her chest. "What are you talking about, Rachel?"

"Oh, Mama, I meant to talk with you and Papa about it, but this is great news. If Seth is going to Texas, I really want to go. What an adventure it would be!"

Seth hugged Rachel and lifted her off the ground. "That's great. What fun it would be to have my little sister around. It would keep me from being lonely for sure."

Rachel laughed. "With the scarcity of women in the town, you might need me to keep you company."

Mama raised her hands. "Hear now. Let's not be planning any such trips until Papa and I can discuss it. Of course, you must go, Seth, as it's your calling, but you, my dear Rachel, will have to wait and talk to your father."

Seth winked at her and bent low to Rachel's ear. "If you really want to go, I'll put in a good word with Papa." Then he leaned back. "I'm going over to the church to share the good news with Papa."

"But he'll be leaving soon to come home for supper. You can wait until then."

He kissed Mama's cheek. "Then we'll walk home together. I can't wait to tell him." A moment later he was gone.

Mama blinked her eyes and breathed deeply. "Well, I must say this has been a most unexpected turn of events." She peered across at Rachel. "I don't know what to make of your ideas. Having you move away was something we knew might happen, but for you to go to Texas unmarried is another matter entirely, and one that will take a great deal of thought."

"Yes, ma'am, I understand." Excitement began as a tiny drop of hope in her veins, then traveled full blown through her body to explode with anticipation. "But wouldn't it be wonderful for Seth and me to be together to help spread the truth of God's love and mercy?"

"Yes, but have you considered what will happen if Nathan returns and you are not here?"

"I have, but it's all so uncertain. A trip to Texas will give me something to look forward to." Nathan had been uppermost in Rachel's mind, but if he did not return soon, she'd go ahead with the plans now formulating in her mind.

Before Mama could respond, the clock chimed the hour, then rang out five strikes. Rachel pushed back from the table. "I had no idea of the time. Daniel and Abigail will be here shortly after six. I must get dressed."

"Of course, dear. This will be quite an interesting evening. I'll mention your desires to Papa tonight, and we'll see what he has to say."

Rachel hugged her mother. "Thank you for your listening ear. You always know just what to say to help me sort out things."

She left Mama in the kitchen and hurried up to her room to change clothes. Daniel had tickets for the evening at the new playhouse in town. Afterward, he planned to treat Rachel and Abigail to a late dinner at the Marquis Hotel. If the town kept growing at this rate, in a few years Briar Ridge would have almost as many conveniences as Hartford. She'd better enjoy them while she could because most likely Texas had nothing like Briar Ridge or Hartford had to offer for entertainment.

Just as she finished dressing, a carriage arrived. Rachel rushed down to greet Daniel. When she opened the door, he stood there with his hand raised to knock. His eyes opened wide, and he dropped his hand to his side.

Rachel laughed. "I didn't mean to startle you. I'm all ready."

Mama greeted Daniel. "This will be such a nice treat for the girls. Enjoy yourselves, and I'll look forward to hearing all about it later."

Rachel kissed her mother's cheek. "We will, and you'll get a minute-by-minute account of it all." She grasped Daniel's elbow as they made their way to the carriage where Abigail waited. Daniel assisted Rachel to the seat across from his sister.

Rachel arranged her skirt and smoothed the silken fabric. "Isn't it exciting that Briar Ridge now has a theater as well as a concert hall?"

"Yes, and I'm so glad you wanted to share the evening with me tagging along."

"I have some news too. Seth is going to Texas to be the preacher at the church in the same town where Sarah and Donavan live. He leaves May 21, and if Papa approves, I think I might go with him. Wouldn't that be exciting?"

Daniel cleared his throat. "Hmm, Rachel, may I dare ask if you've given much thought to how much you'll miss if you go to the frontier?"

Rachel's mouth dropped open. Of course she'd thought about leaving all this behind. "I'll miss it, but a lot will be going on out there, and we'll be doing so much good that I won't have time to really miss it."

Abigail frowned. "Rachel, are you sure this isn't just another passing fancy? I'll miss you so much if you go."

"I'll miss you too, but I think this is something I really would like to do." A tiny tendril of doubt wound its way to her heart. Could she truly give up all of her friends, her church activities, and the love of her family to go clear across the country? She still had a few weeks to make up her mind. And, of course, she needed to talk to her parents about it in more depth.

Daniel reached for her hand. "Rachel, I know you so well, and you wouldn't do this if you didn't truly believe it's what God wants you to do. However, I also know how you've felt about Nathan Reed, and I question your motives for this trip west."

Rachel pulled away sharply. "I really haven't had much time to think about him these days, Daniel. Church activities and helping Mama keep me very busy." That wasn't exactly the truth. Thoughts of Nathan interrupted her at the oddest times, but not as frequently as the first weeks after his departure.

Daniel leaned forward. "Rachel, don't be hasty in deciding to go with Seth. Please be absolutely sure it's what God wants you to do. I know Nathan cares about you, and he will be back if it's at all possible."

"Then why hasn't he written to me?" She had asked herself this same question too many times to count. His silence made no sense to her. Now was she running away because she didn't want to stay here and discover that Nathan didn't really care about her and didn't plan to return to Connecticut? A dull ache began in her temple.

Later that evening her parents called her into the parlor after she arrived home. Papa spoke first. "Rachel, this idea of your going to Texas is a bit premature in our opinion. Have you truly thought it through?"

In her mind she had, and now with Daniel and her father both doubting her, she became more determined to follow her plans. "Yes, Papa, I have, and it's the only way I can really get on with my life. Briar Ridge holds no future for me. With Sarah and Seth both in Texas, it won't be like I'm off all alone. In fact, I would really prefer to go with Seth when he leaves."

Mother leaned forward. "But what about Nathan? You care about him, and he may return at any time."

"Yes, I do care, but with no word from him in these months, how can I keep counting on his return? If he does come back, then of course I'll stay."

Papa peered at her for what seemed to be an eternity before he finally spoke. "I'm not sure this is in your best interests, but if you'll wait and go with Sarah and Donavan later in July, and not with Seth, then we'll allow you to go. But only if Sarah agrees and only for a visit, mind you. After you've spent a few weeks in Texas, we will reassess the situation."

Rachel was relieved that her father had come up with the perfect compromise. "Yes, Papa," she said, beaming. "I will wait until July."

CHAPTER
TWENTY-FIVE

*N*ATHAN STARED AT Daniel's letter. It was postmarked May 12 and had come the day he boarded the train back to Connecticut. A vise clamped his heart as he reread the news once again. On May 21, just three days hence, Rachel might leave with her brother Seth to go to Texas.

His train was due to arrive in Hartford in ten minutes. Although late on a Friday, Mr. Fitzpatrick would still be at the office. He'd check with him and let them know he'd return to work on Monday. Then on Saturday morning he could make his way to Briar Ridge. That should give him plenty of time to arrive in time for the church's anniversary celebration and persuade Rachel to stay in Connecticut.

If she didn't love him, he wouldn't stop her, but he refused to accept that possibility. God was in control, and Nathan would rather believe that Rachel was indeed very much a part of the future God had planned for them both.

Guilt for not writing to her at least once ate a hole in his heart. Had it been stubborn pride or shame that kept him from declaring his love? It didn't matter now, because if he didn't make the effort immediately, he'd never have the chance.

The business with his uncle and Theo had taken longer than expected, but all had been pleased with the final outcome. Until Daniel's letter arrived, Nathan figured he'd still have plenty of time to court Rachel.

As soon as Nathan alit from the train, he headed for the law firm and found the senior partner in his office. "Mr. Fitzpatrick, I have a matter to discuss with you."

The older man waved Nathan into his office and grinned broadly as he reached out to shake Nathan's hand. "You don't know how happy I am to see you back. Seems your reputation for honesty and diligence has made the rounds. Just this afternoon I had another inquiry about you when I was over at the courthouse. They've all been as anxious for your return as I have."

Relief flooded Nathan's heart. At least he didn't have the job to worry about now. "I'll be in on Monday, but first I must go back to Briar Ridge on a most important matter."

Mr. Fitzpatrick's eyebrows arched, but he waited for Nathan to continue.

"You know how we discussed marriage as a sign of stability? Well, I've met the girl I want to marry if she'll have me. But if I don't get to Briar Ridge, she may be lost to me."

"Well, now, it's good news you've found someone with whom you wish to settle down, but how could you lose her? Isn't the affection mutual?"

"I don't know. I think she cares, but I haven't let her know how I feel, and since I've been away for so long, she is planning to leave on a trip westward with her brother. I want to get there and persuade her to marry me instead."

Mr. Fitzpatrick grinned. "I see, my friend. You need to leave posthaste to take care of the affairs of your heart."

"Her father's church is planning an anniversary commemoration tomorrow, and I want to be there for that. I thought perhaps I could leave in the morning, but I have just decided to start out tonight. I'll stop overnight at the Anderson farm, then get to Briar Ridge early tomorrow."

The senior partner stood and came around his desk to reach for Nathan's hand again. "Good luck, young man, and I pray this young lady is the one God has chosen for you. If she is, then everything will work in your favor."

Nathan thanked him and headed for his flat to leave his bags and trunk from his trip home and repack his valise for the trip to Briar Ridge. Within an hour he rode toward the Anderson farm. In another few hours it would be completely dark, but with the lantern he'd brought, he could make his way for the distance to the Andersons. With all the talk about thieves and highway robberies, he didn't intend to ride long after sunset.

While Baron trotted along, Nathan began planning his approach to Rachel. Or should he seek Reverend Winston first? No, he'd find Rachel, since her father already knew Nathan's intentions. He prayed he would not be too late.

The sun sank behind the trees, creating a brilliant golden orange glow in the western sky. The tree leaves rustled with a cooling breeze of late May. If he picked up his pace, he'd be at the Anderson home at the edge of night. His mind filled with the image of Rachel. If only he had not had to leave her for so long. No wonder she had tired of waiting and made other plans for her life.

Leaving Mother and his sisters had been difficult, but they understood his need to return here. He'd promised to let them know as soon as he knew what the future held. Beth and Theo even promised to come up for the wedding, but they didn't think it wise for Mother to make the long journey.

If he and Rachel did marry, their wedding trip would be to North Carolina. He wanted her to meet his mother and Evelyn and the rest of the Reed clan. Then his joy would be truly complete.

Rachel helped Mrs. Bivens and the other ladies decorating the tables for the dinner on the grounds to be served the next day. All would be ready for the ladies to bring their best recipes cooked to perfection to be laid out on the tables. The sun lowered in the sky as the committee wrapped up its duties.

Children ran between the tables, and Micah joined them. After another few minutes of tag and playing, they would be called inside for the evening. The memory of her own childhood and the fun of such festivities skittered through her mind, only to remind her that on Monday Seth would be leaving. She almost regretted agreeing to wait until Sarah and Donavan visited, but in the end that decision was probably for the best.

A sudden chill coursed through Rachel. *Have you completely sought My will for your future?* The words echoed in her brain and stopped her in her tracks.

Miriam pulled on Rachel's sleeve. "What's the matter? You look sick all of a sudden."

"I'm not sure, but I need to go to the church and pray. I'll be back in a minute."

She went into the church and sank onto a pew. With her head bowed, she murmured aloud, "Lord, what am I to do? Have I been making my own plans without really thinking through what You want me to do? I thought if I had options, You'd show me the one to choose by closing doors, but I'm still just as confused as I was months ago. Is going to Texas what You want for me, or is it just what I thought would be the best option if Nathan didn't come back?" She bit her lip and clutched at her skirt.

Peace would not come. Her rambling words only served to add to the confusion filling her heart and soul, and only the Lord could sort them out. What good were any plans she made if they weren't what God willed for her?

Bible verses memorized over the years tumbled through her mind like water splashing over stones in a brook. One from the Book of Proverbs stopped and shouted at her. *A man's heart deviseth his way, but the Lord directs his steps.* Where was the Lord directing her now?

Just after sundown Nathan rode into the yard of the Anderson Orchards. He alit from his horse and approached the house where the family lived. As he knocked on the door, he breathed a prayer that they would accept him as an overnight guest.

Jonathan opened the door. "Nathan Reed. I didn't expect to

see you here this evening. Come in." He held the door open wide for Nathan to enter. "Ma, we have company."

Mrs. Anderson bustled toward them. "Nathan Reed, it's good to see you."

"Thank you. I'm on my way to Briar Ridge, but I didn't want to continue in the dark."

Jonathan nodded his head. "I understand that. We've had a number of robberies along that road the past few months. I take it you need a place for tonight."

"Yes, I do, but I don't want to impose on you."

Mrs. Anderson waved her hand. "Not a bit of trouble. Supper will be ready shortly. You can share a room with Jonathan here."

"You're sure you don't mind? I do need to get on to Briar Ridge as soon as possible tomorrow." A warm bed and a good meal would go a long way in making the rest of the journey bearable. As long as he was in Briar Ridge before the celebration ended, he'd be in time.

"I don't mind at all." Jonathan gestured for Nathan to have a seat. "Tell me what you've been up to since we last saw you."

For the first time in a long time, Nathan didn't mind telling about his trip and his family. A sense of peace and well-being filled him. "I've been to North Carolina to visit with my family. I hadn't seen my mother or sisters for several years. We had a good visit, and I was there when my uncle and cousins needed some help with their business."

"Now, that was a long journey. What brings you back to Briar Ridge?" Jonathan asked.

Nathan grinned. "A certain young woman I believe you know, Rachel Winston."

"Oh, yes, I remember your taking some apple trees to her

father just before that horrible storm we had. We really worried about your making it when the snow became such a blizzard. Then when Reverend Winston returned the wagon, he told us about your ordeal. God sure looked out for you."

"Yes, I was very fortunate in how God arranged everything at just the right time. Of course I was ill for a while, but during that time I realized how good God had been and that He hadn't forsaken me after all."

"I'm sure there's more to that story, but I see Ma getting ready to call everyone to supper, so it'll have to wait." Jonathan stood, and Nathan followed him to the table.

Later, as he lay in bed, Nathan considered his good fortune. Ever since he'd made a new commitment to the Lord, his life had taken a turn for the better. Mother and Evelyn had both sent him off with their love and made him promise to return.

That's exactly what he planned to do if Rachel would come with him. He wanted to get to know her better, and he wanted her to know the whole truth regarding his family. With the complete contentment of a heart at peace with the world, he turned to his side and fell asleep.

Chapter
Twenty-Six

RACHEL WASHED HER face, trying in vain to erase all traces of her sleepless night. She'd wrestled the sheets and her conscience all during the dark hours. She'd dreamed of life with Nathan and then life without him. Just as dawn colored the sky with the rising sun, the answer had come. She would wait here for Nathan as long it took for him to come back. She had only to believe and wait. Here and not in Texas.

The vivacious but simple song of a robin resounded in her ears. Not as musical as the thrasher, but still the red-breasted bird sent forth his pleasing voice. She loved to hear the bird's melody, and this morning it echoed the joy of her decision.

What would Papa and Mama think of her and the reasons she listed for deciding to stay home? She almost dreaded the celebration today. After all her talk about wanting to go to Texas with Seth and how much help she could be to Sarah, she'd have to tell Papa she'd changed her mind.

Even if the dream didn't materialize and Nathan never

returned to declare his love for her, she would go on with her life. God promised to answer her prayers, but this time she'd make sure her prayers were in the right direction. If she set all her plans based on what God wanted her to do, those plans would succeed. The ones so far had been her own.

"Rachel, we're going to be late if you don't come now."

Mama's tone sent Rachel scurrying to gather her belongings. Displeasure was one thing she didn't want at the moment from her parents. Enough of that would come later.

She climbed up into the buggy next to Miriam. Papa drove the horses this morning and cut a glance back at Rachel before snapping the reins and moving to join the line of buggies and wagons heading for the church. More vehicles than usual filled the yard today for the celebration. Women carried plates and baskets of food to the tables they'd set up the evening before. Their happy chatter and greetings filled the air. Soon they would partake of the noon meal and then gather for the speeches and other activities planned.

Despite her concerns about telling her parents, peace filled Rachel. They would understand.

After they climbed down from the buggy, Miriam linked her arm with Rachel's for the short stroll to the churchyard. "Isn't it a wonderful day? The sun is shining, and everyone is happy." She peered up at Rachel. "Are you feeling better after praying last night?"

"Yes, I am."

"Good, because I'd rather see you laugh and smile than cry." She pulled closer to Rachel. "Besides, I'm going to miss you terribly when you leave with Sarah and Donavan."

Rachel hugged her sister close. "You won't have to miss me

because I've decided not to go. I'm going to stay here and wait for Nathan, no matter how long it takes."

A squeal of delight split the air, and heads turned in their direction. "Shh, now. I haven't told Seth or Mama or Papa yet. Don't start celebrating too soon." If they found out before she had a chance to tell either of them, things would not go well for her. Of that she was sure.

"Oh, I'm so glad you're not going. We need you around here."

"Yes, I'm sure you do, but if I get married, I'll likely be leaving you to move somewhere else." And she prayed that place would be Hartford.

"But not as far away as Texas." Suddenly Miriam stopped in her tracks, her mouth open.

Rachel followed her gaze and found Jimmy Turner in her line of vision. She leaned down and whispered, "Do you want to go over and talk to him?"

Heat rose in Miriam's cheeks. "Oh, no, I'd die of embarrassment. He can come talk to me if he wants to, but I don't think he will."

Even as she spoke, Rachel noted that Jimmy turned to stare at Miriam a moment before dropping his ball and marching toward them. Miriam's hand tightened on Rachel's arm. "He's coming over here. What will I do? I'm leaving."

If Rachel hadn't grabbed Miriam's hand, her sister would have been gone in no time. Once Jimmy stood before them, she relaxed her grip. "Good morning, Jimmy. It's nice to see you," Rachel said.

He answered with a nod, but his eyes never left Miriam.

"Well, I must see to the tables. You can come help later if you'd like, Miriam."

Miriam said nothing, and the two continued to stare at one another. Rachel suppressed a laugh as she walked away. Seeing her young sister so smitten with a boy who seemed as equally smitten with her warmed Rachel's heart. Miriam had grown up and soon would be having more young men seeking Papa's approval to call upon her.

Rachel spotted her parents standing by the stage set up for speeches later in the afternoon. She hurried over to them. "Papa, Mama, I have something I must tell you before all the speeches begin." She blinked her eyes and then burst out with her words. "I've decided not to go to Texas."

Neither said a word for a moment. Then Mama smiled and hugged her. "I felt that was what has been troubling you. We've prayed for you to make the right decision."

Papa nodded. "It's well that you are staying here. I did not want to tell you that you couldn't go, but I believed your decision was made without thinking it through."

Relief swooshed out in a flood of air. "Then you're not angry with me for making a commitment I'm not going to keep?"

Her father squeezed her hand. "It wasn't a true commitment if it wasn't from your heart and in God's will."

Rachel hugged him. "I have always known you only had my best interests at heart. I'm glad I didn't let you down now. Thank you." The burden of her decision lifted as though a thousand weights had been taken away. Her heart sang a new song as she followed her parents over to greet a few former members who had returned for this homecoming.

Nathan awoke in the strange room and blinked. Then he remembered he was at the Anderson Orchards and still a good two hours away from Briar Ridge. He rose from the bed and noticed that Jonathan was already up and gone. How late was it?

He found his pocket watch and gasped. It was already past nine. Nathan washed his face in the basin on a nearby table and pulled on his clothes. He ran his hand along his chin. A shave would be necessary if he wanted to look his best for Rachel.

After taking care of that chore, he chose a clean shirt and donned it before stuffing the other one into his valise. He hurried downstairs to find Mrs. Anderson setting a place for him at the table.

"I heard you stirring up there, so I fixed your breakfast. You can't leave for a two-hour horseback ride without food in your belly."

"Thank you, ma'am." She was right, of course, but Nathan almost resented the delay until he smelled the aroma of fresh biscuits and bacon.

In a few moments she set a plate before him along with a dish of fresh butter and a jar of apple butter. Nathan devoured the food as quickly as good manners would allow.

By a little after ten, Nathan was on his way after thanking the Andersons for their hospitality. If he kept a good pace, he'd be in Briar Ridge soon after the noon hour. The first thing he planned to do was to find Rachel and persuade her to stay in Connecticut. The next thing would be to make sure Reverend Winston still approved of his courting Rachel. From there he'd depend on the Lord to take care of whatever happened.

Nathan breathed deeply of the fresh air and the blossoming trees. When spring came to Connecticut, it did so with a burst of color and a myriad of scents. Any other day he would have stopped to admire the beauty of God's handiwork, but beauty of another kind beckoned him forward.

Rachel's beauty had been the first thing to attract him, but as he had come to know her, it was her loving spirit that drew him. She never failed in wanting to help others and putting her family ahead of her own desires. Her love of the Lord inspired him; he had never met one so young who had so much faith.

When the church spire of Briar Ridge came into view, Nathan's heart beat faster. He nudged his horse to a faster pace, anticipation filling his soul.

When he arrived at the church grounds, his eyes opened wide. He hadn't expected this many people. How would he find Rachel in this crowd? He alit from his horse and tied the reins loosely around a nearby tree. When he scanned the crowd again, a familiar figure appeared.

Miriam stood at the edge of the crowd and jumped up and down, pointing to the church. He waved and headed for the main building. Miriam nodded and raced into the crowd, presumably to find her parents.

He stepped inside the dim room to see a figure arranging flowers on the altar at the front. The young woman he'd pictured in his dreams for many months now stood before him. His heart in his throat, he slowly made his way toward her.

Rachel bent over the flowers, oblivious to anything but their beauty. Everyone else was gathering for the noon meal, but she had gone into the church to enjoy a bit of quiet and to check on the flowers for tomorrow's service. This time of year brought a profusion of blooms, and today thick, heady blooms of pink and white peonies filled the vases and drooped toward the altar.

Just then a faint sound reached her ears. Footsteps. She turned slightly, then heard a familiar voice call her name. Nathan! Was it possible? She whirled around to see him standing in the aisle just inches away.

He spoke her name again. "Rachel, I've come back."

Rachel fairly jumped the short distance separating them. "Nathan, it really is you!"

He smiled and held out his hands. "Oh, Rachel, I thought I'd lost you. I tried to get here sooner, but—" He looked at her with guilt and shame written all over his face.

"Shh. You're here now, and that's all that matters." She took his hands. "I can't believe it's really you. When I didn't hear from you at all, I decided you weren't coming back."

His eyes searched hers. "Is that why you decided to go to Texas?"

Rachel gasped. "How...how did you know about that?"

"Daniel wrote me and told me you planned to leave soon with Seth." He grasped her hands. "Please don't go. Stay here and give me a chance."

Tears sprang to Rachel's eyes. Of course he didn't know of her decision to stay. Before she could answer, his finger caressed her cheek.

"Don't cry. I understand if you can't change your plans now, but do know how much I want you to stay."

Nathan had come back, and he wanted her to stay! Before she could speak, her father and mother rushed into the room.

"Nathan, Miriam told us you had returned." Ezra extended his hand, and Nathan shook it. "I was afraid you wouldn't make it."

"I was too, sir. But I've come to persuade Rachel to stay here and to see if you will still grant me permission to court her."

Papa glanced at her, and Rachel shook her head slightly. She wanted to tell Nathan, not have Papa do it.

"I see. You have my permission, but I think you and Rachel need a few more moments alone." He turned and grasped Mama's arm, who gazed at them with smiling eyes. "Come, Mrs. Winston. These two young people have much to discuss."

Once they were alone again, Nathan grasped her hand and led her to the front pew to sit. "Rachel, I must tell you why I had to go back to North Carolina and what happened there. If after you hear my story, you still want to leave for Texas, I won't stop you."

Rachel wanted to throw her arms around his neck and promise she'd stay, but she sensed the need in him to tell her his story. She nodded and sat still. "I'm listening."

As he talked, Rachel's thoughts flew all around her head like a whirligig. First her mind rebelled at such a horrible truth, and her heart hardened at such atrocity. Then, as she listened, her heart softened at the thought of a little boy seeking his father's love and not getting it. As a young man, he'd sought approval and never found it. No wonder he believed God had forsaken him. If Nathan couldn't please his earthly father, how could he ever expect to please his heavenly one? Rachel's heart swelled with gratitude that Nathan had at last learned the truth of God's love.

At the end of the story, Rachel's eyes again filled with tears for all the pain he'd endured. Love filled her heart until she thought it would burst. There was so much to know and to learn about this man who sat before her.

"If after all that, you don't want to stay, I can't keep you here." Nathan looked straight at her now, worry in his eyes.

This time Rachel let all propriety fly out the window. She flung her arms about his neck and buried her face in his chest. "I'm not going anywhere. I'm staying right here where we can get to know each other and let our love grow."

His arms came around her back, and his cheek lay on her head. "My dear Rachel, those are the most wonderful words I've ever heard."

She lifted her face to gaze into his eyes. As Nathan's head bent toward her, Rachel closed her eyes. His lips met hers, and all the love she had harbored in the past months flowed through her as she returned the kiss. Complete peace and contentment filled Rachel. This time she had listened, and God had given her His answer. Her dream of a life with Nathan would come true, and God would be the center of it all the days of their lives.

COMING FROM MARTHA ROGERS

IN OCTOBER 2011,

AUTUMN SONG,

BOOK 2 OF SEASONS OF THE HEART

CHAPTER ONE

August 1889

"KATE MULDOON, I simply can't understand why you haven't found yourself a husband among all the eligible men in this town." Sarah picked up a book from the table. "Hiding yourself away to read and study all the time will not help you find the right man."

Kate grabbed the book from her sister-in-law. "I don't need a man." Marriage and family ranked last in the things she wanted out of life. Her words rang in the air, and Kate fought against the swelling tide of anger that had landed her in trouble on more than one occasion.

Still, why did everyone think a woman's only role was that of a wife and mother? Sarah meant well, but then she loved living on a ranch and taking care of her husband, Donny Muldoon.

Sarah believed everyone should be in love, as did her other sisters-in-law.

"Sarah, I do not intend to marry a rancher or anyone connected with cattle. I was born on a ranch, grew up on a ranch, and have lived around cattle and horses all my life so far, and I don't plan on spending the rest of my life on one." Despite the love of her large family, the ranch held no pull or fascination for her as it did others in the family. Kate hugged her textbook to her chest. "Why do you think I've studied everything about Florence Nightingale and nursing and moved into town to help Aunt Mae?"

"I don't know about that, but I do know Auntie Mae's boardinghouse is full of men who are not ranchers. Why, there's my cousin Seth, who just moved out here to pastor our church, and then there's Doc Jensen's nephew who came to town to assist his uncle with the infirmary. They're both unattached. Sometimes I think you're just too picky."

Picky wasn't exactly the word Kate would choose, but preachers and doctors held no interest for her other than as people she could work with. She did enjoy working with Doc Jensen and his nephew, Elliot Jenson, but they were teaching her to be a nurse.

Even if Sarah did think twenty-three was long enough to go without marrying, it didn't mean Kate was a spinster. "I'm learning all I can about nursing and treatments so I can work more with Doctor Jensen. He lets me help with some of the lighter cases and says I'm getting good at recognizing symptoms. Besides, I was thinking that the preacher would make a wonderful match for Erin."

Sarah shook her head and turned to leave. "That might not

be a bad idea now that she is of marrying age. Erin would make a good wife for Seth and a good mother for their little ones. She loves little Jeremy and has been a big help to me in taking care of him." She stepped through the doorway to Kate's room. "You should think about that too. I'll look for you Sunday at church and then afterward for dinner out at the ranch."

Kate waved her hand in the air to say good-bye. Dinner with the Muldoon clan meant much food and lots of laughter, but it also meant another boring afternoon listening to talk of cattle drives and auctions and horses by the men and babies and mothering by the women.

Three older brothers had ranches of their own, and that's all they talked about. The fourth brother, Cory, had his sights set on being a lawman and had moved into town to be a deputy for Marshal Tate. Erin, the baby of the family, still lived on the ranch. She'd just turned nineteen and was by far the prettiest of the Muldoon clan.

Kate welcomed Cory's company and his presence at the boardinghouse. At least he wasn't interested in finding a bride, and he didn't pester her about finding a mate. He had his sights set on being a marshal himself one day and figured that job too dangerous to take a wife. Kate snorted. So it was OK for a man to be unmarried at age twenty-four, but not a woman.

She laid aside her book and sauntered down the hallway to find the mail from Aunt Mae's boarders. Two trains came each day, one from the west and one from the east. The afternoon from the west would be picking up mail headed for the East Coast. The morning train had dropped off its delivery, and that mail waited for her now.

One of her jobs at Aunt Mae's included taking care of the

mail. With a start, she realized she'd have to hurry to get there before the afternoon train arrived. Ever since the railroads had been completed, Kate had seen more men coming to town to work the ranches around the area as well as find their own land and start farming or ranching. All the land around Porterfield belonged to ranchers and farmers, but in a state as big as Texas, there seemed to be plenty of land to go around.

The Grayson General Store and Post Office beckoned her from across the street. When she stepped into the store, the balding proprietor grinned and tilted his head. "Is that mail from the boarders at your aunt's house?"

Kate plopped them on the counter. "Yes. We had two new faces at supper last night. One came to work with the newspaper, and the other one is helping at the livery. They're sending letters back home."

Mr. Grayson affixed a two-penny stamp to each envelope. "How many boarders are there now?"

Kate closed her eyes to vision the count. "Counting Cory and me, there's seven. All but one of the rooms is filled, and Aunt Mae is happy as a lark. For some reason men come to this town, like it, and stay."

Mrs. Grayson joined her husband. Her blue eyes sparkled as she gazed at Kate. "And when are you going to choose one of these men here for your own?"

Heat rose in Kate's cheeks. Everyone thought they had to ask that question. "I don't plan on marrying anytime soon. I'm studying to be a nurse, and besides, who'd help Aunt Mae take care of the house and all the meals if I wasn't around?"

The plump, rosy-cheeked Mrs. Grayson laughed. "She'd do fine without you, and I've seen how Mr. Fuller over to the bank looks at her. Wouldn't surprise me if she takes a husband one of these days."

"If she does, then I'll take over the boardinghouse." The very idea of her aunt with another man after the love she shared with Uncle Patrick caused Kate's insides to quiver like the branches of a just-felled tree. Aunt Mae did have a few of the men, including Mr. Fuller, looking her way, but she paid them no mind. However, if Aunt Mae decided to marry, Kate wouldn't interfere, but she'd have no part in bringing about that possibility.

As soon as Mr. Grayson dropped the envelopes into the outgoing mailbag, he headed outside and toward the depot. Mrs. Grayson handed her mail from the boardinghouse box.

"Looks like Eloise Perth has a letter from her sister in Philadelphia. Must be hard living so far away from friends and family."

Kate slid the envelopes into her pocket. "I've often asked Sarah about that, but she says loving my brother more than makes up for it. Then, of course, her cousin came out to be our preacher, so I guess it's not really the same." She wiggled her fingers at Mrs. Grayson. "Bye, now. It's time to get things started for dinner at Aunt Mae's."

On her way back to the boardinghouse, the idea of Aunt Mae marrying danced through her head. Except for the fact that Kate's cooking skills left something to be desired, running the boardinghouse might be just the thing for Kate to get her family off her back about marrying, but it would also mean an end to her nursing ambition. Aunt Mae was family, and family came first.

Daniel Monroe finished his letter and sealed it in an envelope. In a few days he'd leave for the greatest adventure of his life, and he wanted Seth to know when to expect him. He reread the post from Seth Winston telling him that the mayor was more than willing for Daniel to come to Porterfield, Texas, and practice law, as they had no lawyers in the town. If lawyers were needed in Porterfield, then that's where he'd head.

Seth Winston had gone to Texas last year to pastor the church where his cousin Sarah and her family were members. The idea of going to Porterfield had grown more appealing as Seth had described it when he'd returned to Briar Ridge for his sister Rachel's wedding this past spring. True, Texas was a long way from Connecticut, but images of the untamed West and all the adventures he could have outweighed the distance.

He envisioned cowboys, gunfights, saloon brawls, and train robberies. Images of the tales he'd heard about Texas rolled through his mind in an endless stream of pictures. All the action and excitement sounded much better than the quiet town of Briar Ridge, where he spent most of his time writing wills and taking care of legal documents for land sales or contracts for service.

He'd already reassigned all his clients to other lawyers in Briar Ridge, and none had truly complained, which only served to emphasize the fact he wasn't really needed here. Daniel cleaned out his desk and put it all in a box to carry home. He planned to have the desk, a gift from his parents, shipped to Texas. Now all he had to do was purchase his train ticket and say good-bye to family and friends. Since his parents, especially his mother, didn't approve of the move, he didn't expect a going-away party.

Father seemed on the verge of understanding Daniel's desire to travel to new frontiers and make a life for himself. Mother, on the hand, wouldn't and couldn't accept the fact that her only son wanted to leave home and move thousands of miles away. His sister Abigail would hardly speak to him, but that did not keep Daniel from planning and making arrangements to leave. At the age of twenty-four, it was time for him to get on with his life, and Texas seemed the best place to do just that.

On the way home he stopped at the depot and purchased a ticket that would begin his trip. He'd have stops in Philadelphia, St. Louis, Oklahoma City, and Ft. Worth before the last leg of the journey to Porterfield.

The ticket agent handed Daniel his passage. "That's a mighty long trip. I take it you're heading out West to join Seth Winston. I can see the need for a preacher out West, but what's a fancy lawyer like yourself going to do there?"

Daniel laughed. His mother had asked the same question. "Not sure, but I hope to help tame some outlaws." How he'd do that he had no idea, but it sounded good when he said it.

"Well, now, just don't go and get yourself shot by one of those outlaws."

"I don't plan to, Mr. Colley." He tipped his hat and walked back out to the rig he'd rode into town in this morning. At least he did know how to ride a horse well. With all the many long trips to Hartford by horseback, he figured he'd have no trouble riding one in Texas. The rig today was simply a convenience for carting home his personal belongings from his office. Tomorrow the desk would be crated and shipped westward.

Daniel entered the foyer of the comfortable, two-story home he still shared with his family. At his age most other men had places of their own, but Ellie's cooking and the free lodging had tempted him to stay. Although he'd miss the cook's great meals, the excitement of adventure to the unknown lured him westward.

After handing over his hat to their butler Stevens, Daniel turned toward the voices he heard and made his way to the drawing room on his left. He knocked, then pushed open the doors. "Good evening, Mother, Father."

His mother stood and hurried to him. She wrapped her arms around him and hugged him. "Oh, Daniel, please tell me you've changed your mind and are staying in Briar Ridge. I can't bear for you to leave us."

He patted her back and glanced at his father, who simply lifted his gray bushy eyebrows and shrugged. "I'm sorry you feel this way, Mother, but I purchased my train ticket on the way home this evening and will leave the beginning of next week."

She pushed back from him and held a handkerchief to her nose. "I simply can't believe it. I don't understand why you have to go all the way to Texas to practice law. New Haven and Hartford are much closer. Why, even Boston would be better than way out West."

"We have a multitude of fine barristers in the cities here in the East. As I've said many times, this will give me the opportunity to travel and see what is happening in the rest of our great country." No matter how many times he explained, his mother would never truly understand his desire to move on. She had grown up in this town, as had his father, and she would never leave it or her beautiful home.

Stevens appeared in the doorway. "Mr. and Mrs. Monroe, dinner is served."

Mother hooked her hand in the crook of Daniel's arm. "Thank you, Stevens. Tell Ellie we'll be right in." She patted Daniel's hand now resting on hers.

Although she held her head high, Daniel noted the slight tremor in his mother's voice as she spoke. "I had Ellie prepare your favorite meal tonight. She'll be serving all your favorites until your departure." She swallowed hard as she walked beside Daniel into the dining room.

Abigail bounded down the stairs but stopped short when she saw her parents and Daniel. Her next steps were much more sedate. "Good evening, Daniel. I didn't know you were home."

Father waited to escort her into dinner. "And what is your great hurry, my dear girl? Is Ellie's food that tempting?"

"No, Father, I'm just happy about my trip to see Rachel and Nathan in Hartford next week. I haven't seen her since the wedding, and I'm anxious to visit and talk with her."

Daniel assisted his mother in her chair at the table. "I'm sure you two will have much to talk about. What's it been? Two, three months since the wedding?"

She turned to glare at him. A month ago she wouldn't have minded the teasing, but since his decision to leave, she had been less than sisterly. "Three, if you must count, but it may as well be three years." Abigail dismissed him and turned to her mother. "I truly miss having Rachel here in Briar Ridge."

Father held her chair while she seated herself. He bent and brushed his lips across her hair. "Then I'm glad you will have this chance to visit Rachel in Hartford."

After his father said grace, Ellie brought in a platter

emanating the most delicious aroma. His favorite roast beef, as Mother had promised. Along with it came perfectly creamed potatoes, buttered asparagus, carrots, fresh baked bread, and his favorite sweet pickles. "What, no soup tonight?"

Mother pressed her lips together. "You said you didn't care for soup at every meal, and since this is your meal, we skipped it."

"Thank you, I prefer to fill up on the main course and not the first one." He glanced over at Abigail who scrunched up her nose as the asparagus was passed to her. "Not to worry, dear sister. After I'm on my way to Texas, you won't have to worry about asparagus. Ellie only cooks it because she knows how much I like it."

"Humph, that *will* be one good aspect of your leaving." She placed two stalks on her plate and handed the bowl to their father.

As his parents began discussing their day, he noted the total lack of reference to his leaving the coming Monday. His mother believed if she ignored it, that perhaps it wouldn't really happen. Father cast a wistful eye Daniel's way a few times, as though he wanted to talk with his son. Perhaps after dinner he and Father could have a conversation. Daniel gazed around at the opulent surroundings. Sparkling crystal, fine china, silver cutlery, and damask tablecloth and napkins reminded him of his parent's wealth. He would find nothing like this in Texas.

Then he glanced again at his mother and swallowed a lump in his throat, along with a potato. He didn't want to hurt her, but he could see in her face and the way she only moved the food around her plate without actually eating it that he had done just that.

How could he make her understand his need to move away

and seek a new life? Somehow between now and Monday he must convince her that God had called him to the frontier. Many hours had been spent in prayer over this move, and now he gladly embraced the future and all it held in the grand state of Texas.

LIFE AND LOVE IN THE OKLAHOMA TERRITORY

EXPERIENCE EVERYDAY LIFE AT THE TIME WHEN OKLAHOMA WAS DRAWING HOMESTEADERS TO ITS TERRITORY WITH THE **WINDS ACROSS THE PRAIRIE SERIES.**

BOOK 1

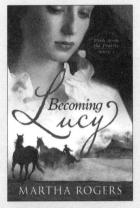

978-1-59979-912-4 / $10.99

BOOK 3

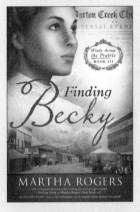

978-1-61638-024-3 / $12.99

BOOK 2

978-1-59979-984-1 / $10.99

BOOK 4

978-1-61638-193-6 / $12.99